I0598948

THE IDES OF MARCH

GREGORY TOWNES

<u>ACKNOWLEDGEMENTS</u>

First and foremost I give God thanks. I would also like to thank my readers, with a special shout out to Lawrence Ballard whose well wishes and prayers were especially comforting. I would also like to thank one of my favorite authors, Tina Brooks-McKinney for her tireless efforts to see me back in print! Special shout out to Ragan Whiteside, my designated reader. Thanks to my family, friends, and my first grandbaby, Sade for reminding me that the world is *still full of magic.*

<u>PROLOGUE</u>: Cypress Point.

For the seventh straight night I woke up screaming. The green LED numbers on my alarm clock read 3:15 am. The same time I woke up yesterday, and the night before that and the night before that. Seven straight nights of being ripped out of my sleep by a bloodcurdling scream and not being able to remember what the hell had scared me so badly.

I got up and threw on my robe. I would not be able to get back to sleep tonight. I went to the bathroom, relieved myself and gargled with some salt water to take the sting out of my swollen vocal cords. I tried to calm down, but nothing worked. After the third night I had started taking sleeping pills, hoping I'd make it through the night, but no matter how many pills I took I woke up at 3:15 in the morning screaming at the top of my lungs and not knowing why. I sat staring at the walls for the remainder of the evening. Too tired to get up and too afraid to go back to sleep.

The telephone rang at 6:30 and it startled me, because I wasn't expecting to hear from anyone, *especially* this time of the morning. The ring was so loud it made me jump. Still groggy from a lack of sleep, I stared at the phone as if it were an odd thing that had just appeared in my bedroom. After several rings I answered it.

"Hello?" I asked, trying to keep my voice steady.

"This is Western Union; is there a Mr. Ezekiel Johnson there?"

"Yes, I'm Ezekiel Johnson," I answered, feeling my stomach tie up in knots. "What is this about?"

"We have a telegram for you, sir. Can you come to the nearest Western Union and pick it up? We show one near you at—"

"Who's it from?" I cut in. My palms became very sweaty and if I were not sitting, I think I would have fallen. I believe there are moments when the psyche senses trouble before it arrives. This was one of those moments.

"It's from Cypress Point, sir. We show the nearest Western Union—"

"I know where it is. I'll be right there!" I stammered. Cypress Point was my hometown and upon hearing the name I instantly knew something terrible had happened.

The man on the other end of the phone gave me a number to recite when I arrived at the office. Although the nearest Western Union was only three blocks away, it seemed to take me forever to get there.

The man behind the Plexiglas was huge with a full beard and no mustache. I recited the number to him and he looked through a stack of envelopes until he found it.

"I have to tell you," he said, staring at the envelope in awe. "You bout the first one *ever* to come in here for a telegram! Now we mostly just send and receive money for people! I don't think I ever saw an actual telegram and I worked here for what seems like forever! What with the telephone and those damned e-mails nobody sends a telegram anymore! These things been obsolete for years!"

"Thanks," I answered with my hand waiting impatiently in the small well under the Plexiglas. "Can I just have it? I'm in a hurry."

"First one I've seen in all the years I've been here! Nobody sends telegrams anymore! Telephone took care of that!" He held the envelope up to the dull florescent light trying to read through it.

"Look, if you knew the people of Cypress Point, you'd understand." I placed a ten dollar bill in the well and gestured for him to give me the letter.

"Cypress Point. That's all it says. From Cypress Point." He gave me the letter without taking the money. "No zip-code, no state or nothing! Just Cypress Point! Hey, mister…where is that?"

"Someplace you'd never want to go," I mumbled and the hair bristled on the back of my neck. "Believe that, mister. *Someplace you'd never want to go.*"

I hadn't heard from anyone in Cypress Point in over six years. The odd thing was I hadn't *thought* about anyone from Cypress Point in that time, either.

I didn't have the nerve to read the telegram in the office, so I put it in my pocket and ran back to my apartment. I put the telegram on the table and poured myself a drink, trying to prepare myself for what I figured at the time to be the worst news imaginable.

"Okay, Ezekiel old boy!" I mumbled, feeling the scotch warm my insides. *"Let's see how bad it is!"* I opened the envelope and read what would prove to be the beginning of the worst nightmare of my twenty-four year old life.

I dropped the envelope on the table and the glass to the floor. It shattered, but I barely noticed it. I read the message over and over...

COME HOME...stop...ALL OF YOUR BROTHERS ARE DEAD...stop...YOUR MOTHER NEEDS YOU...end.

I was in shock, trying to rationalize what I was reading. The letter was so cold and aloof. *All of your brothers are dead.* Just like that, with no more warmth than a train conductor announcing the next stop. What kind of person would send such a tragic message in such an impersonal way?

"Mother needs you," I mumbled, tracing the words with my fingertips. My eyes burned from a lack of sleep and I had the strangest feeling that my sudden insomnia was somehow related to the telegram.

"Six years I've been gone," I groaned. "Six years away from that hellhole!"

When I was eighteen I won an essay contest that led to a full scholarship in a New York City college. I studied Journalism and managed to get a job working for a major publisher. The pay isn't much compared to what some ballplayers and rappers earn, but I'm happy with what I do.

If I were asked to define Cypress Point the first thing that would come to mind would be a hangman's noose. When you're young in Cypress, the noose is loose and non-threatening. In fact, you view it as a jump rope or a toy, but the older you get the tighter the noose becomes until it chokes the life and dreams right out of you.

Most young men in Cypress dream of becoming ball players or entertainers, which are the only two realistic venues open to them. Unfortunately anyone who shows even a glimpse of hope or promise in either of these areas becomes hooked on drugs, or killed over a girl or an unfortunate roll of the dice.

The women fare a little better, but you would be hard put to find a virgin over the age of thirteen. By the time the average Cypress Point woman hits thirty, she has at least six kids by four different men. Three of which are usually in jail or dead.

5

Beauty is a fleeting thing to Cypress women. Most are ruined before they realize the full blossom of womanhood. It's a vicious cycle. Young girls see the older women in their neighborhood use their bodies as tools and weapons, and they grow up thinking that prostitution is a rite of passage.

It's the type of place where any sane person would be embarrassed to say they came from. The population is about twenty-eight hundred, although the town really seems much smaller. Everyone knows everyone and if you're not known, you're an outsider.

Sixty percent of the town can't read above the ninth grade level. Most people are functionally illiterate—that includes my family. Like most Cypress mothers, mine figured she could get a check from SSI if she had my brothers play crazy in school, and like most Cypress children my brothers weren't playing.

They all dropped out of school at about the eighth grade and by then they were labeled with mental and behavioral problems. When I graduated from high school I was one of nine kids—that was the size of the entire senior class. I was one of three boys who graduated that year. One boy's name was Billy Freeman. He was supposed to get a full athletic scholarship for basketball. Billy was totally amazing on the court; he could swish the ball through the net from anywhere it seemed. He picked up the nickname Radar for his uncanny ability to make shots from the wildest angles.

There was no doubt he was NBA material, and I personally felt he could have been one of the greatest basketball players of all time. His mother had big dreams of Billy putting her in a large house by the sea once he made it. Billy was my best friend in the whole world and we both made promises to get the hell out of Cypress and never look back.

He was killed at seventeen years of age; they say he overdosed on heroin, but I knew Billy. He wouldn't use drugs.

The old folks said he was a victim of the Cypress Curse. Some old mumbo-jumbo bullshit they used as an excuse for people being lazy, shiftless and totally without the slightest desire to better themselves.

Someone killed Billy; they killed him because they knew he had a real chance to escape. Whoever that someone was, there were a lot of them. I mean it was probably one person that stuck him with that needle, but everyone who knew about it was just as guilty in my opinion. Billy was found dead in the back of an alley. He had been there three days, and the only reason they found him was because a dog's barking alerted the neighbors that the smell stifling them that hot July week wasn't the usual road kill.

It was Billy, decomposing out in the midday sun with flies and larvae feeding off his flesh like rotten meat.

There was no investigation, no public outrage, just another dead Cypress dream. Everyone was so quick to write Billy off. So quick to believe he was on drugs although there was never any evidence of it.

I believe the town killed him out of pure malice and jealousy. They would rather see death than one of their own make it. No doubt I would've been dead too if I hadn't kept my dreams to myself. By the time everyone found out I was leaving— *I was leaving.* Not even my family knew I was going until that morning.

And now I have to go back...

My hands trembled as I picked up the phone to make arrangements for my return to Cypress. I compared it with asking a free man to willingly return to slavery. What would I find there? Had the people changed?

I stared at a picture my brothers and I had taken right before my oldest brother, J.B died. I remembered the sadness and excitement I felt, secretly knowing I would be leaving Cypress Point for good in just a few days.

My fingers touched each face in the picture and I felt a pang of grief and remorse. J. B. (Jim Bruce, but no one ever called him that), Richie, Danny (Danny-boy), Tom (also known as Tom-Tom), Henry (Mookie, although I never figured out why anyone is called *Mookie*), and Peter (Petey-Wheaty).

Their odd nicknames befit their character. Each in his own way represented what was wrong with Cypress, but strangely enough each represented what was right with Cypress too. They each held as much potential as anyone who ever succeeded. All they needed was an opportunity to build on that potential. If they had been born anywhere else they could have been something other than the thieves, pimps and dope peddlers they became.

They probably tried to rob a bank or a number spot and were killed by the police or in a shoot out with other gangsters. I could just imagine the rest of the town labeling them as *bad asses*. I packed my bags and prepared to make the trip.

My mother would need me.

———   ———   ———

The richest person in Cypress is a woman called Evangelist Washington, the funeral director…

Cypress is known for its beautiful funerals.

Chapter I: The Flight...

I decided to fly to Cypress Point. It was the quickest way to get there and I wanted the entire trip behind me as soon as possible. I flew coach because it had the only available seat left. I was glad that I got a window seat. A woman sitting next to me started making casual conversation.

"First time flying?" I asked her, it was obvious she was nervous.

"No...second, but I'm a lot better this time than last time!" she chuckled. I figured she was in her mid to late twenties. I could tell she was very attractive maybe five or six years ago, but the years of drinking and partying were finally catching up with her.

She continued her conversation with a man in the aisle seat. I took the opportunity to relax. The flight was over six hours long and I didn't want the hassle of trying to maintain polite conversation.

I bought a gin and tonic and gulped it, quickly ordering another. Usually I'm not a heavy drinker, but I was trying to get as tipsy as possible as *fast* as possible. The liquor warmed my insides and I felt a misty glow come over me. Memories seeped in through my closed eyelids and painted a picture on the canvas of my mind.

Suddenly, I was nine years old and back in Cypress.

It was a hot summer day and the sun had baked the air into a thick unbreathable sponge. It was too hot to be any place that didn't have air-conditioning, but Petey-Wheaty and I were playing baseball by the old Getty gas station. It had been abandoned and dry for over two years, but there were still enough gas fumes to make me lightheaded and I secretly worried about the sun causing that dried gasoline to spark.

I told Petey we should've played somewhere in the shade, but once his mind was set on doing something it pretty much got done.

I had to lug Petey's glove and ball, not to mention my catcher's mask. At least I didn't have to carry the bat; Petey never let anyone touch his bat. He carried that bat the way the Peanuts' character Linus dragged his blanket. I started protesting from the time we left the house, but my protests were muffled sighs mumbled under my breath. My brothers, like my father, were all athletically gifted, able bodied and extremely strong willed.

The complete opposite of me; sometimes I think I was adopted.

Petey's dream was to one day play for the New York Mets. According to Petey the Yankees were the rich man's team, poor people rooted for the Mets. I threw what I thought was my best spitball, and he hit what he called an *asskicker*. I saw the seams of the cowhide split as the ball rocketed into the sky. We ran for what seemed like forever, following the ball in the sky as it completed an impossible arc and landed in Evangelist Washington's yard. I remember thinking that ball would have cleared both Shea and Yankee stadiums.

"I can't frickin believe it, Petey! I can't frickin believe it! You hit that ball so hard I saw her skirt split!" I gasped staring at the distance. The ball bounced twice then rolled with its skin flapping until it settled comfortably in a patch of grass.

"You *are* gonna play for the Mets! Man, that ball must be hurtin inside! You knocked the skin right off it!" I blushed, looking at him in that way little brothers do. At that moment I thought Petey-Wheaty could've played for the Mets right then, with no warming up in the Bush Leagues.

I stared at the ball through Evangelist Washington's fence in awe, trying to mentally calculate just how far Petey had hit it, and on the first swing too—when it suddenly dawned on me where the ball had landed.

Evangelist Washington's yard!

She had the biggest house in town (it's an estate actually). Her house looked like an old spooky museum, like one of the haunted houses in an old black and white movie.

"*Ooh crap!*" Petey yelled. "*That's my only baseball! Ezekiel, you gotta go get it!*"

"Petey...no! *If she catches me...*" My eyes pleaded with him, and I had to use my eyes because the words were stuck somewhere in a pocket between my brain and tongue. This was worse than him dragging me to play ball in the hot sun, smelling nasty gas and wanting to vomit.

This was putting my head in the lion's mouth.

"She won't! You're young enough to get over there and back in a hurry! 'Sides, the Mets'll want proof that I hit the ball that far. I gotta show it to 'em!"

"Petey! A busted baseball won't let them know how *far* you hit it! I can tell them! I can—"

"Zeke, just do it! Don't make me git mad on you!"

The hair on the back of my neck and arms bristled as my body shook with fear at what I had to do. The only thing scarier than venturing over into Ms. Washington's yard was the beating I would have taken from Petey. He could really lose his temper sometimes.

Don't make me git mad on you!

Petey once beat a kid so bad they had to wire the kid's jaw shut. I never forgot the maniacal look that came over Petey's face as he almost beat that boy to death. I was always secretly scared of Petey after that, glad that he more often took to hitting baseballs than he did people.

Why did I have to be the youngest? Petey wouldn't dream of telling J.B to hop that fence. I was the only one in the house he could beat; in fact I was the only one in the house that *everyone* could beat.

I gave him one last look that pleaded—*begged* him not to make me go. Seeing that this was akin to playing with fire, I swallowed hard and started to climb the fence. The last thing I needed was for him to hit me *and* make me go. Petey held on to his bat and stared at me coldly. I'd get more sympathy from whatever was on the other side of that fence than I would from him.

The wind stopped blowing and everything just got quiet around me. My scrawny limbs trembled as I threw myself over into Evangelist Washington's yard. The grass was brown and dry on her side of the fence and I thought nothing could live on that side.

It was the side reserved for the dead.

I looked back at Petey, somehow hoping he would tell me to forget the ball and get back on the right side of the fence, but I knew that wasn't going to happen. I had committed myself when I touched down on her property.

"*Go on, Zeke! Go git it!*" Petey urged. I could hear the fear in his voice. My legs felt as heavy as tree-trunks, but I managed to get them to move. The ball had landed right by the cellar door—where the dead bodies were kept for preparation.

Although the ground was dry and parched, it was unusually soft, like walking on thick sheets of cotton. I thought the entire yard would give way and I would fall into the cellar. Right into the waiting arms of some decomposing corpse.

I tried to entertain myself with thoughts of Petey playing for the Mets. Mom would be so proud and the papers would read *Cypress Boy makes good! Plays for Mets!* They would take pictures for the paper and there would be all sorts of important people there. I'd be there and Petey would hold me up in his arms and I would hold the ball up high so everybody could see it and know that my brother *knocked the hell out this damned ball!*

These thoughts carried me; thoughts of Petey helping the Mets to win a pennant and then the Holy Grail of baseball, the World Series. I imagined Petey with his own baseball card and all the kids would want one. Petey-Wheaty Johnson's card would be worth three or four of everyone else's.

Of course I would have crates of them to sell and trade and—

A light breeze tickled the sweat on my neck and blew a soft kiss in my ear, snapping me out of my daydreams and back to the task at hand. I could hear wispy voices warning me not to venture closer to the house.

Warning?

Or laughing?

A cold, hard, crisp smell assailed me. It brought to mind the emergency room in Cypress General on Saturday night. It was the smell of blood soaked sheets and sutured wounds. The smell of pain so great you'd wish for unconsciousness, but they won't let you sleep—because if you did, there'd be no waking. It was the smell of heartbeats tethered to life by the slimmest gossamer thread. It was the smell of the dying and that scared me more than anything, because the funeral home isn't supposed to hold the dying.

Only the dead.

The breeze blew its cool breath again, drying the sheen on my neck. The smell grew stronger. This time there was no mistaking it. It was the hospital. My mind was flooded with visions of sharp, shiny, terrible tools—tools whose sole purpose was to cut the insides out of little boys. There was something else about the smell, something terribly antiseptic like the alcohol gauze that douses your arm right before the needle.

It was the smell of what was to come.

I wanted to bolt, to run and grab the ball and to get back over that fence as fast as possible, but my legs would only move at a snail's pace. I kept feeling someone was watching me, waiting until I bent over to pick up that ball and then they would pounce on me. Or perhaps hands would reach up from the ground, like on that old Creature-Feature TV show.

"Go on, Zeke! Hurry the hell up! Git the damn ball!" Petey screamed again. I could hear the fear dripping in his voice. He was scared for me, but not so scared he would leap the fence to save me.

I etched closer to the ball—willing myself to move faster, but my limbs wouldn't obey. The ball sat in its parked space of grass mocking me, daring me to get any closer to it. The sod beneath my Converse softened; I could feel my feet sink deeper and deeper into the earth. I looked down and saw my ankles were now covered in what a moment ago was solid ground.

"Petey!" I yelled back, "I'm stuck!" My voice was raw and draped in panic. My feet were stuck in the sod like quick drying cement. I couldn't turn around and by now I was convinced I was going to die. No—I was convinced that what was going to happen to me would be worse than death. I clawed at the ground in a futile attempt to free myself, flinging chunks of dirt into the air like a madman.

"Petey!" I screamed, "Something's got my foot!" Dirt got in my eyes, further adding to my panic. I was blind, thrashing in absolute chaos. Every hair on my body bristled and I felt something tickle my ear, like an incessant fly buzzing around my head. Only, this was no fly—this was something out of every young boy's nightmare.

This was the thing with no name or face. The thing that made kids pull the covers over their head at night when they've heard a noise in their closet, or when the shadows created monsters that were invisible to all adults.

"Petey! Petey! Come help me!" I shrieked. I felt like I was screaming underwater. My movements slowed to a surreal pace. I could hear Petey's voice, hoarse and thick with phlegm, screaming for me to *"Get back on the other side, before I git dead!"*

Something had me. Strangely enough even as a child in the midst of blind terror I *knew* what it was.

Cypress had me.

Somehow, the horrible creature that grabbed my sneaker, that dreadful monstrosity that lurked just beneath the surface of the soil, was the embodiment of everything wrong in my neighborhood.

The sky and ground seemed to blend in a collage of bland colors. Reality became a swirl of blurry sights and sounds. I felt myself being pulled down hard, deep into the earth. A light blinded me, but not a light from any source I recognized. This light was as small as the head of a pin, yet as powerful as the sun. A scream bubbled from deep within me, a blood curdling cry with the power to wake the dead…

"Mister…*sir*? Are you okay?"

The flight attendant. I was back on the plane. I could feel the gawks and stares of the passengers around me. They no doubt labeled me as a weirdo and I agreed with them. Here we were *thousands* of miles away from Cypress and I was already having nightmares.

"I'm fine, Miss. Just a bad dream."

"First time flying? Can I get you something?"

"No. I…I'm sorry if I disturbed the rest of the passengers."

She stared at me for a second, a stare that told me she was really concerned about me and not just because she thought I was weird. You have to be very careful on airplanes nowadays. After the September 11th hijackings any slight disturbance on a plane can get you a ticketed trip to the nearest FBI office with your face plastered all over the news for being a suspected terrorist.

"Nonsense," she said smiling. "You just relax, we'll be landing in a few hours."

She turned and walked away, leaving me to the stares of the other passengers.

"Man! Maybe you shoulda drove!" the woman next to me grinned. "I thought I was bad!"

"I—I'm sorry…I just had a nigh—"

"Don't be sorry, baby!" she said, holding my hand way too seductively. I politely excused myself and went to the lavatory. My face was flushed and dripping with sweat. I ignored the stares and smirks as I made my way down the aisle. All I needed was a Sky Marshall thinking I had an underwear bomb or something.

Staring into the small mirror in the restroom, I tried to regain my composure. The memory of Cypress had me all but ready to leap from a perfectly good airplane. I knew—I mean I *knew* Cypress was going to be bad news.

My mouth was as dry as cotton and I couldn't stop my hands from trembling. I stood staring at myself in the mirror seeing traces of that scared little boy who crossed into the funeral home's yard after a baseball.

"Pull it together! Keep it tight!" I pleaded with my reflection. I had not realized how long the scar of Cypress was. Like most people with a traumatic childhood, I'd buried certain memories deep within myself. So deep that I managed to keep a large portion of my childhood blocked. The incident in Evangelist's Washington's yard for example, I could never remember what came after that. I had no idea how I got out of that yard. And it's not just events that are blocked; there are *years* that I simply can't remember. Well, not exactly—after leaving Cypress I simply ceased to think about my childhood. I had no idea as to what I had forgotten, because I simply didn't think about it.

It wasn't until the telegram that I had given more than a moment's thought to Cypress Point or my brothers. I sent money home every month, but it was always detached like donating to a charity. I never associated the check with an actual person called Mother.

I don't know if there is clinically such a thing as selective amnesia, but anything before I turned eighteen is spotty at best. As far as my memory was concerned, that was the year I was born and I didn't try to challenge it.

"I'm not that scared little boy anymore...I'm not scared of you, Cypress. My mother needs me!" I hissed through teeth clenched so tight my jaws ached. My hands gripped the small basin so hard my knuckles were about to pop.

In my sophomore year of college, my journalism professor told me something that had a profound affect on my thinking. He said, "Home is both the soil of our dreams, and the roots of our nightmares." I think of Cypress like that. It was the terrible things I'd seen in that dreaded town that fueled my need to escape, but not through the conventional methods of drugs and alcohol. I wanted to escape to prove the elders wrong.

I had to prove the Cypress Point Curse was just a hoax.

I tore myself from the mirror and made my way to my seat, ignoring the murmurs of the other passengers. How many of them would have braved going into that yard? Not many I think. In many ways, Evangelist Washington's yard was like a microcosm of Cypress—the side reserved for the dead.

"You okay?" the woman next to me asked.

"I'll live," I answered, trying to smile. "Just had a bad dream, that's all."

She held my hand, gently tracing the lines of my palm. There was something soothing about her touch.

"My name is Tamara, *and you are?*"

"*Zeke-Ezekiel,*" I stuttered. Her palm rubbing was giving me a painful erection. I shifted and placed a magazine over my lap, both heads throbbing furiously when I suddenly thought of an old joke that women in bars often say about men:

A man could have a bullet in his foot, his hair on fire and still be thinking about pussy!

"Well, Ezekiel...I don't think you'll have any more nightmares on this flight. What about you?"

"No, I don't think I'll fall asleep again." I squirmed in my seat, trying not to show my embarrassment.

"Good!" she said, releasing my hand. "Where are you going?"

"Cy—Cypress Point," I mumbled, trying to hide my erection. "You probably never heard of—"

"Oh, I've heard of it. I've just never heard anyone say they were going there."

"I see. *You've been there?*"

"Have a safe flight, Ezekiel," she said sarcastically. Her mood changed drastically—totally. The look that came over her face when I mentioned Cypress was one of disgust. She turned and put her headphones on, ignoring me for the rest of the flight. I stared out of the window, feeling a bit silly that I still had a massive erection.

The clouds below us looked like milk colored tufts of cotton candy. A welcome diversion from the cold shoulder I sat next to. I remembered being young and staring up at the sky for hours waiting to see an airplane pass over. Wondering where the passengers were going, and if they knew that thousands of feet below there was a small boy named Ezekiel Johnson, who was going to bed hungry and scared that night.

I ordered another drink and felt an alcohol induced haze fall over me. The pilot announced we would be landing soon. *This is it!* I thought. *It'll all start soon!*

And I have never been more right.

We landed without a snag and other than my rude outburst and Tamara the Ice-Princess, the ride went smoothly. I picked up my luggage and walked to the nearest Rent-A-Car. An extremely obese gentleman with a nametag the size of a DVD Player greeted me. His smile was bright and wide. *Affable fellow*, I thought. He seemed happy with himself, despite his weight.

"Hi! I'm Patrick! Welcome to Luxury Rentals! How may I help you today?" He said this with a sincere sort of enthusiastic charm. As if he were genuinely happy to see me and really interested in how he could help. *Well, Patrick*, I thought smiling. *You could go to Cypress Point for me and tell my mother her only living son is too much of a punk to make the trip!*

"Well, Patrick, I'd like a car. That's why I'm here."

"And you've come to the right place, sir! Would you like to view a list of our very fine auto—"

"A Mercedes. Six-Hundred Series." I pulled out my American Express Platinum Card and watched his eyes bulge from their sockets.

"*Yes, sir!* How long will—"

"Let's make it a week, and give me all of the deluxe options." I forked over my driver's license and signed all of the necessary paperwork.

"Good call! We just got a Mercedes six hundred this morning! I see you're a man that knows his machines! It's black and gold—a treasure of an automobile. Is the color satisfactory?"

"I'm from Cypress Point, Patrick. Anything other than casket slate gray will impress the natives."

"I see. Might I ask—mister...*Johnson is it*? Are you traveling on business?"

"No, Patrick. I'm going to Cypress Point to bury my brothers."

"My deepest condolences, Mr. Johnson. Here is your paperwork along with my card. I will say a prayer for the souls of your brothers, and—"

He grabbed my hand and stared deep and hard into my eyes. Something powerful went through me when he grabbed me. Not quite electrical, but shocking—like touching a raw nerve.

"I will say a prayer for you, too, Mr. Johnson."

He shook my hand firmly and I had to gently pull away from him.

"Th-thank you, I guess I'm gonna need all the prayers I can get. *All the prayers in the world…*"

"The ways of the righteous sometimes seem foolish to the wicked," he said with a Confucius-fortune-cookie type wisdom.

His eyes followed me as I left the counter. I was unsure as to whether he had a psychic epiphany or if my sex appeal now extended to obese male customer service workers.

Nonsense! He was just happy about the type of car you rented. He probably gets a commission. As for the shock, well you were standing on a carpet and the rest is second grade science!

I walked out into the parking lot to pick up my car and noticed hulking thunderclouds had amassed. The sudden darkened sky was the only warning of the torrent that was about to be unleashed. I put my bags in the trunk, removed my suit jacket and settled comfortably in the driver's seat.

"I'm not the same little scared boy who chased that ball into the yard of the funeral home. I'm not the same young man who spent terrified, sleepless nights worrying about the Cypress Curse getting me. I am not afraid. I am a grown man—an *educated* grown man, with a well paying job, a beautiful co-op and a good life. Whatever you have to come up against me, Cypress, *I'm better than it!*"

The rev of the car's powerful engine echoed my statement and my words reinforced my strength.

I drove through the labyrinth of the airport's parking lot and saw Tamara in front of the terminal trying to hail a cab before the rain fell. It was an exercise in futility. There were too many people and too few taxis. I parked and watched her for a moment, admiring her figure and remembering the incredible hard-on she gave me on the plane. Seeing her standing there, her hips wide and her waist pinched, her breasts large and round and still very firm I changed my original assessment of her—she was still a very attractive woman. I pulled the car around slowly

18

lowering the tinted windows. I wanted to see the look on her face when she saw me in a Benz.

"Can I give you lift?" I asked.

"How far are you going?" If she was impressed with the car, her expression didn't show it. I might as well been on the back of a mule.

"I told you, Cypress Point. Can I drop you off somewhere?"

Her lips curled slightly as she looked around. Convinced that she wasn't going to be able to get a cab before the storm hit she grabbed her bag and got into the car. Thunder shattered the sky, but the clouds held their peace.

"Where can I let you off?" I asked, somehow knowing what I was about to hear.

"I'm...*going to... Cypress Point, too.*"

I didn't say anything. I didn't even look at her. I merely started the car and pulled off.

"Nice car," she mumbled.

"Thanks. It's a rental, but I have a six hundred at home. Different color of course."

"Pretty fancy for a *Cypress* man...ain't it?"

"I am not a Cypress man. Fuck 'em if they can't take a joke."

"Cypress isn't known for jokes. Jokers, yes. Jokes, no."

"I know what you mean."

Thunder exploded again, but this time the clouds saw no reason to be polite. Instead of rain, hollow hailstones the size of golf balls fell. I would've been disappointed with anything less.

So now it starts. Fitting omen, I thought.

<u>Chapter II</u>: **The Wheel of the World!**

Tamara and I did not speak for what seemed like hours. I sensed her unease at returning to Cypress Point. Maybe she thought I was playing some sort of joke on her while we were on the plane when I said I was going to Cypress. Although we didn't speak the silence was comfortable. I don't think either of us were in the mood for conversation.

I played my CDs, allowing the sultry voice of Sade to relax me. I silently kept repeating my mantra over and over again to myself. I was not the same little scared boy from Cypress, I was returning a success. Last year I crossed the sacred threshold of the two-hundred and fifty thousand dollar-a-year salary and that was before the bonus.

I will bury my brothers, and pour a little wine over their graves, honoring their memory, but celebrating my emancipation. I will try to assuage the grief my mother feels by letting her know her baby son has become a success. I will take her out of Cypress and move her to New York with me. I'll put behind me the garbage of the Cypress Curse and most of all I will tell whoever doesn't like it to kiss the crack of my ass in Macys' store window during the Thanksgiving Day Parade.

Lost in these thoughts and floating on Sade's smooth silk-smoky voice as the six hundred pierced the road like a laser, I almost missed a diner on my right hand side. Tamara cleared her throat and flicked a well-manicured finger toward the sign.

"I'm hungry. Nowhere else to eat for a long while."

I pulled the car into diner's parking lot, taking a hard look at the place. The building seemed a breeding ground for Botulism. Moss and Crab grass covered the driveway and the windows looked as if they hadn't been washed in months. I expected to see a sign advertising Ptomaine poisoning. The air outside the diner had a damp cavey smell that reminded me of old dilapidated buildings after a hot humid spring rain.

A smell I knew only too well.

It reminded me of the old building in Cypress I called home. Where the halls held the dank, rotten remains of too many broken dreams. It was a smell that cloaked the walls of a young couple's first apartment; where the wife swore they would live no more than a year—just long enough for them to put away a little nest egg and move up and out. The smell that no matter how much the wife scrubbed and cleaned she couldn't erase or mask. The same smell that remained years later, after the dreams of newlyweds have long since faded with all of the other fairy tales of youth.

Funny, how those smells never quite leave you. They lie as dormant as memories, waiting for any lame excuse to pop up. And it's not only the smell, oh no—the smell brings the rest of the nightmare to life. The smell is the conductor on the *Bad Dream Express*. The smells invoke images and voices of ethereal monsters with beefy forearms and groping hands. Hands that clutch at private rooms in a little boy's soul, hands that hurt and smother dreams like infant candidates of crib death.

Thought yo' stupid ass was a big shot, huh? So you wanna rent a Benz to show off—huh, Noo Yawk? Well, Ezekiel we got sumpthin for yo' ass! Round here we don't coddlin to edumacated sissies with FANCY suits and FANCY cars! Round here we liable to grease yo' cornhole up and stuff it proper!

I swooned and had to hold on to the car to steady myself. This was going to be harder than I imagined. That smell…it brought back not just memories, but images. It conjured up thoughts of hundreds of faceless, hopeless people, all moving nowhere fast.

"Square up, quick! If you can't handle this how we gonna make it to Cypress?" Tamara hissed, snatching me away from those terrible inner voices. Her hand on my shoulder forced me to focus. The look on her face was one of genuine concern—and rightly so. This ugly diner with its smell of terrible childhood fears would be the Litmus Test.

If I could get past this, there was a chance I could handle Cypress.

I stood looking at the diner, remembering that I was driving a Mercedes. Remembering that I paid more in taxes than any six men in Cypress earned legitimately, but most of all that I was the youngest brother of six of the most ruthless, baddest men to ever walk the face of God's green earth.

My breath stuck in my throat. The air around me had hardened to Jell-O. My lungs in their pride and arrogance refused to inhale that stench and staged an instant strike. I stood rigid, unable to move as that smell invaded me like bacteria. Tamara nudged me; her fingers clasped my shoulder like a vise.

"You don't expect me to eat in that outhouse, do you?" I blurted.

"If you're going to Cypress, this is probably the best of the pickings!"

I stood remembering how my brothers weren't afraid of anything that walked on two legs or four. I used this memory to force the inner demons back into the stygian depths of my subconscious.

There were at least a dozen truck driver types and a smattering of local redneck hicks. The Jukebox blared with an ancient blues song, something about a man threatening to beat his woman with a lead pipe for not doing right.

Immediately all eyes fell on Tamara and I, like pigeon droppings on a new cardigan. Being dressed in an eighteen hundred-dollar suit I stuck out like a roach on a white wall. I ignored them and concentrated on moving closer to the counter. The voices started bubbling again, writhing like hot liquid steel in the pit of my stomach.

Why'dja come back, Ezekiel? You knew what'd happen! You know you ain't strong enough to handle this! You're brothers are dead. DEAD! Nothing can bring them back! Why'dja come back?

BECAUSE...

One step at a time toward the counter. Tamara is right behind me.

MY MOTHER...

Her hand is on my shoulder, gripping me. Keeping me grounded and focused.

NEEDS ME!

That's why...

I stood at the counter; Tamara walked to the far end of the counter and lit a cigarette.

"*What may I get for ya, fancy youngin?*" the man behind the counter asked. He placed his palms down on the counter and his upper lip curled slightly as he spoke.

He looked to be in his mid-seventies, but it was hard to tell. All of his teeth were missing and his skin had deep pockmarks in it. There was a large confederate flag suspended from the wall behind the counter. The counterman wore a faded tee shirt with a Bald Eagle blazed across the front. The eagle held an M16 in one claw and the American Flag in the other. Underneath, the caption read: *If you don't speak the language,*

22

stay the hell out the country! He smelled of used oil and sweat. There was the faintest hint of stale urine about him, like he didn't take the time to shake himself properly after pissing.

Behind him on the grill were cheeseburgers, sizzling in grease. A deep fryer to the far left boiled lard soaked French fries. A wide, melodic ceiling fan whipped the putrid oil throughout the diner in a thin mist, coupling it with the thick fugue of cigarette and cigar smoke. The menu was placed under the countertop glass, but it was barely readable through the stains. Nothing about this place looked remotely sanitary and the food looked as disgusting as it was inedible. My eyes searched up and down the counter and then I saw it.

A glass pie holder.

A pristine, sparkling clear, crystal glass pie holder that held the most delicious looking Boston Crème Pie. It seemed so out of place in a Choke-N-Puke like this. Although the pie holder looked airtight, I could still smell the pie above the rank. The aroma pierced through the heavy greasy air and tickled the hairs in my nose.

I held my breath, relishing the pie's smell and feeling my stomach growl. Half the room's eyes were on me. The other half were gathered at the window marveling at the Mercedes.

"Let me have a slice of this pie and a cup of coffee. Decaf, if you have it." I was amazed at how steady my voice was. I half expected a broken gasp to escape but instead a strong, deep resonant voice emerged.

"Sure you don't want a *café-latte,* Mr. Fancy britches?" the counterman asked snottily. He lifted his palms off the counter and took a half step back. I didn't know if this move was an advance or a retreat. Instinct told me that I scared the counterman. His step back was a cue to the other yokels.

"Just the pie and the coffee. Decaf if you have it."

"*Zat yo' car?*" another man asked me. Judging from his dental work, he could have easily passed for the counterman's son.

"Yes," I answered without looking at him. "I'd like the pie and the coffee to go, please."

"*Mercedes ain't it? It's a beaut! What a car like that run nowdays?*"

"*Too darned much if'n you axed me! Why we 'Mericans gotta buy from our forma enemies is beyond me! An anybuddy drivin' some shit like dat should have dey ass shaved an hoss whupped!*" the counterman said. His eyes were as cold as steel and I noticed a grease covered picture of him in an army uniform. Underneath the picture the caption read *World War Two vet! We saved the World!*

All eyes were on me now, as a sea of red and blue plaid lumber jackets and politically incorrect baseball hats (one of them read, I ain't killed a Liberal yet, but the day is still young and another read, kill them all. Let God sort them out.) that covered the sediment of society washed toward me. I pulled a ten-dollar bill out of my pocket and placed it on the counter, ignoring the man's question.

"*Cream and sweetner?*" the counterman asked sarcastically. The grin on his face was all the evidence needed to let me know that strangers with *fancy britches* couldn't just come and mosey up to his counter, order their food and leave. At least not when he had a good dozen men behind him. Oh no, I couldn't just order my coffee and a slice of pie and leave with my lady friend.

I had to be humiliated first.

"Black. No sugar," I replied without looking at anyone. My movements were slow, calculated. I didn't realize it just then, but I had taken a defensive stance at the counter, subconsciously creating a circle around myself. My feet set apart, lowering my center of gravity. I was glad that something stuck out of all of the self-defense classes I took.

"*Why didn't I guess it!*" the counterman smirked. He picked up the bill and examined it—the way people usually look back into the toilet before they flushed, to make sure they didn't let out anything vitally important. The rest of the patrons slowly moved toward me. My fancy car, fancy suit, fancy diction and now *fancy money* made me suspect. Someone cut off the Jukebox and the sudden rustling of feet blended with the cadence of the ceiling fan's metallic whoosh.

"*Where you from, boy?*" another man asked, staring at me menacingly. They were like a pack of wild dogs, carefully sizing up their prey. To them I was an outsider and all outsiders were either troublemakers or trouble bringers. Either way they deserved whatever they got and what they usually got was trouble.

Here it comes, Ezekiel! They're gonna do you like in that movie Deliverance!

I stood my ground, jaw locked and set for just about anything. This would be my baptism by fire. I wanted to say something but that molten river of steel had now crept its way up into my larynx. The silence hung heavy in the air. I could hear the counterman's raspy breathing, and out of the corner of my eye I saw his hands slowly reaching below the counter—

"*Him from CYP-ress Point. Him turnin' home.*"

It was Tamara. Her dialect and inflection were purely Cypress. A bittersweet wave of nostalgia went through me when I heard her speak that way. I had not heard that accent since I had left home. The crowd backed away, still eyeing me suspiciously, but there was a reluctant acceptance slowly growing.

"*Where him git da car? CYP-ress boys don't dress an ride fancy,*" the counterman stated hotly, returning the accent. His hands were now locked below the counter and I had little doubt as to what they were locked on. "Him don't got the looks of Cypress. Him got the looks of *foreigner.*"

The way he said *foreigner*, like it was the worst thing in the world to be from someplace other than this hellhole. He stretched the word, pronouncing each syllable with emphasis.

The tension in the room grew into a hard, scaly claw and was poised to swipe.

Tamara sashayed over to me. The air stood as still as a photograph. Everyone's eyes were on her. Her hips swung and thrust forward with every slow and deliberate teasing step. It was the walk of a Cypress woman—sexual, daring, arrogant. She put her left hand on her hip and threw her hair back mockingly, placing her other hand on my back.

"*Him no hafta 'splain nuthin to likes a you. Him CYP-ress. Him turnin home.*"

The counterman nodded slowly and without taking his eyes off us placed my coffee on the counter and gave me my change. The other patrons went back to their usual inane chatter. Someone cut the music back on and now the jukebox singer crooned in remorse about the girl leaving him, causing him to brain her with the lead pipe until she was dead, and mourn over her remains.

The counterman walked over to the pie and removed the glass case. The top was heavy, judging from the way the muscle in his arm jumped.

"Which piece him want?" he asked softly.

"Dis piece," Tamara said, pointing to a slice of the pie. "Bring 'im dis piece, and the coffee to the back booth. And bring me a tuna sammich and a cold root beer." She rubbed her finger along the counter and smirked at the grease.

"*An it betta be clean!*" she whispered.

She placed a finger through my belt loop and led me to the rear of the diner. There were six high back booths, offering total privacy from the rest of the place. Tamara chose one next to the window with the best view of the Mercedes.

Although still a long ways away, I knew then in that diner, I had returned home.

CYP-ress—said that way to invoke pride and a sense of intimidation. Cypress Point men were known to fight to the bitter death at the slightest hint of disrespect. I once watched my brother Mookie beat a man into a coma because he refused to apologize for stepping on Mookie's shadow. A Cypress man's shadow was supposed to be his only true bodyguard and friend. It was said in Cypress that your friends and even your family may run, but your shadow will always be there.

If you asked a Cypress man how he was doing, he's apt to reply "We doin' fine." The "*We*" being the man and his shadow. Stepping on a man's shadow and not apologizing was the equivalent of spitting in his face.

Cypress women usually did most of the talking for their men in an altercation. The men stood silent, strong. Only getting involved when they felt the moment warranted complete violence. Words and arguing were for women. Tamara's reaction to the men in that diner was exactly what was expected of a Cypress woman and my reaction was exactly what was expected of a Cypress man.

If Tamara had not been with me, that scenario would have ended much differently. Namely with me being buried behind the diner and the Mercedes being stripped for parts that none of them could have ever used.

"Thank you," I whispered, staring deeply into her eyes.

"Don't *thank* me, Ezekiel. Just don't ever put me in that position again. *I never want to have to act like that again!*"

"Tamara, let me ask you…did you grow up in Cypress?"

"That's a *stupid* question. Does anyone *move* to Cypress? Of course I grew up there! Why do you ask?"

"Because I don't remember you. We look to be about the same age—same generation at least. I would have at least seen you in school or knew your sister or brother."

"I don't want to talk about it."

"I understand, but I'm on my way back to Cypress because I got a telegram stating that my six brothers are dead. I mean—it took something *like that* to bring me back to this hellhole. Why are you coming back?"

"What part of *I don't want to talk about it* didn't you understand?"

"I didn't mean to pry."

"I know... it's just that...well—just because you gave me a lift doesn't mean I owe you my life's story!"

"Touché."

"And don't think hard of me for the way I spoke back there! I'm not one of them Molly girls!"

"Actually, that never crossed my mind!" I said honestly.

Molly girls were the lowest women in Cypress. Called that because most of them came from the Molina Houses, which were notorious for whores. A Molly girl was the type of woman who would sleep with a derelict for a swallow of wine. There was very little (if anything) sexually that a Molly girl wouldn't do. Most were scarred and diseased hags before their thirtieth birthday.

"Tamara, I was totally amazed at the way you turned into Cypress like that! You don't come across like a Molly girl or anyone from Cypress for that matter! That's why I asked...you remind me of *me. I wanted to escape that hellhole and now I have to go back!*" My voice betrayed me. The plane ride coupled with the fact that I came so close to dying at the hands of an ignorant mob overwhelmed me in that moment. Right as the counterman brought the pie and coffee. I stifled a cry and bit my bottom lip hard, forcing the mist threatening to cloud my eyes to dry up.

Crying was for pussies and I was now, for all intents and purposes, a CYPress man.

The counterman left without looking Tamara or I in the face. She placed a hand gently over my wrist.

"*It's going to be okay, Ezekiel,*" she whispered sipping her soda and staring at the *sammich* on her plate. "I know how hard it must be to come back to a place like Cypress, but

27

sometimes we have to finish what we start. Sometimes, we have to come home…you know?"

"Yes, I know." I sipped the coffee and marveled at how good it was. Rich and aromatic. It was easily the best coffee I had ever tasted. The pie was even better. *Funny*, I thought. *How a dive like this could have pie and coffee this good. Looks can be so deceiving!* And the smell was gone. The counterman must've washed his hands before he brought the food, because I no longer smelled the rank on him.

Or maybe I just got used to it.

Tamara ate quietly without looking at me. When her sandwich was finished, she played nervously with her napkin, folding it in half and then in fours and so forth. When it got too thick to fold, she'd unfold it and start again.

"Ezekiel, do you believe in God?" she asked me softly.

"Yes," I answered wondering where the question was leading.

"I mean…the way the Bible says that God is. You know—how He can be cruel sometimes."

I thought about her question. From the time I was a child I was brought up in church and we all had to say a Bible verse before dinner. The Bible was one of the first books I learned to read. I remember shuddering in fear and disgust at parts where God would order people to kill other people, or have she-bears tear little children apart for laughing at a prophet's bald head. I once saw a picture in a Sunday school book where a little boy was up to mischief in his parent's study. He was trying to pull a large book off a shelf and in the corner of the ceiling there was a huge single malevolent eye staring at the boy. The caption underneath the picture read:

God sees you!

That picture scared the hell out of me. For months, I kept looking up into the corners of ceilings, expecting to see that eye. It's amazing how a small thing like that could make such an overwhelming impression on the mind of a child.

There's a room deep within us all where we bury our childhood dreams and fears. A mental Pandora's box padlocked by the maturity of adulthood. We never quite get over our fear of the dark, or the Boogey-man. As boys, we're taught not to cry and to stand up straight and tall. Don't be afraid.

Be brave. Be a man.

"No, I don't believe in *that* God," I replied. "That God is a figment of a warped and sadistic imagination. I think people misinterpret God—the church has misled the masses. I believe in a loving and just God. A God who doesn't require the blood sacrifices of children or small animals. A God who could care less about rituals and cares more about us. Most of all…a God who doesn't play favorites."

In other words, the complete opposite of the Evangelist's God.

"I used to think that. I mean…I used to think it was stupid to have to give all of your money to the church and wait for God to fill your cupboards. The Evangelist told me…she told me…"

"It's okay, Tamara. Take your time. Believe me, I know it's not easy."

"*You're going back to bury the dead…but I'm going back to save the living,*" she whimpered, looking out of the window at the Mercedes. Her voice was low, but even. She spoke in slow rhythmical tones. Much the same way my movements by the counter were. Measured and precise.

"*I told you I'm not a Molly girl, and I'm not…but I've done a lot of things in Cypress I want to forget. See…a while back…*" her voice faltered and she took a sip of her root beer. The release of the sarsaparilla and Boston Crème filled the booth. I squeezed her hand, letting her know that I understood. "*A while back,*" she continued, "*I made a deal…a deal to get out of Cypress, but I didn't…I didn't uphold my end of the deal.*" Another sip of the root beer. This time the cubed napkin rushed up to her lips to hold back a gasp. "*I have to see the Evangelist…to ask her to set me free…to let me live.*" The napkin was pushed deeper, pass the lips and almost stuffed into the mouth, to keep certain words from escaping as words are wont to do.

Evangelist Washington was head of the Chamber of Commerce, the church, the city council, the school board and the owner of the local newspaper. Hell, by now she probably owns all the air in Cypress.

Legend had it she was the devil's first wife and she nagged him so much that he set her free. She scared everybody.

One of my rare childhood memories (besides the ball going in her yard) was when I saw her in the basement of the

29

church one Sunday right before service. I had to pee ever since we left the house and my mother kept telling me to hold it until we got to church. I pleaded with her to let me go near a tree and relieve myself, but she insisted that I hold my water and not take a chance on ruining my good church pants. Mookie, Danny and Tom-Tom kept teasing me making references to waterfalls and leaky faucets. They kept giggling and tickling me, trying to make me wet myself. They thought it was pretty funny, until my mother slapped Mookie so hard his ear turned red. Then they looked at me coldly—like it was my fault Mookie got hit. I knew later on Mookie would hit me as payback, and I hated the fact I was the youngest.

It felt like my abdomen was filled with urine and it was backing up into my brain. It took all of my will power and bladder control to stay dry until we got to the church. Not to mention the fact that had I wet myself my mother would've beat all the water out of me and then Mookie would've beat it back in.

The men's room was in the church basement. I never liked going down there alone because it was a creepy place with large looming cobwebs and floors that creaked loud and long. The overhead pipes always whined and sputtered, making noises that sounded like a little girl's screams. Sweat from one of the pipes had shorted out a few overhead light bulbs, making the basement hall that much gloomier. The corridors reminded me of a Greek myth I had read about a labyrinth. So many twists and turns, that the hall seemed to go on forever.

I took a wrong turn and instead of the bathroom, I walked into Evangelist Washington's private office. A thick soupy haze covered the floor. There was a lingering odor of mildew and something I couldn't quite place, but it made me think of road kill. A low humming sound reverberated in the walls.

Her back was to me, but I could see her face in the wall mirror. Her eyes were turned up in her head and drool hung off her lips in thick threads. She was hunched over a table that held a dozen or so strangely shaped candles. The wax was twisted into the shape of snakes and deformed arms. She was mumbling something under her breath, but I could tell it wasn't English.

I was mesmerized listening to the unnatural chants of the Evangelist, and watching the flames dance on the wicks of the ghoulish candles. I first thought she was praying, being in a church and all, but then I somehow *understood* what she was saying. Her voice entranced me. I suddenly understood the wails and moans that underlined the ghastly sounds she made. I subconsciously began to make the same wailing sound.

My breath became as heavy as a rock, stretching my lungs until I had to inhale in short bursts of fever filled air. The sound of my bladder emptying and soaking my good suit pants snapped me out of my trance. I carefully backed away from her office and ran back up stairs to the church. My mother looked at my ashen face and my wet pants with a combination of disgust and concern.

"*A rat*," was all I could mumble to her. I must've looked pretty shook up, because even Mookie was worried about me.

"*I wet myself because a rat ran past my foot.*"

"*Excuse* me?" Tamara asked, bringing me back to the diner snapping me away from the memory. "Are you even listening to me?"

"Yes…it's just that the mere mention of the evangelist makes my testicles retreat back in my stomach. Sorry to be so crass. It's just that I've tried to forget…I mean I did forget a lot of my past—my childhood." She looked at me strangely. I wondered how I looked to her, from my outburst on the plane up to that moment.

"Tamara, there is a large—and I mean a *LARGE* part of my childhood that's blank. Sometimes someone will say something to me, or I will hear a song or see a picture and suddenly—*poof!*" I snapped my fingers; "it's like I'm transported back to the past."

"Is that what happened to you on the plane?"

"Yeah, really strange memory of being in her yard going after my brother's baseball. I never can remember whether I got the ball, or how I got out of her yard. Something happened to me in Cypress. Something so terrible, I won't let myself remember it."

"Even now? With you on your way back and everything?"

"Even now. Sometimes I think I'll dream something. I say I think, because I wake up screaming a lot."

"I know a lot about bad dreams. She haunts me until I can't stand to fall asleep. Once I pay her, everything'll be okay."

"Is that it? What, do you owe her money? How much?"

"You know she don't want money! *She wants me*! I'm going back to ask her to set me free...to set a price and set me free."

We stared into each other's eyes and something passed between us—something strong and foreboding. A sliver of the terror that was yet to come. Her eyes held a light and beauty, that with the exception of very small children I had seldom seen in

Cypress. And like me she was willingly, or unwillingly walking into a place that was all but guaranteed to remove that beauty and light.

"Maybe we can help each other," I murmured. "Do you have a place to stay when you get to Cypress?"

"I have money," she shrugged. "I figured I'd rent a room at the Barrett."

The Barrett was about as close as you could get to a decent hotel in Cypress. It was clean and catered to a better class of people. In Cypress that usually meant people who didn't piss in the elevators and puke up Bluetrain wine all over the carpet.

"You don't have to waste your money. If push comes to shove you can stay with me."

"Where you stayin'?"

"Probably at home with my mother, help her make the funeral arrangements."

"She know you comin'?"

"No, oddly enough the phone was disconnected and the operator could find no listing for her number. It's just as well. That explains why she sent a telegram instead of calling me."

"When was the last time you spoke to her?"

I stopped and thought about that. When *was* the last time I spoke to my mother? I sent money every month, but that was impersonal—distant. My mind raced backwards over the last six years. I hung my head in shame as I realized I had not *spoken* to anyone from Cypress Point since I'd arrived in New York to make my fortune.

"I...I never called her. I only wrote...a few times. I've sent money though, and every year I've sent birthday cards and Christmas cards. I know how it sounds, but I guess I wanted to block out everything about Cypress. God, I feel like a total idiot! What kind of son *am I?*" This time the tears were there and I furiously rubbed them away. I had not even thought about my mother or brothers until I received that telegram. How could I have not thought about my mother? Even the cards I sent were separate and cold. There was always some corny Hallmark line like, *Thinking of you on your special day.* Or, *with best wishes, this holiday season.*

"Don't be so hard on yourself. I think you're the first person other than myself to actually get out of Cypress. Your mother must've known this. I imagine it was hard on her not having you around for Thanksgiving and all, but I'm sure she was proud of you just the same. Which is more than I can say about my family."

"Rough, huh?"

"Home was always someplace I came to wash up, change my clothes, and sometimes sleep. Some days I really believed no one would notice if I disappeared and never came back."

I thought about how I would brag to my mother and tell her I was going to get out of Cypress and not with a basketball or a record deal. I was going to get out by using my mind. I was going to single handedly put the lie to the Cypress Curse.

"You do just that, Ezekiel. You get out of here anyway you can, you hear?" she'd tell me. *"Your father always had high hopes for you. He'd say 'that's the one with the brain' that's what your daddy'd say about you, Ezekiel, and it's true! So you go ahead and dream your dreams, cause it ain't all make believe."*

My heart filled with an ache that felt as if someone dropped a stone in it. I was overwhelmed with the idea of seeing my mother again. Determined to bring her with me to New York. Going to Cypress took on a new dimension; I would bury the dead and renew life.

We finished eating, and I left a considerable tip for the toothless counterman. The other patrons regarded us impassively. The hailstorm gave way to rain, but now the wind had picked up considerably.

"We better be careful!" Tamara said as we got into the car. "This is still tornado season!"

"I don't remember any tornadoes in Cypress!"

"Yeah well, you yourself said there's a lot you don't remember!"

True, I thought, *but tornadoes? How in the hell do you forget tornadoes?*

Cypress Point wasn't on any of the maps I had bought. It was just as well; small towns like Cypress don't appear on maps. They're like weeds—they grow wherever they damned well please.

By some arcane knowledge I knew just where to turn and what private dirt road to take. This inner compass guided me so long as I didn't give thought to it. I simply drove—the car did the rest. Sade crooned how my love was king and she'd crown me in her heart (she has always been the epitome of sexy in my opinion) and I relaxed with her voice filling my mind, underscored by the wind's howling outside and the rhythmic *Whoomf-Whoomf* of the car's tires eating at the dirt road.

"Probably should've rented an SUV," Tamara said lazily, but I barely heard her. I was about to lapse into one of my *Memory Spells* again.

I am in the park and Radar is there playing ball by himself. Always practicing. Lost in his game he hadn't seen me duck through the slit in the chain link fence. The sun had not quite set and the sky is a beautiful mixture of burnt orange holding up dark purple clouds. I watch in awe and pride as Radar does a crossover dribble, spins around and throws the ball with one hand behind his back from the three-point line.

Swish!

Nothing but net.

"Man, I don't think Lebron or Kobe could mess with you!" I remark, slapping him high-five.

"I just hope I can make the money they get one day," he gasps, trying to catch his breath, wiping the sweat off his face with his towel. He lays the basketball down and sits on it. He practices so hard, but he doesn't need to. Basketball is his gift— that much is evident.

"What brings you to my Empire, baby?" he asks and sitting on that basketball he does look like a Emperor surveying his kingdom. That will be his moniker. They'll call him the Emperor!

"I got some news for you! You know the NBA is starting to recruit out of high school, right? I think I might be able to get somebody down to this little feces factory to come see your game!"

His eyes bulge wide. He's hesitant, thinking I will yell— GOTCHA, at any moment.

"If'n you jokin, don't. This my dream and I don't let nobody play with it!" He holds the basketball close to his chest guarding it, or is it guarding him? "This my shadow."

"No, Radar! This is your light! Your way out of here! And I am not joking with you. My writing and your game are our gifts, and we will get out of Cypress!"

"One way or the other," he chuckles.

"What's that supposed to mean?"

"It means nobody gets out of here without the Evangelist sayin it's okay." He goes back to shooting the ball, confident that I am not playing with him, but still oblivious to the chance he has. The fulfillment of his dream in his mind is still a long way off. The idea that it could happen NOW *is too outrageous to entertain—unless the Evangelist says it's okay.*

Swish! Swish! Swish!

The rim of the basket must be magnetized. He can't miss! Why should such a talent—such a gift *depend on the whims of one insane old woman?*

"Forget her," I say angrily. "Forget that old skank! We're getting out of here! Do you hear me? Do you hear me, Radar? My books will be on display at Barnes and Noble and you will be on a Wheaties box wearing sneakers with your name on them!" I grab him roughly, forcing him to stare at my face. I am seething in anger now, seething that he has placed so much faith in someone other than himself and God...and me. After all, we made this plan together. We were going to escape, and nothing would stop us. Nothing would—

"Who's in this park cursing the holy name of God's messenger as His sun sets? Who dares provoke His holy wrath?"

Every muscle in my body turns to flaccid putty as I hear that voice. Waves of disgust and fear shake me. I turn and see the Evangelist walking—no, gliding toward us. Her feet covered in a misty haze.

A cloud, I think. She's riding a cloud.

She is wearing the same snow-white gown she sometimes performs baptisms and funerals in. Her eyes glower with a hatred that is incomprehensible—an unfathomable maniacal loathing. Her lips are covered in a deep red lipstick and I gasp in shock when I realize it's not lipstick, it's blood. Her hands reach for us; her fingers are splayed out from the palms clutching the air like poison filled pincers. She stands about ten feet away—glaring with her lips drawn back, revealing teeth that look as sharp as knives. Her pupils close to slits. There is a smell that accompanies her, her robes are perfumed but they hide a deeper smell that I immediately detect. My mouth fills with water and my stomach bubbles in violent waves. I know what that smell is.

It is the stench of the funeral home's cellar.

"Well?" she asks, still reaching with fingers that resembled claws, though coming no closer. "Which of you blasphemed?"

Radar stands behind me, his basketball clutched close to his side. I can feel his heart beating like a jackhammer. There aren't many things a boy like Radar is afraid of, and the Evangelist is at the top of the short list.

"I said it," I croak, trying to find my voice. "I didn't mean any disrespect toward you, but Radar and I are leaving Cypress and that's the gospel truth." My voice grows stronger as my chest heaves up and down in a combination of rage and determination. She can't stop us! I think angrily. We have a right to leave—to make it!

"We have a—"

She laughs, which scares Radar even more (me too, but I don't let her know it) and he drops his basketball. I watch as it bounces once, twice, three times and then it rolls about five feet before it explodes. Now I am really scared for Radar, because his basketball is a symbol of his gift—it's the only thing his father ever gave him. It's like Samson's hair.

"No! Oh God, no! Ezekiel, tell her sorry! Oh God, no! Not my ball! Tell her sorry!" Radar is hysterical as he picks up the flat plate of rubber. Tears streak down his face and mix with snot. He blubbers uncontrollably, holding that dead basketball like it held all of his talent—all of his dreams.

"Zeke, tell her sorry! Please! MAKE HER GIVE IT BACK TO ME!"

I have never heard this type of pain. It's not a physical pain—it is a pain of the soul. The type of deep wound that never heals, the type of pain you lock in a room and pray that no one is ever stupid enough to walk into it.

The type of pain that makes a man answer voices that only he can hear. Voices that can only be silenced with the sleep that comes from strong liquor or a drug filled needle in the vein.

I stare at him briefly and in that moment, a thousand memories flood my mind, breaking a mental dam. I see Radar daring to hope—daring to dream that he can escape this circle of lunacy known as Cypress Point. I hear him scream and I remember the screams and chants of young girls and adults who watched him play in this very park—his Empire.

I hear him scream, and I know all of that is gone. The Evangelist has taken the light out of his eyes. The Rhyme is gone from his mind and the fire is out of his blood, as my father used to say about the mentally ill.

Poor Radar.

The Evangelist smiles wide, showing all of her snuff and blood stained teeth. She eats the dreams and hopes of children. She is the spoiler, the car accident, the split second mothers turn their backs while small helpless children pull pots of hot water off stoves and irreversibly mar themselves.

I spit in her face without thinking, reacting on pure reflex. What she has done to Radar is as much sacrilege as cursing the Holy Ghost. Once done, I take a deep breath and hold it, my small chest full of pride soaked air—whether she kills me in this moment or not is inconsequential.

I ain't no punk.

"Forget you, you old wicked skank! We're getting out of Cypress and there's nothing you can do to stop us!" I say this defiantly, hoping that Radar will come to his senses and help me. Hoping that he will realize that flat dead basketball is not the holder of the magic—he is. But Radar continues to howl in indescribable pain. His mind is wafting on a cloud of smoke and shadow. In his arms he holds his dead savior and he mourns. The umbilical cord that fastened him to hope has been cut. Samson has been shorn, a pitiful thing to be ridiculed and mocked now.

I run to him, to harness him back to the womb of reality, but he is too far gone. His mind is now hidden deep in some hallucinatory cavern. Radar believes the Evangelist's threats.

I've always viewed her as a grownup bully and after what she did to Radar's ball, I know it is true.

My brothers said the only way to deal with bullies is to stand right up to them. Right up to them and spit in their faces, because bullies only pick on the weak and the helpless and in the immortal words of my brother Mookie, "Ain't no punks in our family!"

"Ain't no punks in our family!" I shout again, swallowing fear and anger. Feeling them combine to make a deadly concoction that slides down my throat in a hard lump and settles deep in the pit of my soul.

Radar is my best friend in the whole world and the Evangelist has made a deadly enemy out of me this day.

She takes a quick step toward me (step? No— a quick glide). The smile still etched across her face. The wind moves with her. She controls the breeze. When she speaks the crickets stop chirping and a dead heavy silence soughs in the air.

"You're Eliza and Uriah Johnson's youngest, aren't you?" she asks rhetorically. There isn't a person in Cypress she doesn't know—from vixen to visitor. A cold chill goes through me when she says my parent's names—especially my father's.

"Yes," I reply, trying to keep the fear-anger down. She's a bully! She's a bully and all bullies are cowards. All bullies are cowards and there ain't no punks in my family!

"Well, little Johnson seed. There is a custom in this country that the youngest son doesn't go off to war, has to be there to carry on the family name and so forth. I gave the eulogy over your father and I'm pretty sure I'll do the same for you!"

"Don't talk about my father," I fume at her. My father died when I was twelve years old. He worked himself to death in the Evangelist's casket factory. "Don't ever let his name past your lips. I mean it! I—"

"SILENCE!" she screams. Her voice booms like thunder and echoes all around me. Her voice feels like a living thing, pushing the air into my head. All of the other natural sounds in the park cease. My heart skips a beat causing my pulse to race like an out of sync drum and it takes several seconds for it to regain its normal cadence.

"I've had just about enough of you! Johnson's little boy...so impudent just like his father. He thought he was special, too! You have brothers, don't you?" she rubs her chin and the blood on her teeth glows in the waning light. The street lamps are now coming on, accentuating the grin and vicious look on her face.

"Don't threaten my brothers! My brothers could kick your ass and not lose a minute's sleep over it! They could bust your flat ass and watch the ball game right after!" I scream so *loud my head shakes like a tuning fork. All I can see is the white of her gown. That gown seems to fill everything now and somewhere in the far distance, I am aware of a basketball hoop with my best friend weeping inconsolably under it. His mind has shattered like the fine porcelain plates my mother only takes out on Christmas.*

"Is that so? Well, perhaps they could and perhaps they can't. I'll let the future be the judge of that one. Okay, little Ezekiel Johnson. You want to leave Cypress so badly I'll let you. Just don't ever come back here, because the Wheel of the World spins when I tell it to! The Axle of the planet tilts in my direction. All things, both great and small serve the Evangelist!"

Her voice drones on in my ear, paralyzing me. Radar howls in anguish and I can feel things in the wind biting me, inside my mind; eating away at my determination. The biting things laugh at me. They keep repeating the same thing, "The Wheel of the World!" I try to fight them, but God help me the pain is so great. The pain is everywhere and I can't focus. The biting things are inside me and they pick and bite from the center out. I hear laughter, over my screams and over the screams of Radar. It's the Evangelist laughing, she's laughing at me and her eyes are spinning around and around like two giant windmills.

"The Wheel of the World...the Wheel of the World...the Wheel of the World...the..."

"—Wheel—Watch the *wheel*, man!" Tamara screamed turning the steering wheel just in time enough to keep us from being formally introduced to an oak tree. I fought to regain control of the car as we barely missed the tree and slipped into a thick brush of weeds. The headlights were blocked and entangled with vines and foliage. We were traveling blind in total darkness. The Mercedes slipped off the non-road onto a lower embankment. Tamara pulled her feet up in the seat and covered her face. Thick branches whipped the windshield as the car bucked and turned like a wild steer. My body shivered in waves trying to shake the vision of the Evangelist out of my head. I could still smell her in the car—that sickening scent of her perfume that barely masked a rotten, potted-meat smell. I could hear her telling me to never come back to Cypress Point. I gripped the steering wheel with all of my might, fighting to regain control. Tamara now had her face completely covered, crying in her blouse. I tried to stop the car, but we were on too steep a hill. Lightning flashed across the sky, giving me a brief look at the dense forest that I was banging the Mercedes into.

Good thing I took out the full insurance plan! The Wheel of the World...what was it about the Wheel of the World?

The Wheel of the World turns for the Just and Wicked alike!

I don't know how that came to me, or where I first heard that, but it calmed me down and somehow it slowed the car down. I felt the tires grip the road and the wheels were back in tune with the steering column. Also, that smell was gone. Thick green leaves draped the windshield, brushing it like the rough-buff of the local car wash. I floored the gas pedal and felt the Benz leave the ground. We soared through the air and all I could think about was the line that just popped into my head like the suddenly found piece of a stubborn jigsaw puzzle.

The Wheel of the World turns for the Just and Wicked alike!

The car landed in a clearing, just as soft as rain. The road ahead was bright and unobstructed. I continued up this path. Tamara slowly climbed out of the fetal position as she noticed the smooth ride.

I cut Sade back on, letting her ask me if it was a crime that she still wanted me and that she wanted me to want her too, because her love was wider than Victoria Lake and taller than the Empire State.

The storm finally let up and I saw an old weather-beaten handwritten sign that read:

Welcome to CYPRESS POINT! Come stay awhile

I didn't drive the car here...the car drove me here!

I slowed to a crawl as I approached the sign. Tamara let out a low moan that released the fear. We squeezed each other's hands without saying a word and I drove past the sign.

"The Lord is my shepherd, I shall not want..." Tamara started. I have never considered myself a religious man (after that incident in church you'd have to drag me screaming and kicking to go back) but I whispered the Psalm along with her. The wind blew violently; I could feel the car shake and shimmy, the windows rattled. I pulled over, thinking we were in the middle of the tornado that Tamara spoke about earlier. She kept quoting the Psalm.

"And I will dwell in the house of the Lord, forever."

As soon as she finished, the wind died.

"Amen," I mumbled. A chill went through me, as I realized those exact words were engraved on the front of Evangelist Washington's funeral home.

"We're home," Tamara gasped.

"Yes, we're home. *The soil of our dreams and the roots of our nightmares.*"

Chapter III: The Black Lights

We drove about a quarter mile before I saw anything that was vaguely familiar. My memory was worse than I suspected. Buildings that I could have *sworn* were on the left-hand side of the street were now on the right hand side. And it appeared that the street signs had been reversed on some blocks; instead of Wickens Avenue facing Chandler with the house numbers going *up*, it now faced Vine Street where the numbers went down.

The fruit stand now faced the poolroom instead of the cleaners, and old man Shelton's pawnshop—which was *supposed* to be in between the Fish-n-Chip restaurant and Harry's Hoot-n-Hooch (the local name for the Cypress' cheapest liquor store) was now all the way at the opposite corner of the block.

All eyes followed the Benz as it cruised down the block. I could see second and third floor windows open as people popped their heads out to stare. A group of teenagers all covered in the same color bandana gawked at me. I pulled the car up to the curb and parked. Exiting the car, I searched up and down the street. I stared back at all of it oddly; something was wrong. Tamara looked at me, worried.

"Why park here? You know anybody on this street?"

"No, but let me ask you something—did Mr. Greenway's fruit stand used to face the poolroom?"

"Wha—"

"This block is all wrong! I mean everything is here, but it's not in its right place! Look!" I pointed to the street signs and buildings drawing invisible lines with my finger, oblivious to smirks and stares around me.

"You've been away from Cypress for a long time?" she asked while we walked up the block.

"Six years. I left the year my oldest brother was killed. He died on this corner over two dollars." I pointed to the corner just ahead of us. I hadn't noticed that I'd pulled up to block J.B died on until that very moment. "Something's not right...this isn't the way the block was—"

"What happened to you back there? I mean when the car went out of control."

"I had some sort of flashback...I was remembering the Evangelist...in the park. Radar...*she blew up his basketball.*" I rubbed my brow and frowned. My head hurt badly now, too many memories—too quickly.

This is all wrong! The block is turned inside out, like a mirror image! No—like a deck of cards that's been reshuffled! The wheel of the world has turned and the dust has settled wrong!

"I remember Radar. He was a good basketball player. Too bad about him using drugs. You don't look so good. Maybe you had a bad piece of pie at that diner. You wanna go and see if the fruit stand has some Pepto-Bismol?"

"No...not my stomach—my head! I just need a second to take all of this in. We're going into the poolroom; somebody there'll know my brothers. They'll tell me how they died."

I wanted to hear it from a stranger first. I wanted to be able to shush my mother and tell her I knew how her six boys went home to Jesus—to spare her having to recite whatever the story was. I wanted to tell her not to worry, because the Prodigal Son had returned home and for her to pack her things and we'd leave Cypress Point behind us forever.

"Don't go in there mentioning anything about the Evangelist or what you just told me. Let's keep that between us, okay? Cause I can't do for you *here* what I did for you at the diner, okay?" There was an underlining message in her statement. Part command, part pleading.

"I didn't *think* I looked *stupid,*" I sarcastically replied. "I didn't need you to tell me tha—"

The word stuck in my throat as I stepped on the curb. The same curb J.B was shot to death on. Suddenly the air was full of his smell—Newport cigarettes and CK1 cologne. It was as if someone had taken a paintbrush and redid the scenery. The corner was empty when I walked up to it, but when I stood in a certain spot—

—The spot where he died. The spot where his lifeless body collapsed, cold and removed from this world—

I could see him standing on that corner, shooting dice against the side of the building. His fedora tipped to the side, totally covering one eye like a patch. I could *see* him, standing there looking at nothing and yet seeing everything.

—Cool ass J.B. My mother's firstborn, my big brother—

43

I could see the children playing in the street, little girls turning Double-Dutch and boys chasing each other up and down the block. Three guys are shooting dice and J.B had all but cleaned them out. Somewhere in the distance, a boom box blared with Evelyn Champagne King singing *I'm in Love.* It is mid-march but spring has kissed the streets early with its warm breath.

"You gonna play em or lay em? We ain't got all damned day!" one guy shouts. He is serious, but there's no malice in his voice.

"I'm gonna do whatever I feel like doin! *Anything else would be uncivilized!*" J.B replies, using his best British accent. The guys around him laugh and pass a brown-bagged bottle between them. He rolls the dice and everyone moans. He has won again.

"You cheatin!" someone barks. A loud fierce looking man picks the dice up and studies them suspiciously. "You cheatin an I'm not payin!"

"You payin and that's the end of it. I don't want to have to whip you over two dollars, but it's the principle of the matter. If I let you get away with it, then anybody'll try me. If you ain't got the whole two dollars now, I'll take something less, but you'll owe me the difference."

There is no fear in his voice as he speaks but every nerve in his body is alive—*aware.* He stares the man in his eyes. My brother is a tiger, the streets are a jungle and in the jungle, *the tiger is the last one to starve.*

"I ain't givin you nuthin! You cheated!" the man spits. His pulse is racing, his eyes twitchy. He's dangerous, because he's scared. Never leave a person scared of you; J.B has always stressed that to me. Leave them *respecting* you, but not scared. Let them fear the consequences of crossing you, but don't let them fear *you.* A scared person will kill you.

My brother remains calm. His breathing is slow and steady. The man's eyes dart back and forth in a sweeping motion, but J.B locks in on him and only him. He reaches into his waist, but my brother has already anticipated this move. Before the man can get his hand *near* his gun J.B has his out, aimed at the man's head.

"Street rules say I kill you now. Street rules say never pull a gat unless you're gonna use it. Now, c'mon, think about it! Is two dollars worth dying over?" He disarms the man, pulling his gun out of his waistband and tucking it into his pocket.

"I'll just keep this until you pay me my money." J.B turns to walk away. He is sixty dollars and one gun richer for his efforts. His would be victim is shivering in fear.

Never leave anyone scared of you!

Everything is quiet; someone has turned down the boom box and the girls have stopped their jump rope chanting. There is a pregnant pause, the only indication the streets are about to give birth to a deadly violence.

Across the street, a charcoal-gray Electra 225 with dark tinted windows peels off, burning rubber and snapping the air with a piercing screeching wail. J.B turns and in one fluid motion fires at the car, hitting the driver's side of the windshield, shattering it. The report of the pistol echoes throughout the block. Now there is random chaos, children scream and run in a blind panic. Mothers are calling for their children with soul splitting cries of worry. There is going to be a death—of that there is no doubt. The only question now is *who* will be the Grim Reaper's choice?

J.B is oblivious to the screams and shrieks around him. His eyes are focused on one thing—the Electra 225. Although the windshield has collapsed from the bullet, he still cannot see into it. The inside of the car is cloaked in darkness—even though it's broad daylight. The color seems to be bleeding out of the street. The car is somehow sucking the tint out of the world.

This odd occurrence serves as J.B's undoing. The guy he took the gun off of has a back up piece. He draws his weapon and with a calm that contradicts his nervous jittery demeanor, fires at J.B.

J.B whips around, the bullet barely grazes him. His eyes are still glued on the Electra 225, although it has not moved since having its windshield shattered. Pulling the other gun from his waistband, both pistols in hand, he proceeds to fire at both the car and the dice thrower.

The next series of moves happen in a surreal fashion. The colors have now been washed down to a bland tone nearly matching the car's gray hue. J.B weaves and dodges bullets with the grace of a Chinese Acrobat. He fires simultaneously at the man and the car's engine. He strikes the man in the face; the bullet lodges just above his left cheekbone. I see the man's head fly back in a coned shower spray of blood. Convinced that the man has gone the way of all flesh and is no longer a threat, J.B turns and repeatedly fires at the car. The bullets speed into the blackness of the open windshield and land with a dull thump.

There is a look of sheer determination in my brother's face. He empties both guns into the car's blackness and for what seems like an eternity the block becomes silent again.

Then it happens.

The inside of the Electra 225 pulses and the darkness from its interior spreads out in black splayed tentacles. There is no noise; just an eerie silence as everyone—children and adults alike all instinctively look away from the car. The black beams pierce J.B like bullets, but instead of imbedding themselves in his flesh they pass silently through him. His body is a riddled pincushion. He looks two-dimensional—like a piece of Swiss cheese. The corner is drenched in his blood and the Electra 225 drives away.

I see him fall, his eyes an eternal blank stare of night. His body lands with a hard thud. There are no shell casings from the car, no evidence that he was shot. My eldest brother lay there, looking as if someone took a giant paper-hole puncher and went to work on him. I could see daylight through him.

He had more holes in him than a sieve.

The beams of black light crushed his bones into a powdery, almost pancake-like mixture. If not for his clothes holding some semblance of his corporal form together, he could've been washed off the street with an ordinary garden hose.

"No bullets," I mumbled. "The black-lights. The black-lights killed him!" Upon hearing myself say the words *black-lights*, I snapped out of the trance-like vision and found myself lying on the ground, in the exact spot that J.B died on.

"*Will you get up from there!*" Tamara said through clenched teeth. A small crowd had gathered around me—children mostly, snickering and trying (not too hard) to hold in their laughs.

I ignored them; the vision of what happened to my brother was still fresh in my mind. It played over and over again like a haunting refrain. Like a really disturbing horror movie that you can't shake out of your head.

I stood up and brushed myself off, looking around in a wide-eyed panic.

"It wasn't bullets. It was the black-lights that killed him." I said this aloud, but to no one in particular. I stared at the ground that soaked up J.B's blood like a sponge, still seeing flecks of his flesh; wondering what the black-lights were and who was driving that spooky car.

"*Think about where you're at, man! This is Cypress Point. You're putting us in dangerous in a situation! You're...*"

Tamara whined on and on, but her voice became low and insignificant. I was more interested in what the corner had to tell me. I heard voices. Low, whispery, but they came in clear and unobtrusive—like elevator music at the department store.

Voices telling me to—

Tamara shook me and the voices fell silent.

"*Are you with me now?*" she asked. There was a look of worry and exasperation in her face and I understood why. Here she was, getting out of a Benz with a guy and I suddenly start babbling about black-lights after writhing around on the ground like a drug-addicted moron.

"Yeah," I grumbled holding my head. The crowd around me dispersed. I guess they thought I was drunk and once my lady friend got me up to my feet I was all right and therefore the show was over. "I guess you want to get away from me as quick as possible. I just want you to know that nothing like this ever happens to me in New York." I expected Tamara to take me up on my offer and walk away. After all, if I kept flipping out like this I was a severe liability.

"I know that," she said and touched my cheek gently. "You still wanna go in the poolroom?"

"Yeah." I was glad she didn't walk away.

We could hear the raucous laughter from three doors away. The poolroom was a combination bar and fish joint. You could shoot a game of billiards, get drunk and eat all in the same place. We walked in and I heard a cacophony of dirty jokes and boisterous laughter mixed with the thunderous cracks of cue balls breaking the pyramid of pool-balls. They almost spoke English here.

"—Main, you shoulda seen the way I freaked that girl! I melted her cheese!"

"—I had two a them! Freakin' them both at the same time!"

"— I had ta buss tha' candy-boy upside his haid ova a swalla a beer! Ain't dat sumpthin!"

"—So I gets her inna room an come find out she gotta bigger joint than me!"

The jukebox blared.

This was the type of place I had frequented as a child (although if asked prior to that moment I would've had no recollection of it) bringing J.B a pack of cigarettes, or running an errand for someone else to make myself a dollar or two.

Cigarette smoke suspended overhead and hung like a low cloud. Tamara and I made our way to the bar. I felt a lot more comfortable in this place than I did in the diner. Although the reactions I received were the same, no one could accuse me of being a *foreigner.*

A very large heavyset woman walked up and asked me for a light with enough bass in her voice to make Isaac Hayes envious. Tamara hissed at her (hissed—just like the sound a cat makes when it's angry) and the woman walked off. It took me a moment to gain my bearings from that and another moment still when I realized the woman was no woman at all—but a very ugly man in a dress.

I made a mental note to thank Tamara later.

I raised a hand to get the bartender's attention, which was unnecessary since all eyes were on us since we walked in.

"*What can I get ferya?*" the bartender asked, wiping the bar with a towel that had seen better days.

What the hell, I thought. *At least he didn't call me fancy youngin*!

I was about to order when Tamara stepped in front of me and pinched me lightly on my hip.

"Him an me want two gin and tonics, lime twisters." Again she spoke with the Cypress accent, only this time softer, more natural. The tone and inflection of her voice was steady and calm. Nothing like the clarion call to war she made back at the diner. She spoke as if we'd been in this poolroom together a thousand times, surprised that the bartender would even address me directly.

After all, I was a *CYP—ress* man.

She dusted off the barstool and I sat down. I would have to remember to let Tamara do all of the talking and that was hard—not because I'm chauvinistic, but because I am a *thinking* man (at least I *think* I am.) and having someone always speak for you is like having someone *think* for you. Here I was at a bar, and it was considered unmanly for me to order my own drink when I had a woman with me.

Sitting there in that moment an epiphany hit me. I suddenly understood why the women did all of the talking. Why the women in Cypress were the equivalent of the Secretary of State or ambassador.

The Evangelist.

In my graduating high school class there were only three boys: Radar, Neil Brachman, and myself. And this was the norm. Girls learned to read and write, to count money and to pay the bills. Men learned to go to work in factories (which is what Neil did immediately after graduation), hustle, pimp, or sling drugs. But it was the women in Cypress who went to court to speak up for the men, the women who made the payment agreements with the utility companies. The women who either started or diffused the violence that plagued the town like a leech.

All because the Evangelist ordered it that way. I don't remember when she did. It was probably many years before I was born, and they don't teach you that in weekly or Sunday school, but I knew it was true.

Tamara sat down on my left and gently rubbed my thigh under the bar. I didn't know if it was a sign that she was feeling amorous or a cue to observe something that was happening.

I quickly scanned everyone in our direct vicinity, there were at least fifty people surrounding us, some simply chatting, some trying to get to the bar to place their orders, and some with nothing more on their minds than to test me.

The bartender brought our drinks and sat them in front of me. I reached into my wallet and pulled out a twenty, closed the wallet and laid the money on the bar by Tamara. Her lips curled in a slight grin.

I was finally getting the message.

Tamara picked up the money and handed it to the bartender. She then picked up the drinks and sipped from both glasses. A look of concern came over her face as she took a moment to examine the glasses carefully. She gave me one glass and kept the other for herself. I sipped from my glass and it took all of my strength to keep from reeling back on my heels at how strong it was. It was like drinking pure fire. My throat burned and pulsed in flaming waves of pain. My chest locked up on me and I had barely swallowed a good sip. My top lip quivered and I could feel sweat bead in my scalp, oiling my hair. I looked down into the glass and saw that the lime had curled into a shriveled worm-like thing. The alcohol had bled all of the green out it until it was a sickly jaundiced yellow slug floating in my glass.

As strong as my drink was, I knew Tamara had taken the stronger one. I remained silent although I wanted to reach across the counter, snatch the bartender and break his ass bone into three equal parts. Whatever was in that glass had to be well over a hundred and fifty proof. My eyes watered and it took a moment for me to catch my breath, but somehow I managed to do this without moving. I was staring at myself in the mirror behind the bar and my expression had only slightly wavered.

Tamara's hadn't wavered at all.

"I'll be danged and hanged! Last man I saw that took a sip a the pantha piss had ta have a kidney removed! Ain't that right, Buford?" The man on the right hand side spoke. His voice was a high-pitched screech that required a full burst of breath for each and every syllable he spoke—the obvious result of too much malt liquor and severely diminished lungs. He spoke in a slow and labored nasal cadence that reminded me of the old smooth pimps I would see my brothers imitate sometimes.

"Last cat had a big ole triangle head, too! Look like one a them box-head boys from Beacon Street! Ain't that right, Buford? He had little hands, but a big ass—ass like a Molly girl. Ass was so big he almost got the wood put to his doo-doo maker. Matter a fact— his ass was bigger than Lucille's. Ain't that right, Buford? He came up in here and took a sip a pantha piss and got down right indignant! Ain't that right, Buford? He got his ass kicked up in here that day, though. Me and my man Buford had to regulate the ballistics on that box-head farm-boy! Ain't that right, Buford? "

Buford was a large man who sat on the opposite side of the man who spoke and merely nodded when he heard his name and went back to his drink. The only thing holding Buford up was the will to finish what was in his glass. Other than that, nothing else really seemed to matter.

"My name Slim-Ron, the poor hoe's don. This my man Buford Thrilla the ladies' killa." The man held up his right hand for me to shake. There was a badly tarnished silver ring adorning his pinky. He had a crude but jovial way about him. He reminded me of the class clown, the guy who was invited to every party because he was guaranteed to make a fool out of himself and no matter how ugly the girls were, no matter how bad the food and the music, there would always be Slim-Ron to talk about the next day.

"I'm E.J—Ezekiel Johnson." I don't know what made me introduce myself like that. No one ever called me E. J, except—

—Except for J.B...

You be better than good at it! You hear me, E. J? You bout the only one with a real chance, so you be better than good at it!

That was the last thing I remembered him saying to me, right before he left to go and meet his friends on that corner and he—

"Pleased to meetcha. You in Cypress Point! Passin boots or layin' down roots?"

—died.

"A little of both, I guess. I'm here for the funeral."

Everything got quiet. It wasn't sudden; there were still a few random sounds of pool balls crashing into each other, but the momentum of their crashing was a lot less intense. I was aware in that moment that everyone was listening to me. I knew I'd draw a lot of attention to myself, but I expected to drum up a conversation with the bartender. Bartenders knew everything that went on and would most likely be my best source of information. Normally, the bartender would ask me all of the questions, where I was staying and so forth. He would do this with the smooth and subtle grace of a con artist. But the bartender simply placed the drinks down and walked to the far end of the bar.

"What funeral might that be, friend?" Slim-Ron (the poor hoe's don) asked suspiciously. "I don't know nuthin bout no funeral. You knowed bout a funeral, Buford?"

"Naw," Buford mumbled in a deep voice, the complete opposite from Slim-Ron's whiney falsetto. "Don't know nuthin bout no funeral."

The air around me became sharp as the situation took a drastic turn for the worse. People who had money riding on pool games abruptly abandoned the tables and walked over to me. I didn't think my voice carried that far, but apparently it had. Either that, or someone close to where I sat gave everyone the cue to approach. I could feel Tamara's hand on my thigh. She was right; she couldn't get me out of this one like she did at the diner. This was real and the patrons played for keeps.

You in Cypress Point! Passin boots or layin down roots?

I stood up, took a healthy gulp of the *pantha-piss*, reached into my pocket pulled out a twenty-dollar bill and held it high over my head.

"This is E.J.! J.B, Ritchie, Danny-boy, Tom-Tom, Mookie, and Petey-Wheaty were my brothers. I'm just getting home and I got twenty-dollars worth of drinks for any man who can tell me what happened to them!"

I looked in the wall-length mirror behind the bar and saw people dropping their heads, covering their faces and going back to their games. This, I was not prepared for. I was sure that at least dozen shriveled liver alcoholics would give me the bum's rush for the money. A guy announcing free drinks and no one takes advantage?

Not very likely in Cypress. Not very likely at all.

I slowly slinked back to the barstool and put my money on top of the bar—almost daring someone to claim it. What had my brothers gotten into that no one would want to talk about it—even for money?

"Now do you know which funeral?" I turned to Slim-Ron and scoffed through tightly drawn lips. Slim-Ron looked around nervously; his eyes kept darting back to the twenty. Although the poolroom went back to its usual level of chaotic noise, there was something different; I felt that people were discreetly watching Tamara and I. Listening. The bartender was at the other end of the bar, but every time my eyes met his, he would hurriedly look away. No one wanted eye contact with me, but everyone was secretly staring.

"I can't talk to you here. You're gonna have to meet me later and make sure you don't tell nobody. Bring the money with you!" Slim-Ron said in a voice so low I barely heard him. *"Meet me in the back alley, in about ten minutes. Get up and walk out this place and act like me and you ain't got no dealins!"* Slim-Ron took my drink and in one gulp finished it. He then got up off the barstool and walked over to one of the pool tables.

"I got next game," he whined in that snively chalkboard-raked voice of his. He placed a dollar on the edge of the pool

52

table took a cue-stick off the rack. Someone mumbled something and gestured in my direction. Slim-Ron merely shrugged and chalked his cue-stick.

Tamara looked at me in the bar mirror and motioned to the door. I nodded slightly and after about three minutes, we left the poolroom.

On the way out, I noticed that Buford Thrilla (*the ladies' killa*) stared at Slim-Ron with a cold hard intelligence. It was a look that startled me, because not even two minutes before Buford looked like your average alcoholic simpleton—the type of guy who could only entertain two or three thoughts at one time: drinking, using the bathroom and getting something to eat.

The primal man's urges.

I walked around the corner to the back alley of the poolroom and waited for Slim-Ron. Tamara quickly followed behind me. The back alley was filled with empty liquor and wine bottles. There were crates piled five and six feet high. In the far back of the alley a solid brick wall separated this street from the next. The shadow of the building cast the back wall into perpetual night. The smell of spoiled food and decomposed cats and rats stapled the stink to the air. I covered my nose and fought the urge to vomit, but Tamara didn't seem bothered by it at all.

Whatever happened to my brothers must've been *really* bad for no one in the poolroom to speak on it. I kept trying to think of a plausible explanation for everyone's reluctance but my mind drew nothing but blanks. Their deaths would have been the biggest news in Cypress Point since…*well,* since ever!

I paced anxiously back and forth waiting for him. The minutes crawled past from five to ten to fifteen.

"Where is that jerk? He said ten minutes!" I said angrily.

"I know! Something doesn't feel right out here."

"Tell me about it! Since we got off the plane things have been getting weirder and weirder! Why would he have to meet me back here to tell me something? What could've happened that no one wants to talk about it? I mean my brothers were known all through Cypress Point!"

"I know. It's pretty creepy. Let's get back inside."

"Give me a minute. That *pantha piss* is playing havoc with my bladder." I walked deeper into the alley, being careful where I stepped. Hypodermic needles and thick cheesy goop swallowed the ground. I should have held it; I should have waited until I got back into the poolroom and used the men's room there. But my bladder was about to explode. When I felt I was far enough away from Tamara to be polite, I unzipped and gave the back wall a good washing.

"*Hurry up!*" Tamara whispered. "*This place gives me the—OH MY GOD! HELP, HELP! SOMEBODY CALL THE AMBULANCE!*"

I turned to see what she was screaming about. The back of the alley was suddenly flooded with light. The sun just peeked from behind the clouds. Tamara's mouth hung open in a wide O. Her face looked pale and weak. She was staring at something behind me.

My bladder emptied (her screams put the faucet on full blast) and I zipped up and turned toward the wall. I looked up and saw it.

Slim-Ron.

He was naked, suspended about twelve feet above us and nailed to the back wall in the crucifix position. His eyes had been gouged out of their sockets and his tongue had been torn out, replaced with a twenty-dollar bill; his throat had been slit from ear-to-ear and someone had gutted him, pulling his intestines out like rope. There was a sign over his head written in blood that read:

SLIM RON THE POOR HOE'S DON!

KING OF THE FOOLS.

Other than the sign, there was no blood.

Tamara tore out of the alley in a blind panic covering her mouth. I stayed, looking up at Slim Ron wondering just what did he have to tell me that was so bad someone had to kill him.

Slim-Ron was a small man; he stood at least five-four, five-five at the most. He couldn't have weighed more than a hundred and twenty pounds. Still, it would have taken at least two really strong men on ladders to carry him up there and pin him to the wall like that. His hands and feet were nailed with railroad spikes embedded deep into the brick. Only a nail gun could have drove those spikes that far.

And then there was the blood, where was it? The wounds that were inflicted on this poor simpleton should have made pools and pools of blood and yet other than the neatly painted sign there wasn't any. The twenty-dollar bill in his mouth was an obvious warning to any one else; I was not to be spoken to. Whoever killed Slim Ron did it to make an example of him.

That would explain why he was stripped naked, to humiliate him. He had broken a code or a promise by agreeing to talk to me. His words kept going through my mind: *I can't talk to you here.*

His intestines swung back and forth like an out of sync pendulum, dangling in the breeze. The corners of his mouth were frozen in an eternal sneer. It was an obscene sight, seeing a human being hung like a piece of meat in a butcher's freezer.

I stared at him wondering if anyone would mourn Slim-Ron. I stood, wondering what he wanted to be when he was young; what were his dreams and hopes, his goals and aspirations. Wondering if he had any idea when he woke up this morning he would wind up stripped naked, butchered and spiked to a brick wall.

There were so many things that didn't add up, but I kept searching for the logical explanation. I thought about when the Evangelist caused Radar to lose his mind and I spat in her face and stood right in front of her. I did that to show her, Radar and myself that she was just a person. Not God, not Jesus, not an angel, not even Abraham or one of the prophets.

Just a person.

A pang of guilt went through me staring at Slim-Ron. I had not been in town an hour, and I had caused someone to die horribly. My mouth dried up and my hands became slick with sweat.

Someone killed him as a message to me! If they did this to him, what will they do to me?

The wailing sirens of the ambulance and the police approaching snapped me out of my musings. I turned and saw the crowd from the pool hall standing at the mouth of the alley, but no one came in. Not even Buford, Slim Ron's friend came to see what happened.

"Twenty dollars! The man died over twenty dollars!" I screamed at the crowd. In New York twenty dollars was a twelve-pack of cold beer, and an Instant Scratch-Off Lottery game ticket. Here, it was someone's existence.

"I'm not the same little boy in her yard!" I said, remembering the nightmare on the plane. "You can't scare me away!" I endured the stares and gawks of the onlookers, aware that I probably looked like a raving maniac. After all, my brother had died over *two* dollars so why couldn't Slim Ron die over twenty.

The ambulance had CPVA stenciled across its side and it took me a moment to figure out the letters meant Cypress Point Volunteer Ambulance. The police arrived and politely shoved me out of the way. They brought ladders and a couple of claw hammers (how convenient) and pulled Slim Ron off the wall. His body was quickly placed in a black bag and hauled off. The ambulance attendants worked with about as much medical professionalism as sanitation workers.

The police didn't question anyone, take fingerprints, pictures, or even bother to stop and scratch their heads and say, "*Hey, how'd he get up there?*" For all intents and purposes, they probably ruled his death as a suicide. Two cops carried the ladders back to the police van and one of them ordered the crowd to disperse, because as he so aptly put it, "The show's over, folks!"

I saw Tamara sitting on the car waiting for me. She was visibly shaken, wide-eyed and trembling. Her pampered hair-do now hung in a limp, listless clump over her tear- streaked face.

"You okay?", I asked lighting a cigarette for her. Her hands were shaking too badly to hold the match.

"No, I am not okay. We have to get out of here! You see that don't you? I can't go to the Evangelist now—everyone's seen me with you. She must hate you! She's going to kill anybody who talks to you! Look what she did to that poor man! Imagine what she'll do to me! We hafta go! We gotta get back! We gotta—"

I grabbed and held her tightly. She was hysterical, crying and speaking at the same time. Her words came out in small explosions. The glue of her sanity was slowly losing its grip.

"Now you listen to me and *you listen good*! I know what we just saw is terrible enough, but *some gangsters* killed Slim Ron! Maybe even the same ones who killed my brothers; this is the acceptable, logical, educated person's way of thinking. The Evangelist had nothing to do with it, unless she was down with the gangsters. She might have *ordered* them to do it, but she did not kill him! There is nothing supernatural about Slim-Ron's death."

"You really believe that?" she asked through tear soaked eyes.

"Yes, I really do."

"Then you're as good as dead! If there wasn't anything mystical about his death then answer me this: how did he get past us into the alley? What happened to all of the blood that would've came out his body? How could someone kill him like that so fast? When we left the poolroom he was still in there. Still in there! It didn't take us but a minute to walk around the corner! How—"

"Maybe the moment we left the guys in the poolroom did it! Maybe they opened a backyard door, brought out some ladders and a bunch of them sick twisted fuckers carried him up and power-nailed him to the brick wall! This is scary enough without either of us going off on a tangent!"

She looked around, her body pulsed with waves of fear, but she was starting to calm down. Maybe something that I said penetrated. I held her close to me and gently kissed her cheek.

"Can we get away from here? Can we just go and see your mother?" she whimpered.

"That sounds like a damned good idea!"

I opened the car door on the passenger side for her. As I walked around to the driver's side, I noticed a note under the windshield wiper. Casually I picked it up and put it in my pocket without reading it.

"Don't worry about anything, Tamara. I'm not going to let anyone hurt you. I promise you that."

"Ezekiel, if there's nothing supernatural going on…then why has your behavior been so bizarre since we got here? And what was it you said about the black-lights killing your brother?"

"I know, but there's a logical explanation for everything. I have to hold on to that, because if I don't, I'm just as crazy and just as backwards as everyone else in this town. I'll admit, things are strange here—things have always been weird here, but that doesn't mean it's something mystical."

"You keep telling yourself that shit. Maybe you can convince yourself you're right, but I know there's something here that defies anything natural."

Although it pained me to even contemplate that idea, a part of me knew she was right.

"I believe in the power of the mind. People go to church and claim they receive the Holy Ghost because they've worked themselves into a frenzy. People place a great deal of faith in voodoo workers and nonsense like that. Because they do, it works. The mind is a powerful tool. It's like if you believe something hard enough—you can *make it happen*."

"Did you know that was the same alley your friend Radar was found dead in?"

"No, I didn't. But even that doesn't mean anything. It's just a coincidence."

"*Yeah*, okay."

I started the car and headed for my mother's house. *Mother needs me*, the telegram read.

Chapter IV: The Revelation

I drove around for over a half hour looking for my old building. Nothing made sense. The streets were all backwards; house numbers were now placed at random. Familiar streets now ended early and turned into unknown blocks. All landmarks were displaced.

I pulled up in front of an abandoned building and decided to read the note that was left in the windshield. It was written on a plain white piece of paper and the handwriting was crude but legible. The note read: *Go see the old woman Ophelia. She can explain everything to you. Don't try to talk to anyone else but her. It's death if you do.*

"How much further to your house, man? I want to wash up and change my clothes, not to mention take a nap!"

"Not much further, I think. Not much further at all." I folded the unsigned note and put it back in my pocket.

I relaxed and let the car drive me. I felt the same inner compass pulling me, but I had no idea where I was going.

I remembered that Ophelia was an old bag lady, regarded as crazy by most of Cypress Point. It was said that she got into a terrible argument with the Evangelist and afterwards lost her mind. Prior to this, she was a respected nurse who worked in Cypress General. I saw her once, right before I left Cypress. She reeked of old wine and urine. Her clothes were tatters and her head and feet were wrapped in aluminum foil. She carried a sign around her neck that was written in an indecipherable language. If asked, she would tell you her I.Q was one of the highest in the world and only a person of similar or superior intelligence could understand (or *cipher* as she put it) the message that hung around her neck.

The car pulled me toward Vine Street.

"I *know* you don't live up here!" Tamara said, remarking about the area. Vine Street was a strip of flophouses, transient hotels and abandoned buildings. This area was once full of private houses and thriving small businesses, but there was a terrible storm that flooded out the sewers; the pipes were laid sometime around the end of the nineteenth century and just gave way. The result was a throbbing wave of sewage that flooded everything and imbued the street with a permanent fecal smell. Prominent businesses left after the Evangelist said there was no money in the coffers to repair the area. People lost their jobs and their homes. Soon after property values plummeted, the Evangelist came in and bought everything dirt-cheap. She then razed the houses (in the name of God, of course) and built slum tenements that looked dilapidated a week after they were finished.

The Molina Housing Projects.

This was considered the Red-Light district of Cypress Point. Everything was for sell here; any sick and depraved want or desire could be found and the price negotiated. Men, women, boys, girls, or animals—it didn't matter. This area of Cypress was Babylon, Sodom, and Gomorrah to the *Nth* power.

"No," I answered. Choosing my words carefully, "I'm going to be honest with you. There is something very strange going on. I'm not ready to say supernatural, because I hate that word. But the truth is, I can't find my house. I mean the entire area has changed! Anyway, somebody left me this note on the windshield after we left the alley." I gave her the note and watch her eyes widen as she read it.

"The old crazy lady? You're kidding me, right?"

"No, and for some reason I think once we find her it'll all make sense."

"Do you believe in miracles, Ezekiel?"

"Why?"

"Because we're gonna need one. A really big one."

"My father taught me that prayer changes things."

"Well, I hope he taught you some prayers."

"He taught me to PUSH. *Pray until something happens.*"

———   ———   ———

Traffic was sparse as neon signs glowed and throbbed like an infected tooth, invigorating the predators. I turned off my headlights, trying to remain as inconspicuous as possible. I turned my head in disgust as I saw a child, no older than eleven or twelve, approach a car to solicit the driver. Her hair was dyed platinum blond and hung in Shirley Temple curls. Her face was hard though—a weather beaten canvas of terrors that I couldn't begin to imagine. The driver whispered something to her and she hopped into the passenger side. The driver made a U-turn and pulled into an alley.

"*I hate this fucking town,*" I murmured.

Something, an inner voice perhaps forced me to circle this block at least a dozen times before I saw someone with a squeegee offer to clean my windshield for a dollar. My first impulse was to tell him to take a flying leap and then I recognized him.

"*Buford?*" I whispered.

"*Go up one block and turn into the alley. Don't worry about the car. Nobody'll touch it—MOVE!*"

He never looked at me as he spoke. His eyes swept the street like a broom and his voice was low and rushed—dripping with fear, but rational and intelligent. Nothing like the ignoramus I saw at the poolroom earlier. This was a person of daring and grave risk. Just by speaking to me he could easily wind up like his partner Slim Ron.

As I turned up the alley I thought about one thing—there was something that someone didn't want me to know and would *kill* to keep me from knowing, but there were people willing to risk their lives to tell it to me.

I parked the car in the dark alley, using my headlights for illumination.

"*Don't go out there!*" Tamara whispered, worried.

"It's okay. If they wanted to do something to us, we wouldn't have made it this far."

I stepped out of the car, motioning for her to do the same. The night air was as hard as leather and the alley reeked of body odor and waste. People were strewn about, sleeping in cardboard boxes or make shift shanties. The lethargic look on their faces was enough explanation of what drove them to this horrific state—they just gave up. No one in Cypress Point really had much hope of achieving anything anyway, these people had even less than that.

"Look a here, look a here! Ain't you bout the pretty one!" a voice groaned from the back of the alley. I looked and saw a man walk out of the shadows toward us. His movement stirred the air and the scent almost paralyzed me. The man smelled as if he hadn't bathed in years. As if he wore the same clothes day in and day out, regardless of the weather. The smell was so strong and stifling I had to fight the urge to vomit.

"Yes, you are a pretty one!" he continued toward us. At first I thought he was talking about Tamara, and then when he stepped completely out of the shadows into the dim light I realized he was referring to me.

"Tee-hee-hee! Yes, sir-ree! You a pretty one! A pretty boy like you in a place like this…*anything can happen!*"

He stood about ten feet away from me now, wearing stippled corduroy pants that couldn't hold another stain. He wore a coat made of dirty patches of cloth that looked like it came from car seats, pieces of carpet and upholstery. His shoes were flaps of leather wrapped in filthy duct tape.

But as horrendous as the man's clothes were, the *man* himself was a hundred times worse. His skin was so mottled and blanched I truly could not tell what color he was supposed to be. His nose was bulbous, filled with broken veins that resembled a roadmap to hell. He looked pallid, with lesions covering nearly every square inch of exposed skin.

"Yes, sir!" he said smiling and I saw that his tongue looked like a cancerous sausage in his mouth. "Anything can happen!"

He reached for me and I shrank away from him. I could not breathe the entire time he stood in front of me. The dim overhead streetlight shone in my face when he moved toward me.

"Wait a minute!" he gasped. "You're Mr. Uriah's son! You're his youngest son!" The change that came over him was astounding. One second he had the smirk of a lecherous pervert, the next he was shaking in fear. His jaw trembled. He was trying to say something but couldn't get his mouth to form the words.

"I'm so sorry, sir. It's a jest I play sometimes. I'm really harmless! I am! Please fer gimme! Please!" Tears welled in his cyst covered eyes and fell in copper tinged streams down his dappled face. "*Could a man like you find it in your heart to fergive a miserable creature like me?*"

"No…*no harm done!*" I gasped trying not to inhale. "Just let us go!"

"*Ri-ri-right away, sir!*" he said stepping back. "Although I would be honored if you let me sing a song for you. I'll stay downwind as to not offend you. I would be truly honored, sir. *In memory of your father.*"

Before I could answer he started singing. A strong beautiful voice emerged from that blister filled mouth. He sung *The Last Mile of the Way*, an old gospel song that was one of my father's favorites. The man's voice was as clear as a bell, with a range that would put any professional singer to shame. His voice was so stunning that I was moved to tears.

"How could," I wheezed, woozy from not only the stench but at how truly beautiful his voice sounded. "How could a man with your obvious talent live like this?"

"Ah, that's the rub of it, sir! Mine is indeed a tale of woe. I know what I look like to you, young Ezekiel. But I can assure you that I was not always like this—"

"We don't have time to hear this, Ezekiel! Let's get out of here," Tamara rushed.

"I want to hear this. I want to know. Continue," I told him.

"I once owned a club not too far from this street here. It was somewhat successful in that I sang and people from all over Cypress would come to hear me. I met a woman and fell in love, we were ready to have a child. The world seemed to hold nothing but good things back then, Ezekiel. I can tell you now that I have loved and I have felt love as wide and as deep as the sky above us. I had the world on a string then," he chuckled and wiped his lips with the back of his gnarled hand.

"The club grew popular. I bought a new car. House. All of the trappings of success. Then the Evangelist forbade me to ever see my love or my baby again. No reason. Just that it was God's will. She told me if I tried she would kill me and them. Soon afterwards the great flood came and ruined this area...and I guess I just got caught in the shit storm when it hit."

"What's your name?" I asked him.

"Don't rightly remember my given name, sir. Most people here call me Pickle on account of my nose, my condition and my drinkin when I can get it."

I still had the twenty that I offered Slim Ron in my shirt pocket. I gave it to him.

"Thank you, sir!" he said bowing his head. "I'll be on my way now. You have this poor wretch's gratitude for all eternity."

"What the hell was that about?" Tamara asked.

"Beats me! You would never think that a guy like that could sing that well! Man! If he could only get a hot shower, some medical treatment and—"

"People ain't necessarily here because they have to be, Ezekiel. A lot of them messed their lives up and chose to be here. Good thing you didn't let him touch you. He looked like a wet leper."

"You don't think he really had leprosy, do you? I mean in this day and age? It's curable you know! This isn't the ancient bible days where you just discard lepers to a colony!"

"You're in Cypress Point, remember?"

I didn't comment. We walked though the alley, past all the other cardboard box inhabitants. They regarded us impassively; to them I was just another customer. A small emaciated boy, no older than about ten, walked up and led me by the hand down the stairs in the back of the alley. I held Tamara's hand and led her. It took my eyes a few moments to adjust to the dark, but the boy maneuvered the alley with a deft ease.

The stairway led to a basement. We were in total darkness now; not even the outlines of shadows were visible. The boy stopped me and cut on a small pen-sized flashlight, pointing out places in the floor that had totally given away, revealing a sub-cellar beneath.

"*Dough step on nana open pawts*," he ordered.

"Where are you taking us?" Tamara asked. Fear and disdain carried in her voice.

"*Ne'er you mine. The* lady *wantsta see him.*"

We followed in his footsteps, making sure we only stepped where *he* stepped. We walked past rows of doors, each engraved with a strange symbol. One in particular intrigued me; it seemed to glow in the low light. "*What language is this*?" I asked, tracing the symbol. The boy snatched my hand away with a speed and power that contradicted his small frame. He gripped my wrist so hard I could feel the bones in my hand crunch together. My fingertips grew cold from the lack of blood flow.

"*Dough touch nuffin! Dough ask questions you ain't ready foe answers to.*"

His eyes twinkled and scowled at me. I could've sworn his pupils opened and closed in slits—like a cat or a snake. He released my hand and I quickly massaged the flesh in an attempt to get the blood flowing again. He opened a door that led to an unfathomable darkness. There was a cold, deep, unnatural feeling about what was through that opened door.

"*Go in there. She'll be to see you when she ready.*"

"I'm not going in there!" Tamara said sternly and I agreed with her. This was the type of darkness that made *grown men* afraid of the dark. The boy shone the penlight into it and the dark *ate* the puny beam of light. The dark seemed solid.

"Now you listen to me—"

The boy shoved both of us through the door with one hand and slammed it behind us. Tamara held me so tight I thought my ribs would crack. I was sure the boy had sprained my wrist. I looked around, but there was nothing to see.

"Is there anyone in here?" I asked, trying to keep some semblance of sanity about me. The words came out in damp muffled notes. The darkness smothered the sound as well as the light.

"Tamara, you still have those matches?"

"Yeah!" She reached into her purse and lit a match. I saw the sulfur head ignite but it gave off no light. I couldn't even see her fingers holding the match. The flame went out as soon as the sulfur burned. "I'm getting out of here!" Tamara screeched, only it came out as a hollow whine. She pulled away from me, apparently to get to the door. I instinctively reached and barely managed to snag her waist. Together we tried to feel along the wall for the door, but the wall never came. The darkness altered our sense of direction. The room could only be *so big*, but we stumbled on and on never reaching a wall. Never reaching a *boundary*.

"*Ezekiel, please get me out of here, because I'm really scared now. I'm really scared and I want to go home. I can live with the bad nightmares; I don't need to see the Evangelist. Let's just get back to the airport and get on a plane and go back to New York!*"

It wasn't the fear in her voice that startled me. It was the, *this is the final phone call before I commit suicide* tone of how she spoke. It was the, *please come get me before I do something really crazy* aspect of her words. Tamara was one step from a total mental breakdown and she knew it.

"*Hush, we are going to be fine!*" I told her and at that moment I really believed it. Then Tamara told me she dropped her matches and we both bent down to pick them up. That's when we discovered that the *room* we were in didn't have a floor. My hand passed under my foot and came across nothing solid. So what were we standing on?

"Tell me again, tell me again how we're gonna be okay. Just say it."

"We're gonna be okay."
I lied.

———   ———   ———

It's impossible to tell how long we were in that unnatural darkness. My mind raced to try to find a plausible explanation. I kept coming back to an old Twilight Zone episode where a little girl rolled out of bed and into another dimension. That's how I felt ever since we arrived in Cypress.

God, please help us. Please, I whispered to myself.

Call her, a voice said to me. I was unsure as to whether it was my own inner voice or something else, perhaps in the midst of everything I had really gone crazy and developed an acute case of Schizophrenia.

Call who?

Who are you here to see?

"Lady Ophelia! We are here to see you. I know you can see us, if you would be so kind as to turn the lights on we—"

The lights came on at once. Flooding us, blinding us. Tamara shrieked and buried her face in my chest. It took my eyes several blinks to adjust. Ophelia sat in a chair on the far side of the room, behind her was Buford and the little boy who almost broke my wrist. Behind us were a dozen or so people kneeling and praying.

The little boy came over and gently pulled me by my good wrist to where Ophelia sat. She had not changed much since the last time I saw her. She still reeked of excrement, body odor and cheap wine. Her hair had slimy things crawling in it and she was wrapped in aluminum foil. There was a silver spot in her pupils, and the rest of her eyes were covered with a thick filmy coating that suggested that she was losing her sight—if she could see at all.

"See there, Buford? I tole you he'd figure it out."

Buford eyed me suspiciously and mumbled, *"He don't look like much to me."*

"That's cause you see with *eyes,* Buford Thillton, but Ophelia sees with the Wheel," she curled a finger beckoning me closer.

I moved slowly, reluctantly. She put her hand on my head and massaged my scalp. Her hands were covered with warts and scales. Her fingers had dried filth on them.

"So you're Uriah's little boy, all grown up. Glad to see you made it back here. The legend is true; Cypress' time of trouble is bout up. I'll give you whatever help you'll need—which'll be considerable, if'n you believe."

That smell, that dried pong threatened to upset my stomach. At least with the singing bum, Pickle I had the chance to stand downwind of him. Here, I was trapped. I swallowed hard and tried to hold my breath. "Can you...can you tell me what happened to my brothers?"

"Yes, I can tell you that. I can also answer a lot of the other questions that has plagued your mind. Like, where's your mother and your house." Still holding my head, she forced me to kneel in front of her. "But you hafta axe me. Just like you axed to have the light."

"Lady Ophelia...please," *God, the smell! When was the last time this woman washed?* "Please, tell me what happened to my family." I could feel Tamara's hand in my back, trying to reassure me. My body trembled and shuddered in repulsion from Ophelia's touch. There wasn't anything evil about her; it was just...*nasty*, like having to stick your hand in a filthy toilet. Shit washes off, I kept telling myself. *It washes off...*

"Prepare yourself, little Ezekiel. What I am going to tell you will change the rest of your life. Listen well, and do not interrupt..."

Here it comes, I thought. The thing that got Slim-Ron killed and brought me here. I steeled myself, trying to prepare for just about anything.

Anything, except what I heard.

———   ———   ———

"Before I answer your questions directly, it's important you understand the goings on and doings of a lot of things. *Cypress Point* was founded in the third year after the end of the Civil War. Former slaves and soldiers, both black and white founded this piece of land. There was a small tribe of Indians here who welcomed them and I guess for the first time since the Magi knelt by the manger, black, white, and red got along in Christian brotherhood and fellowship.

"The Indians were a small but *powerful* group. They had the understanding of things far beyond mortal reckoning. They had a way of protecting themselves from outsiders, you see. They had *the Wheel*."

The way she said *'the Wheel'* made me tremble. The room was quiet except for Ophelia's voice. I saw a look of awe and astonishment on everyone's face. For some reason it reminded me of how ancient people must've looked at the sky during an eclipse.

"Cypress Point was ruled at that time by three judges: One black, one white and one red. They were good and just men who wanted nothing more than to see peace and prosperity reign. No one called another out of name then, and for a time I guess Cypress Point was about the closest thing to heaven on earth.

"But the Indians had the Wheel, you see. The Wheel was the secret that only the Indians had. Whenever someone became sick or if there was a question about when the rains were coming, the Indian judge had the answer. One day the black judge and the white judge plied the Indian with strong whisky an asked him how such a thing was possible. The Indian told them about the Wheel. Well they decided that the Wheel should be shared amongst the three of them. The Indian judge disagreed and told them they weren't ready to handle the responsibility, that the Wheel was a power that could easily corrupt and taint the town. Besides, the whites and blacks outnumbered the Indians nine to one. The Wheel was the equalizer. They argued for days and nights on end, until the black judge suggested that they at least get a look at this Wheel that had them so riled up.

"Well, against the Indian judge's best instinct, he took the other two men to it. It was set in a cave, deep in the earth. It took them days to travel that far down, but the further down they went, the more they noticed they weren't hungry or tired or thirsty. They didn't need to sleep. Then they got a look at it…at the sheer beauty and power of it; it vibrated and radiated at them."

She stood up, looking at everyone. She pumped her fist and stomped her foot to give emphasis to what she was saying. I was spellbound.

"The Wheel is not of this earth, you see. It is not from this plane of existence. The Indians found it when they arrived here many, many thousands of years ago and it was ancient even then. Well, when the other two judges saw this thing, they told the Indian right then and there that either he agreed to let them share in the power, or they would kill him on the spot. The Indian refused and tried to use the power to protect himself, but it was too late! The black and white judge caught on! They understood what they were standing in front of! They knew how the power worked! Those three men—the best of friends, brothers in different skins fought like beasts for days, gnashing and tearing at each other. They used the Wheel in a blasphemous and terrible way. In the end, the three of them died.

"Now the three judges...had daughters; three little girls that were thirteen years old—all born on the same day and just getting into the realm of womanhood. Virgins and virtuous, the three of them were friends as their daddies were before them.

"They set out on foot to find their daddies, the judges. The Indian girl led the other two to the Wheel and there they saw what was left of their daddies' bodies. The Wheel affects virgin women and children different from men, and women who have lost their maidenhead. The three judges' bodies had been mutilated, torn apart like by an animal that had gone berserk. Blood was everywhere; it soaked the Wheel—forever staining it. The three girls made a vow to keep what really happened silent from the town and they came back and told the town that the three judges had been set upon by a wild bear and rendered limb from limb.

"They swore in the blood of their fathers never to allow the Wheel to come between them. They swore before the Wheel, to keep the terrible power a secret from the rest of the town. Now, Ezekiel...I know you're wondering what this got to do with you an your brothers, but you must hear me out. The girls, they grew up to be strong, beautiful women—but their growing was slowed down considerable. I mean they grew older, but not *old*. They grew maybe a month's time in the course of a year—if that much. Well, after while the town folk got to talking. Somebody figured out that it just won't natural for the three of them to look in their early twenties, when people birthed after them to be in the change of life. At first they were branded as witches, until the white girl...she broke down an told about the Wheel. A dozen men left in the dead of night to find it. They reached the tunnel and clawed over each other like crabs, trying to reach it first. It was a hell of a sight. Men scratching and tearing at one another, brothers biting and ripping at each other like beasts, all to get close to the Wheel. After that the three girls vowed again to keep the Wheel amongst themselves, to use the power to control the town. The three girls became obsessed with the Wheel. They would sit before it for hours and sometimes days on end, studying it...trying to uncover its secrets. Oh, the things they learned in those days, the secrets of this world and many others. Things that have baffled man for years were simple to them. The Wheel uncovered mysteries and revealed things that are unknown even to this day.

"The blood...the blood *stained* the Wheel. The Wheel...made an agreement with the white girl...she promised the Wheel fresh blood in exchange for more knowledge and power. The Wheel taught that trollop all the secrets of life and death.

"The black and the Indian discovered that the white girl's power was increasing, but there was nothing they could do about it. She defiled the Wheel...and the Wheel defiled her.

"Now, the folk of Cypress Point were hard working, god fearing, good people. They scrimped and scraped out a living by the sweat of their brow, and the callous of their hands. They were simple folk, with no high desires of fancy aspirations. A man could hope to marry, have a son or two, work his land and God willing live to see his grandchildren.

"Time passed as time does; wars were fought, the country grew in power and prosperity, but Cypress Point remained outside the sphere of those events. The Wheel, you see, the Wheel protects the town and in a lot of ways...it *curses* the town. No one enters Cypress Point without the Wheel's permission...and no one leaves without it."

I thought about the Evangelist's words that day in the park when she gave me permission to leave...

You want to leave Cypress so badly...I'll let you. Just don't ever come back here, because the Wheel of the World spins when I tell it to! The Axle of the World tilts in my direction. All things, both great and small serve the Evangelist!

Tamara was right; this was beyond the scope of the natural world. There was no sense in me denying it any further; I was up against forces that defied all of my education. The laws of time and space were suspended in this hellhole. I was now the male version of Alice, gazing through the looking glass after falling down the rabbit hole. From the looks on the faces around me, they knew this tale of warped history.

I was the student, cramming for the final exam.

"The white girl was able to predict the First World War, the stock market crash, earthquakes, floods and all other major disasters. Soon, her power among the town grew. People came to her for advice and counseling. The black and Indian were hung in effigy, ostracized and cast aside as charlatans and conspirators against the white daughter.

"You've probably guessed it. The white daughter is the Evangelist. I am the Indian daughter. And the black daughter was named Eliza. Yes, your mother. The three of us are the original descendants of the Cypress judges. I know this is hard to fathom, but the sooner you recognize the truth the sooner we can be free from this curse."

"What do you mean...*was named Eliza?*"

"We are going to go through something together, Ezekiel. You and I are going to mourn in a moment, but before that happens, I have to finish my story and you have to promise me, you will not interrupt again. Promise me!"

"I...I promise."

But what do you mean, 'Was named Eliza?'

"Good. I promise you that when I am through, your questions will be answered. I know you, young Ezekiel. I know you better than you know yourself. There are things about Cypress that scares you, things that happened when you were a child that you buried deep, deep, *deep* in yourself. All of those memories will surface soon, Ezekiel. The prophecy will be fulfilled."

She continued to rub my head, massaging and caressing her hands through my hair. She pounded her chest when she said "deep" and her voice cracked with emotion. Tears streamed down my face. I cried uncontrollably. She pulled my head close to her chest and in that moment the smell was gone. I looked up at her and saw that she was no longer covered in filth; her skin glistened with a healthy radiant hue. Instead of aluminum foil, she was covered in a silver gown that shimmered like fine silk. I stared at her in awe. The crazy bag lady routine was a ruse. The woman in that chair exuded grace, confidence and a wisdom beyond imagining. I grabbed her hand, which was well manicured and smooth and kissed it.

"I believe you, Lady Ophelia. Please continue."

"You see me as I truly am now. Don't you, Ezekiel."

"Yes." Even her voice had changed. Her diction was smoother, more educated.

"Good. As I said the town folk were simple people, a very superstitious people. It became taboo to try to achieve anything other than what was set for you. The story of those men who ventured to see the Wheel became the stuff of legend and folklore, twisted and retold until the gist of it was that any man trying to gain too much would become a victim of the Cypress Curse."

"Eliza and I tried our best over the years to break Clara Washington's grip on the town, but trying to convince the people that the *Evangelist* was a power hungry harpy from hell was like talking to lint and expecting an answer. Over the years, I managed to snag a few; those you see here and a few others, but Clara's power overshadows everything…her strength comes from not just the Wheel, but also the belief of the town.

"She forbade us to see the Wheel or to go near it! She became paranoid, digging deeper and deeper into the occult, playing with the forces of darkness. Eliza and I pleaded with her, we begged her in the name of our fathers to abandon her destructive quest. We asked her to remember the vow me made in the blood of our fathers, but she laughed at us.

"Then, in the dead of night, your mother and I went to see the Wheel. It was heavily guarded by mystic defenses, but no one can fully hide the Wheel if it's sought. We stood before the Wheel. We asked it how we could defeat Clara, and that's where the plan first took root."

"What plan?" I asked, fascinated.

"Hush, Ezekiel. All of your questions will be answered in the course of time."

You could've heard a pin drop in that room. Tamara's hand was placed firmly in the small of my back. I felt a twinge of shame for my earlier feeling of repulsion toward Ophelia. Looking at her now, she was the epitome of grace and honor.

"Of all the things Clara possessed, she lacked the thing God gave to rich and poor alike; she lacked love. No one loved her. The town feared her, but fear is a far cry from love, Ezekiel. Clara's heart was as lonely as it was cold and hard. She went to the Wheel, to try to gain a man' s love.

"When your daddy was a young man, there were two women who fancied him. One was the woman he'd eventually

72

have seven strong handsome sons by, the other is Clara Washington, the Evangelist.

"Clara tried everything in her power to woo your daddy from your mother. But Uriah Johnson had a quality that is rare among men today. He always remained faithful. A woman's heart is a fickle instrument and a woman like Clara isn't easily dissuaded. She tried every underhanded trick to get your daddy to sleep with her, till finally your mother approached her right outside of the church before service.

" 'Clara Washington, why can't you let my man be?' she asked her, right in front of the deacons. Clara turned three shades of red, furious she was. She'd tried to spread a rumor about your daddy; that he wanted her—not the other way round. She spat at your mother and reached to slap her, but Doug Hollands held her back and your mother walked off proud with your daddy waiting for her.

" 'Let me go, Doug! Don't ever put your hands on me again!' Clara barked. Doug let her go and apologized ten ways from Sunday. He explained that he didn't want her embarrassing herself over obvious sinners—that's the term he used. That might have been the end of it right there, if dumb ass Cliff Dixon hadn't said 'I saw the way he looked at you, Evangelist. Any mule can see that man want you. That trollop put a hex on him!' The other deacons mumbled that they saw it too, but it was all lies. All lies.

"Clara became obsessed with your daddy. She wrote him letters and sent him expensive gifts. She worked all kinds of roots trying to capture his love, but true love can't be tricked or perverted. It's as pure as sunlight and twice as bright. Your daddy spurned her openly. The entire town learned of this, it became the hottest gossip. It shamed and blighted Clara; disgraced her in front of the congregation. No one dared speak about it in her presence, but there were rumors and rumors of rumors—such things are soon the basis of what people believe to be the truth.

"As you know, your daddy worked as a laborer in Clara's factory. Your mother never mentioned her past to him, never told him about the Wheel. She wanted a normal life. She wanted to have children, cook dinners and greet her husband at the door when he returned home from work.

"They were married after a year of courting. It was a beautiful wedding, straight out the storybooks. Mrs. Schulman baked the cake; Mr. Gilmore did the decorations. Yours truly performed the ceremony. It was a gala event, as elite as the Wedding of Canna. Over a hundred people came to help your mother celebrate her special day. Clara showed up, too."

Her voice dropped. Her eyes lowered.

"It was supposed to be your mother's finest hour, her special day to remember for all time. When I said the part about if anyone knew a reason why they should not be joined in holy matrimony, Clara leapt up out her seat and screamed to the top of her lungs that Uriah was her man. She accused your mother right then and there of working roots on your daddy. She spit on the wedding cake and turned over the table holding the gifts. She ran to attack your momma, tearing her beautiful dress. Every time I think about it, I get so mad I can't see straight. We should've killed that whore right then and there, your momma and me. I should've taken my shotgun and put her down like a rabid dog, but even that would've been too good for her an I doubt if a shotgun would've worked anyway."

"What do you mean? She's human enough…I mean she doesn't act like it, but she's still just a person. That's something I learned a long time ago," I mumbled.

"Clara…has *power*…I'm not saying she's invincible, but she's not to be taken lightly. I learned that the hard way, Ezekiel. I learned that the hard way. When Clara went into her tirade, hell bent on destroying your mother's wedding, I ran up to her and slapped the taste out of her mouth. We fought like two wolverines, trying to kill each other. Clara saw she was no match for me physically, so she resorted to using her magic.

"That's how it started, she made a wind blow through the hall so strong that it destroyed the decorations. People were slammed into each other. Old man Chandler broke his arm in three places…it never did heal right. Bertha Mathis was crushed and killed, and about thirty other people had to be hospitalized. The screams and shrieks of our neighbors in pain and panic replaced the joy and happiness that filled the hall only moments earlier. I couldn't stand to watch anymore; I stood up to her, forcing the wind back on her, she landed in the wedding cake. Well, let me tell you…*when everyone saw Clara covered in white icing and chocolate cake— child, they laughed so hard some of them peed their pants*!" She laughed and covered her mouth; her eyes brightened for a second and then frowned.

"Well, that just about did it for Clara. She threw a fit when she heard everyone laugh at her. She put a curse on everyone there, everyone who survived that is. What happened after that was the worst I've ever seen. I've lived a long time, Ezekiel and I've seen a lot of things—both good and bad, but what I saw that day was by far the worst. I've seen men behave as dogs because they got a fill of liquor. I've seen women sell their children for drugs. I've seen men sell their manhood and their women, Ezekiel. I've seen a lot of things over the years, but what I saw that day ranks as the worst. Mayhap because I still blame myself—mayhap just because. Anyway, Clara screamed at the top of her lungs…a sound that was *inhuman*— nothing made by God could've made that sound. The doors and windows to the hall slammed shut, we were trapped inside with her. Everyone ran and cowered in the corners, terrified beyond words.

"She raised up and floated about five feet off the floor. 'Those who laugh today will weep tomorrow.' She said, further scaring the guests. I spit at her, watching as she floated to the door. The doors opened and she floated out like a feather on the wind. That's when it happened; the doors slammed back shut. I knew something was wrong—your mother knew it too. We ran and tried to pull the doors open, before it…before it…"

"Go on, Lady Ophelia; go on and tell him"

"Thank you, Buford. It gets hard sometimes to tell this part. I'm going to have to rush through this, because every time I tell it…*I relive it!* The sprinklers cut on…spraying everyone with scalding hot water. I saw Tim Eastman—God bless his soul—covered as many women as he could…*he died…giving his life*. I watched the water boil the skin off that man. His face was as red as a lobster's. Mat Willis and Arnold Nevins were there too. They died trying to get the windows open—they were electrocuted.

"Your mother kept her wits about her, she managed to provide cover and safety for a lot of people by shredding her wedding dress and wrapping it around the sprinkler heads. Only God knows how many people she saved by doing that. It might not have been so bad if the hot water had been the worst of it.

"About forty people died that day, it would've been a lot more if not for your father. God blessed Uriah Johnson with a *powerful* right arm; your daddy pulled that door right off its hinges. Right off the hinges! I swear, I think that man is a descendant of Samson! God knows his sons were as wild as the strongman."

She chuckled and I had to join her, bittersweet memories washed over me. Growing up, I hated being weaker than the rest; I blamed it on the fact that I was the youngest—the shallow end of the gene pool.

It was no secret about my father's strength. I once watched him lift the rear end of our pickup truck to change a blown out tire when the jack broke. What made it even more impressive was that it was pouring rain and my mother and I sat in the truck while he lifted it. Many things about my childhood lay shrouded in obscurity, but that is one memory I will take with me to my grave.

"Ezekiel, I can't think of one couple in all of my years who could have survived that kind of beginning. But your daddy and momma did. Clara failed, Ezekiel—that tragedy didn't tear them apart—it made them *stronger*!

"Your daddy, he worked—I mean, Ezekiel that man *worked*. Whatever he could do—carry coal, lumber, bauxite, he would do it and never complain. He'd work twenty hours a day, six—sometimes seven days a week. Your mother had a dream of saving up a few dollars and moving out of Cypress Point. She wanted to get away from Clara...to...*protect* your daddy. Then the great winter storm came. Work in Cypress has always been scarce, but this winter it was close to impossible for an honest man to find a decent wage from decent labor.

"Things were hard with your mom and daddy back then. They were hard all over, but it seemed that your family was hit harder than others. That's because Clara had put the word out that anyone that helped your daddy would be labeled an infidel. Meanwhile, she would send gift baskets, bread and meats—things like that. She would always send over a Boston Crème pie, your daddy's favorite, but your momma would send it all back and tell Clara to keep her charity. Pride runs deep in your family. Well, after a while hunger over rules pride and soon enough the baskets of food Clara sent was not only accepted, they were anticipated!

"Oh, how Clara carried on! She kept offering your daddy a job in her factory. That was her plan all along, to get your daddy just where she wanted him. Finally, he accepted. His pride kept him from taking handouts any longer.

"Your mother pleaded with him not to work for Clara, but Uriah told her that a man had to tow the line. He said *a man had to stand on his own*—proud man your daddy was. Good man, too.

"Anyway, he promised your mother that he could handle Clara's advances. Your mother never told your father about the Wheel. She...she *covered him* so he wouldn't remember too much about the wedding disaster. We both did...to all the guests who survived...I mean some remembered seeing Clara float on the air, but most don't remember the power your momma and I showed that day.

"Your momma knew that nothing good could come from him working for Clara, but a man has to be in charge of the family. We had watched Clara destroy too many homes by taking away a man's authority.

"Ezekiel, your mother knew nothing good could come of it...but she did little to stop it. It lasted—oh I guess about three weeks before Clara put the moves on him. It was about two weeks before Christmas. She came to your daddy and asked him to work late, '*Uriah*,' she said. '*I'll pay you overtime.*'"

She said this in a shrill high-pitched voice, imitating the Evangelist. Some people snickered and tittered, but hearing her speak in that strident wail made my flesh crawl.

"Your daddy quickly agreed. That overtime would allow your father to get your mother a Christmas present. She told your father that there was a shipment of mahogany wood that was due to come late, and she wanted a man there to help with the count before she signed off on the invoice. Well, that shipment of wood still ain't arrived! It was a trick! A lie to get your daddy alone! She pulled out a bottle of liquor, '*to take the chill out of the night air*,' she told him. I'm almost ashamed to tell it; the liquor she gave your daddy that night was the same whiskey Clara's dad and your granddad tricked my daddy into drinking. She poured and poured and your daddy drank and drank. They sat and made idle chatter, and your daddy had no idea as to the strength of that liquor. Well, when Clara thought she had him good and soused she stripped butt naked in front of him and tried to put her nasty...*well*, you get the picture. She tried every wily and underhanded trick known to get your daddy excited, but Uriah—drunk as he was, remained faithful. 'What's wrong, Uriah?' she said. 'Scared to touch a real woman? Scared that your gonna get confused about your feelings?' Your daddy tried to clear his head, he knew then seeing her naked that he was in trouble. 'Clara,' he told her, 'there's only one woman for me. Put your clothes back on and let's forget about this.' Clara looked him dead in his eyes and switched her bony hips towards him. Well, Ezekiel...your daddy took one look at her and he laughed and laughed and laughed. Ezekiel, he laughed so hard he couldn't catch his breath! Clara warned him, she told him to stop laughing or she'd be forced to hurt him. I don't rightly know what went on in your daddy's mind at that moment. I know that whiskey plastered him, but I don't what he was thinking. Ezekiel, he kept laughing and if Clara's is one thing she's not to be trifled with. She could've killed your daddy right then and there...I think...I think in her *own way...I think she loved him*. I know it's hard to cipher her loving anything, but in her own way...I think she loved him. It was jealously and *pride*, an unholy combination if ever there was one."

Her voice cracked and she covered her face, weeping.

"Go on, Lady Ophelia. Tell me what happened."

She cleared her throat and wiped away tears in her robe. Her face was a mask, trying to hide an indescribable pain.

"She grabbed him...in his...*stones.*"

She formed her hands like claws and clutched at my testicles, but she didn't touch them.

" 'You're a strong but stupid man, Uriah. A mule has heavy stones and a strong back, maybe that's what Eliza sees in you! You want to give her strong babies, Samson? Strong as mule and twice as dumb!' She squeezed your daddy there and mouthed the curse. Well, after that your daddy took to drinking and he couldn't hold a job. He became a *mule*, Ezekiel. His...physical needs grew to the point where your mother gave birth every year for seven years straight. With each birth, Clara became more incensed at your family. I stood as midwife to each of your brothers' births, including yours. The curse, Ezekiel...that witch cursed your family in a sadistic and evil way!"

"What? What did she do? I've listened to you for close to an hour and I still don't know what happened!"

She started crying again and I cried with her. I looked around at everyone in the room; their eyes quickly averted mine.

"What happened? A man died because he tried to tell me! Now you tell me what happened! No more history lessons— no more of it! I want to know what happened to my family right now!"

"Watch your tone, boy!" Buford barked. "This here is the Lady!"

There was a look of righteous indignation on his face. I had blasphemed by raising my voice. Lady Ophelia was an icon to these people and Buford made it known from that look that I could easily end up like Slim Ron for desecrating sacred secrets.

"I'm...I'm sorry, but I have to know!"

"*Ezekiel,*" Lady Ophelia whined. Tears streamed freely down her face and she took deep breaths and held them. She was trying not to hyperventilate, but what ever she had to say would not be said easily. "*Your brothers died from the curse!*"

"What curse!" I screamed, ready to grab and shake it out of her. My nerves were raw and frazzled. Every one in the room jumped; I had no idea my voice carried that loud.

"Beware the Ides of March, Ezekiel. Beware the Ides of March!"

"What in the hell does that mean? What does Shakespeare have to—"

Buford reached to grab me, but Ophelia stopped him.

"Ezekiel, the curse is centered around the 15th of March. The day your brothers were called home to reward."

"But...this is only March eleventh! How did they—"

"Bear with me, son. In the time you have been gone your brothers passed on year after year...on the same day...on the same block...March 15th—the Ides of March."

"I—I don't understand—"

"The year you left Jim Bruce was murdered on March 15th. The next year Ritchie was killed, also on March 15th—on the same corner. It followed like that, Danny, Thomas, Henry, and Peter. All killed in the order of their births, all on March 15th and all on the same corner. Your mother died of a heart attack when she discovered you were coming home. I'm so sorry, Ezekiel but now you know what the curse is. Clara means to wipe out Uriah's entire lineage. Your family worked hard to get you out of Cypress, and now that you came back the only way out is to defeat Clara."

I collapsed at her feet, the wind knocked out of me. I tried to wrap my mind around what she said, but it was too fantastic—too incredible to be true. All of this time I was prepared to hear that my brothers died in a gun battle with the police, that they died trying to rob a liquor store or a number's spot. Not this. There was no way I could prepare for this. I could barely imagine the grief and the anguish my mother endured as she watched her sons picked off one by one—every year on the same day.

I could not imagine a more insidious torture. What kind of sick, twisted hatred could create such a curse? What kind of *evil* could do this?

"I know how you feel, Ezekiel Johnson. It's not everyday a man finds his life torn asunder. As hard as this is for you to believe, if you don't defeat Clara the Evangelist, you will share the same fate as your brothers. Dead, on March 15th, at high noon, on that same corner."

"But how? I mean, were they all shot to death?"

"No," Buford said. "None of them were shot—at least not with bullets. They were hit with—"

"Hush, Buford!" Ophelia ordered. "Let me tell him!"

"Tell me what? About the black lights?" The room swarmed with murmurs.

"What do you know about the black lights?" Ophelia asked suspiciously. I told her about my experience when I stepped on the corner, how I saw and felt everything that happened, how that strange car pulsed with that blackness that speared J.B.

"What was that? It wasn't light and it wasn't darkness…I told Tamara it was the black lights. It was the first thing that came to mind."

"And rightly so. When God made this world and all others He called the light out of the darkness. There is a place where light meets shadow, where the line between reality and illusion is blurred. This is where life and death kiss, this is where you will find the Wheel."

"Will you—will you stop talking in riddles! This man has lost his entire family…who gives a damn about that!" Tamara screamed. She shook as she spoke, her eyes moist with tears that were too stubborn to fall.

"You mind yourself, girlie! Nobody talks to Lady Ophelia that way! You mind yourself or I'll—"

"That's enough, Buford. I can speak up for myself. You're Tamara, aren't you?"

"Yes…I didn't mean any disrespect…I—"

"—Don't want your history read out loud, do you?"

"…*No*…" Tamara gasped and remained silent.

"Well, I've got a few questions! Lady Ophelia, this is all too much to take in. You're telling me that my brothers died in the order of their birth…on the same day on the same corner—"

"A year apart, on March 15th. I know it's a hard thing to fathom, Ezekiel. But it's the truth. Clara must've sent you that telegram…it was her will that you return, to join your father and brothers in death, but if you believe in me…if you trust me, Ezekiel, I can save you! Together we can accomplish what your mother and brothers could not! We can defeat her!"

My mind swirled with a hundred questions and each question led to a hundred more. There was something surreal about all of this. I kept thinking about the past six years, how I never gave more than a moment's thought to Cypress Point. How my childhood memories simply vanished once I left its borders.

I thought about the haunted memories that threatened to drown me since my return, and now this. Finding out my brothers did not die together, but separate—with the timed precision of a metronome.

There was no logical explanation for this. It defied a thinking man's version of reality. I could no longer feign ignorance at these things. There was another world beyond the one I had accepted as real.

A world ran by the Wheel.

"What…what do I have to do?" I asked her, swallowing hard.

"We have such a short time together, Ezekiel. You must complete the plan your mother and I conceived so long ago."

Her eyes glowed with a warm hope and I felt lightheaded at the task I had inherited.

"We all countin' on you!" Buford said solemnly, the crowd all murmured in agreement. I turned and looked at Tamara, her eyes were open portals of soaked fear. She wanted no parts of this and I couldn't blame her. But I had little choice.

"I want to see their graves. I want to know exactly what happened to them," I said, fighting tears of anger, grief and fear.

"You will see and you will know, Ezekiel. I promise you that. You are all that's left of your mother's sons. Your mother died with your name on her lips. She knew this day would come. I cannot begin to tell you how proud I am of you, not for what you have done…but for what you will do."

"Oh yeah? And just what will I do?" I asked, angrily. I felt I was being used in some insane vendetta.

"The Wheel turns for the just and wicked alike, Ezekiel. Only God Himself knows for sure what will happen, but I have faith that you will honor your family's memory and bring justice to those who did this evil. Buford, bring my sign to me."

Buford went and brought back the aluminum foil covered garbage can top, Ophelia's *sign* that I grew up seeing her carry. I remembered the feelings of disgust and revulsion I felt whenever I saw her and that sign. Like most people, I was convinced she was crazy. I felt a twinge of guilt and shame at all of the times I joined kids in teasing her out of ignorance.

Buford passed her the sign, handling it as gingerly as a newborn baby. The room was a silent as a tomb; everyone watched the sign in awe. I half expected it to start singing. Ophelia stared at it, tracing the strange symbols with her fingertips. Then she looked me straight in my eyes, the expression on her face was hard and stoic. Her eyes never wavered.

"Come closer, Ezekiel."

I did.

"Look at this sign carefully. Look deep and look hard, Ezekiel. I've had this sign since I was fifteen years old; the message on it was given to me by the Wheel itself. No one—not me, not Clara, not even your mother could fully cipher it. I want you to look at it and nod your head if you cipher this message."

I stared at the unearthly symbols—marks that were not part of any known alphabet or language. The twisted, malformed characters looked more like the scribbling of an angry child. There was no rhyme or reason to the markings; they were hieroglyphics for stupid people. They were indecipherable scribble-scrabble. They were—

The markings moved! They began to swirl and shift, forming actual words! I stared in wide-eyed amazement as I *ciphered* the message. Every hair on my body stood on end. It was like a veil had been lifted from my eyes. It wasn't a garbage can top that she held, but a beautiful silver disc! My head swarmed with a hundred thousand different thoughts, all hitting me at random. Too much information—all jumbled— overlapping—rushing in. I was drowning in knowledge. I couldn't take my eyes off the sign. I was being psychologically electrocuted—I tried frantically to form some sort of cerebral filing system; to put the influx of information into mentally bite-sized pieces. It took all of my power to look away, and when I did the strange stream of data stopped.

I looked up and saw Ophelia smiling.

"He has ciphered it," she said with pride. "The prophecy is now complete!" She passed the sign to Buford and he took it away. I could feel the stares and gawks of those around me. You would've thought I had pulled Excalibur from the stone.

"Tell no one of what you have ciphered. The time will come when the information you've gleaned will come useful. If you tell anyone what you have ciphered the knowledge will leave you."

"I... don't remember what it said."

"You will, Ezekiel. When the time comes, you will."

Chapter V: Three days to the Ides of March

When we finally left Ophelia's it was morning. Tamara was a nervous wreck and I wasn't much better. We didn't speak or even look at each other until we were both in the car and safely away from Vine Street.

I kept hearing Ophelia's words in my mind. What she had told me was a terrific story, but it was just too wild to be true. All of my life I rejected the Cypress curse as hogwash—total garbage.

"Did you believe any of that, Ezekiel? I mean the part about your brothers dying a year apart and all on March 15th!"

"The whole thing is beyond my understanding. I grew up hearing the fables and fairy tales about the Wheel, but I thought it was like Santa Claus—you know? As for my brothers, I can't believe that. If you knew my brothers, you'd know they would have stormed her house and dragged her out screaming and kicking. They would've smothered her in hot grease and set her on fire! There's no way they'd sit around and wait for the end to come—"

"Maybe they didn't have a choice—"

"You don't know my brothers. They put the B-A-D in bad! There's no way they would've sat around year after year and let her do this to them!"

"*You don't know the Evangelist.*"

"Wait a minute! How long were you gone from Cypress? You had to have known my brothers! You knew they died a year apart, didn't you?"

"I...Ezekiel, I knew *of* your brothers...I didn't know them personally. So many people in Cypress die from bullets and knives. I heard rumors, that's all—I didn't know that the rumors were true."

"What rumors?"

"They used to call that corner the death square. A lot of people died on that corner. I had a friend who was stabbed to death by a man who thought she was cheating on him. He walked up and stabbed her like forty times in broad daylight and no one helped her. She bled to death right there on that same corner, Ezekiel. Another time a guy got drunk and shot like four people, all on that corner. He said they were laughing at his shadow. There's one story about a lady who was pushing a baby in a carriage and slammed the baby on the curb—right there on that corner. There's a lot of stories like that in Cypress. Some of them true, some of them exaggerated. I know it sounds stupid, but a lot of people die in Cypress."

"And it looks like I'm next."

"Listen to me very carefully, Ezekiel. Forget everything that happened back there. Forget it! Just point this car in the direction of the airport and let's get the hell outta here!"

"You don't have to tell me twice! I was just thinking the same thing!"

I squeezed her hand and she squeezed back. I wanted so badly to delete everything that I had heard from my memory. My mother was dead, along with my six brothers. I would mourn later, from New York City. What I would not do is follow the path they led. I would not be this avenging angel Ophelia made me out to be, and I had no intention of being anywhere near Cypress Point on March 15th.

We drove down Wilkins Avenue until it turned into Empire Road. "This should take us straight into Morristown and then we can get to the interstate," I said, trying to sound enthusiastic. So far so good—it seemed that everything was back to normal. Streets were just as I remembered them; landmarks were back in their rightful place.

"If ever there was a time when we needed luck on our side it's now."

"Tamara...I'm really glad you're here with me. I mean I wish neither of us had returned, but I can't imagine going through this alone."

"I know. Remember on the plane, when you said you were going to Cypress Point? Well, it's because at first I thought the Evangelist sent you. I thought you actually worked for her!" She let loose a nervous chuckle and I patted her hand gently.

"When did you realize I didn't?"

"When we were at the diner I knew for sure. I never really believed you could be down with her, I guess I was just being sill—"

I mashed the brakes and swerved wildly trying to avoid the silhouetted figure in front of me.

"The Evangelist!" I gasped in horror. There she was, standing in the middle of the street—just standing there, glowing as if surrounded by candles—almost daring me to hit her. The screeching of the car's brakes ripped through my ears, paralyzing me. I tried to back the car up; I think it was my intention to try to go around her—although I'm really not sure. My mind was blank with fear, my body moved on its own.

"*It's her*!" Tamara rasped. The words scratched out of the throat. Clara moved with amazing speed. Before I could react, she had reached into the driver's side window and snatched the keys out of the ignition.

"It won't do to try to leave, Ezekiel. We have a date together!" She caressed my face and my skin crawled. She leaned in close to me, pressing her cheek against mine; I could smell the apricot flavored tobacco snuff on her breath. A smell that always caused me to retch and heave growing up. Her tongue darted around my ear and my insides turned to cold jelly.

Her breath was hot measured blasts of angry steam on my cheek. I was as rigid as a corpse, unable to even take a deep breath.

"I'm going to teach you about *pain*, Ezekiel. I'm going to teach you about fear. Just when you think you can't be anymore afraid, I'm going to double and triple your fear. I'm going to break you, smart boy. I'm going to stretch the limits of your sanity and have you beg me for death. When I am through with you, you will know that Clara Washington is truly *the Evangelist*!"

Tamara stared blankly out the windshield, one step from total catatonia.

"Hey, Molly!" she said to Tamara, in an almost laughable manner. "How tricks? I see it didn't take you long to pick up another *sugah-daddy*!"

She must've thought that was funny, because she laughed so hard snuff flew out of her mouth and hit me. I sat there petrified with fear; frozen solid as a statue with her spittle dripping off my eyebrows. I had fallen into a deep hole and the top and bottom were connected—swishing me into a mad merry-go-round.

I shut my eyes, trying to imagine something good, something positive to help me survive the moment. My heart pounded so hard I thought it would explode in my chest. I pictured my father, such a simple yet complex man. I thought about the time he worked all night in the lumber yard—during one of the worst snow storms ever, just to make sure he had enough money to purchase Christmas gifts. My daddy wasn't scared of Clara and although standing up to her eventually got him killed, he did so with honor and dignity.

"*Ain't no punks in my family, bitch!*" I managed to whisper. I could barely hear myself over my heart's thunderous pounding.

"I'll give you that much, but truth be told there ain't much a *nuthin* in your family—*now is there?*" Her eyes glared at me and I have never seen such a degree of hate seething in anything. It dwarfed my own anger; as much as I detested her, she absolutely *despised* me.

"Thanks to you there isn't. But I'm back and like you said—*we have a date.*"

"You lack your father's physical attributes," she squeezed my puny arms and her hand groped at my crotch. "But you have his stubbornness, I'll say that much about you. It's gonna be a real pleasure planting you in the ground next to him. Make no bones about it, Ezekiel. Jesus might resurrect you, but I'm going to kill you. There's nobody that can save you, boy. You and Molly over there can go now; I'll see you soon enough—and one more thing, *little boy*: I am the Evangelist—not a bitch. A bitch is a female dog. You'd do well to learn the difference—*while the blood is still running warm in your veins.*"

She threw the car keys in my lap and I saw a hulking figure materialize behind her. As scared as I was of her, I was *a hundred times* more terrified of the person behind her.

"*Lukie!*" Tamara wheezed. I thought she was going to have an asthma attack and die from the way the word rattled out of her mouth. Blank with shock I started the car without thinking. My body moved on its own and it was a good thing too—I was totally incapable of performing the simplest mental tasks. The car started and we peeled out of there as fast as the Benz would take us. About three miles away I slowed down and merged with other traffic. I think it was then that my heart settled back into its rightful place in my chest.

"Are you okay?" I asked Tamara.

"I don't think I'll ever be okay. Of all the people to see, why did it have to be him?"

"Because God is cruel."

The abomination known as Lukie was born Luke Thomas, he suffered from gigantism; a disorder where the body grows and just keeps growing. Lukie stood about six feet tall at age twelve. His body kept growing—his IQ didn't.

His freakish size also gave him freakish strength. I once saw him crush an apple with his bare hand. There was always a dark, evil, perverted aura about Lukie. He would murder puppies and kittens by throwing them against the wall until they were flattened. He'd tear the wings off birds and he once caught a squirrel and set its tail on fire. When asked why he did these things he'd simply reply, "*Just to have sumthin to do.*"

When he first hit puberty, he began raping young girls. He would kidnap and keep them in an abandoned basement, raping and sodomizing them repeatedly. With no food and water, the girls would usually die from shock, starvation and dehydration. Once the girls no longer appealed to him, he simply kidnapped another.

He was able to do this with very little resistance because he only kidnapped whores or girls from the Molina Houses— Molly girls. When the police finally did catch up to him, Lukie had murdered over seventeen young ladies whose ages ranged from twelve to thirty. The bodies were all in the cellar in various stages of decomposition.

Instead of locking him away in an insane asylum, the Evangelist convinced the judge that she would take Lukie as a ward of the church and she would be responsible for him. The judge agreed and Lukie became a caretaker in the funeral home.

The town avoided him, but since he very rarely came out without the Evangelist, memory of what he did to those poor girls faded into one of the usual stories one would hear from the old timers at the bar.

To help sate his voracious sexual appetite Lukie took to masturbation, often spending hours at this until he fell asleep from sheer exhaustion. The Evangelist had to go through great pains to keep him from doing this in public, especially when he went out with her.

Growing up, I would quake in fear whenever he came near me. The mere mention of his name was enough to scare me. The word conjured up horrible pictures of those poor girls, slowly tortured and sexually battered by this monstrous deviant.

When he broke into the elementary school and molested an eight-year-old girl the Evangelist couldn't ignore that— raping and killing Molina girls was something she could attribute to God's holy wrath of all whores, but that little girl really shook up the town. So, she set out to show Cypress Point that Lukie could be forgiven and she decided his punishment: The removal of one testicle courtesy of a hot comb during afternoon prayer service with the deacons as witnesses.

This was Cypress Justice — according to the Evangelist.

He has to be about thirty now. From the scant glance I stole of him he has to stand at least seven and a half feet tall, weighing well over three hundred pounds, rock solid.

He looked like he was chiseled out of stone.

—————   —————   —————

"God is cruel," I repeated looking in the rear view mirror. The sight of Lukie had caused some weird flashbacks. Something happened between Lukie and me, but I couldn't remember just what at the time. And the funny part was I felt my amnesia was a blessing. Where ignorance is bliss, it's folly to be wise.

"You...you...still gonna leave...right?"

"You're damned right about that! She can kiss my ass because that's the last part she's going to see of me!"

Tamara touched my face and gave me a warm look of approval. I turned left on Morristown Road and sighed in relief when I saw the sign that pointed to the highway. We were going to make it. I would leave and mourn my family. I would not be in Cypress Point on the 15th of March. And although Lady Ophelia prophesized a knock down drag out fight between the Evangelist and me, I could still claim victory just by leaving.

I took the ramp that led to the highway and I was kind of surprised to see the streets deserted. This early in the morning there should be some sort of traffic. The ramp seemed unusually long—I sped up, anxious to get on the road—but the highway never came. At the end of the ramp I came out exactly where I entered.

I looked at Tamara and frowned, we both knew what was happening. Though I was loath to give my fears voice, she shouted it out for both of us.

"We're going in circles! We're going in circles! How is that possible? The highway has to be here! It's always been here! The sign is right there, the highway has to be here! Here's the ramp, where the hell is the highway!" Tamara screamed.

"I don't know. I don't think she'll let us leave."

"Forget that! Let's go the same way we came!"

"Do you remember how we came?"

Tamara started crying, little quiet sobs of pain and anguish. I didn't say anything to her. Truth was, there was nothing I could've said.

I cut the radio on, but instead of music all that came out was a loud cackling, maniacal laugh.

The Evangelist's laugh.

We drove around for about an hour, trying to find the service road that I took into town. No one would help or give us directions. No matter which street I turned down, I'd eventually come right back to the place where I almost ran the Evangelist over with the car.

"What are we going to do?"

"I don't know," I said parking the car. "But I'm not giving up! There has to be a way out of here! There has to be!" I wracked my brain trying to think of something. The Evangelist would not outsmart me. She would not outwit me. I was smarter than she was, more educated.

I pulled out my cell phone and cut it on—surprisingly I got three bars showing a full signal. I dialed the area code for New York City and got a blaring busy signal. "I got a strong signal, but I still can't get through! She even has the cell phones rigged! Probably blocking the satellite!"

I walked over to a payphone and tried to dial a friend in New York. I couldn't complete the call; again, once I dialed one-seven-one-eight there was an incessant piercing busy signal. I dialed information and the computer voiced operator answered, telling me to say the name and address of the party whose number I wished to reach.

"Long distance, New York City. Give me the number to—"

The busy signal returned, this time the cadence of it was much quicker—violent.

"What's wrong? Who're you trying to call?" Tamara asked.

"New York. She must have all the phones rigged, but I got a surprise for her Molly ass!"

I walked over to the car and opened the trunk. I pulled my laptop out of one of the bags. "Welcome to the twenty-first century!"

"What are you going to do?"

"I'm sending an e-mail to a friend of mine. Letting him know what's going on."

"I don't understand."

"She thinks she can cut us off from the rest of the world. Well, she's wrong. I have a few tricks up my sleeve, too."

I opened the laptop and tried to access the Internet. I banged the keyboard furiously.

"What's wrong?"

"Look." I turned the laptop around so Tamara could see the monitor. The Evangelist's face smiled back at her, plastered across the computer screen.

"We're going to die, aren't we?"

"Yes, some day we all will. But I don't plan on dying in the next few decades, and it damned sure as hell won't be in Cypress Point!"

I closed the laptop and put it back in the trunk. "Think," I said out loud. "Think! You're smarter than her, you're better than her!" I put my hands in my pockets and paced around the car. I pulled a card out of my pocket and stared at it curiously.

"Providence favors the foolish!" I said smiling. I dialed the number on the card; the phone rang three times before there was an answer.

"Thank you for calling Luxury Rentals, this is Patrick; may I help you?"

"Patrick, I can't remember when was the last time I was so happy to hear some one's voice!"

"Well that's always refreshing to hear so early in the morning! May I ask who's speaking?"

"This is Ezekiel Johnson! I rented the Mercedes six-hundred from you. Do you remember?"

"Yes, of course I do. Your brothers passed away. What can I do to help you, Mr. Johnson?"

"It's Ezekiel. Let me ask you, does Luxury Rentals have a GTS installed in the vehicles?"

"Yes, sir. It's standard for all of our cars."

"Great!" I sighed in relief. GTS stood for Global Tracking System. No matter where I was, Patrick could track me. It prevented the car from being stolen.

"Listen to me very carefully, Patrick. I need for you to tell me exactly where I am—"

"I don't understand. Is the car okay?"

"Never mind that! Now you listen to me! I need for you to come and pick me up! Bring any car you have—"

"What's wrong with the car? Oh my word, I'll be fired if anything happens to that car!"

"Patrick! The car is fine! Besides, you can charge my credit card—remember? Now I need for you to come and get me! I'll make it worth your while…say…a thousand dollars?"

"A thou—I'll be right there!"

"Good! Determine my position from the GTS and bring a mini one with you!"

"Yes, sir! Hold the line and I'll get your coordinates."

Tamara motioned for me to tell her what was happening, I covered the mouthpiece of the phone and told her I'd explain later.

"Sir, are you there?"

"I'm right here, Patrick."

"This is odd…and I have a strange feeling about this, but I'll come—I think you're going to need my help."

"Thank you, Patrick. Please hurry." I ended the call and put the phone back in my pocket.

"Well?" Tamara asked. "What was that about?"

"The guy I rented the car from is going to come here and get us."

"How?"

"The car has something like a homing device inside. There's a computer that tracks the car's movement via satellite. Patrick will track us and when he gets here, we'll leave with him."

"That's a bad move, Ezekiel. You know foreigners aren't allowed in Cypress."

"He's not a foreigner, he's American. Besides, if we play into this by her rules we can't win. I have to use whatever I have to beat her!"

"You know what I mean! Think about what happened at that diner. You could be bringing that man here just to get him killed!"

I hadn't thought about that.

"Let's pray that doesn't happen. As for now, Patrick is our best option. In the interim, I'd like a hot shower and something to eat. If I'm going to die in three days I'd like to be wearing clean underwear and have a full stomach."

"I'm sorry. You're trying to do something and all I'm doing is complaining."

"I'm sorry, too. I didn't mean to snap like that. We're both under a tremendous amount of stress. Let's see if we can find somewhere to eat and then we'll go back to Lady Ophelia's to unpack."

"I don't like that woman. She scares me."

"She scares me, too! But right now she's the only person in this hellhole willing to help us!"

"You think we'll ever see New York again?"

"Yes, I do. I'll make a deal with you—when we get back I'll treat you to a steak dinner at Peter Luger's!"

"Too fancy for me! I'll settle for a televised Knicks game and a six pack of Budweiser!"

"Tall cans! It's a deal!" We laughed and I pulled her close to me. We stared at each other, the smiles slowly evaporating. I kissed her gently on the lips. I tried to kiss her again, more passionately but she pulled back from me.

"I'm going to hold you to your promise, Ezekiel. The one about nothing happening to us."

"I'll tell you what; when we get back we'll have that six-pack over my house...*and I'll make you breakfast*."

"I'll make *you* breakfast—*in bed*!"

We drove until we found a diner that didn't look too slouchy and went in. There were about a half dozen people sitting at the counter drinking coffee and reading the newspaper. I glanced over my shoulder at a man sitting at the counter. He was reading the Cypress Point News and the headline read something about New York City being totally blacked out from a freak heat wave. I thought about that blaring busy signal when I tried to reach New York. According to the article, there was mass looting and rapes and people reported seeing mutated animals roaming the streets.

Tamara and I sat at a table and a waitress came over.

"What can I get for ya this mornin'?"

"Can we see a menu?" I asked looking around, more than a bit leery. The Evangelist's face appearing on my laptop really spooked me. Like she was watching my every move—reading my every thought. What if she had something to do with what was going on in New York? Was she truly *that* powerful?

"Sure!" the waitress replied, handing us two faded hand written menus. I searched the menu for something that wouldn't take too long to prepare and wouldn't be too easy to mess up when I saw it—the same heavy, lead-crystal glass pie holder.

"Is that Boston Crème Pie?" I asked, staring at it. I hadn't noticed when I first walked in, but the entire diner smelled like pie.

"What—oh, yeah I guess George baked it. *Funny, I don't remember a pie being there this morning!* George! George! You bake a pie?"

George was the cook—a gravel voiced man with a stained apron and a tired expression. He popped his head up from the kitchen, surveyed the situation and said with a tinge of exasperation, "Yo' azz ain't cooked it! I'm the onlyist one round here that cook! If'n a pie here then sell it, heifer!"

The waitress sucked her teeth, rolled her eyes, put her hands on her hips and asked me if I wanted the pie.

"Yes!" I answered, reaching into my pocket. "How much for the entire pie and the pie case?"

"George, how much for the pie and the case?" She rolled her eyes again, gave me a look that told me I was more trouble than I was worth and swung toward George's direction.

"If I gotta set the friggin prices what dahell do I need you for? Sell it and come pick up these aigs! *Gon rooin my fuggin bidness!*"

Again she sucked her teeth and turned to me, her patience worn thin.

"I don't know. Gimme what you think it's worth; just make it fair—I don't want George getting mad."

"Is thirty dollars enough?" I watched her eyes light up as I spread the money on the table.

"*Er...uh...let's say ten...and twenty's the tip for me!*" She eyed the money and licked her lips in a slow, seductive way.

"Just get the pie, Molly. *And keep your lips dry!*" Tamara cut in with the sharpness of a scalpel. Her eyes were cold and hard, and not just at the waitress—she was angry with me, too.

The waitress locked eyes with Tamara for the briefest of seconds then hurried away, snatching the money off the table. She placed the pie case on our table and left to attend the rest of the customers.

"You mind telling me what is so important about that waitress and this pie case?"

I smiled. Not only because of how delicious the pie looked, but because I had detected the slightest trace of the green-eyed monster, jealousy.

"There was no need to be nasty to her, Tamara."

"Never mind that," she blushed. "What's this about?"

"Remember when we were in that diner, on the way up here? Well, the first thing I noticed that didn't look like it was infected with food poisoning was a glass pie case—just like this one! Then Ophelia reminds me that my dad's favorite pie is Boston Crème! I'm thinking—"

"That there is a connection?"

"Yes!" I lifted the glass cover off the pie and grimaced at how heavy it was. "Feel this!" I gave her the cover.

"Man! This is heavy!"

"This is lead crystal...it's pretty expensive." I slid the pie onto a plate and groaned out loud when I read the engraving on the glass.

"What's wrong?"

"Read this!" I turned the pie holder around so she could read it.

"To Eliza and Uriah, a couple who were made in heaven; what God has joined—"

"Let no one put asunder," I finished.

"How did—"

"I don't know...but I know that this is my mother's pie case; it was a wedding gift. I know in my heart this is the same glass pie case from that diner we ate at yesterday."

"Then how did it get from that diner to this one?" she asked.

"I don't know, but I mean to find out!" I turned to get the waitress' attention. She walked over with a reluctant look on her face. "Excuse me, can I ask you a question?"

"Look, I didn't mean any harm...it was just my little joke. Don't tell George, he'll—"

"I just want to know where you got this glass pie case from! This was a wedding gift to my mother and I saw it yesterday at a diner right outside of town—"

"I don't know nuthin about that case or that pie. You best ask George about this. I don't wanna get involved with no kinda trouble! George! George!"

"What? I'm busy!" George shouted from the kitchen. He came out and around the counter wiping his hands on his grease soaked apron.

"Whatja want?" he asked. He stood all of about five feet six, he had a massive barrel shaped torso and rail thin arms.

"I just want to know where you got this pie holder."

"Beats the jizz outta me! I never seen it before! Now if that's all I got aigs and bacon fryin for my payin customers. You can give the nice young lady here your order and I'll be more than happy to cook it for you!"

"It was on your counter, George. It didn't just walk in here, *now did it?*" There was perhaps just a trace of anger in my voice. The waitress shook and stepped behind George.

"You trynta start trouble up in here, boy? *Cause I got a remedy for trouble…*"

"You alright in here, big George?" a man sitting at the counter asked. Then, he and three other men stood and walked over to my table.

"You should ask this boy here if'n he alright! He got my dander up now!"

"Look, I'm not trying to start anything! I just want to know—"

"An she called me Molly!" the waitress broke in. "Him carryin a lot a money, George. I sawned it!"

"It's I *seened* it! *Ig'nant heifer*! I don't care what's in his pocket! I ain't no thief! Now, do you wanna order, boy? Or, do you want to test ole Georgie's patience?"

"Look, George—I don't want any trouble. Can you tell me where you got the pie case? I'm sort of in a war with the Evangelist—"

"Don't ever mention that name in here! May she burn in the crack of my dead mother-in-law's ass for all eternity!" There was a fear—an incredible seething dread that threatened to erupt throughout the diner when I mentioned the Evangelist. George reached into his tee-shirt and pulled out a small gold locket.

"Look a here!" He unclasped the locket and it opened to show two small pictures of three little girls dressed like angels.

"It was Halloween…" His voice lowered and the pain was evident. "They wanted to go trick-or-treat dressed like angels—that's what they were—angels!" A tear welled up in the corner of his eye, but didn't fall. "That damned Lukie—"

"Oh my God!" I gasped at the mention of that monster's name. "He didn't—"

"They live, mister. He didn't kill them, if that's what you were gonna ask. He raped them, all three of them. They so messed up now they no good in the head or in the body. Little Bernice, she might not never get normal. I went and got my shotgun, ready and loaded for jail or hell and that tramp that calls herself a preacher and a *Evangelist* protected that rat-fink summabitch!"

The look of anguish that cloaked his face was enough to tear at anyone. How many people had Clara Washington destroyed?

"George, you don't have to tell me twice how evil Clara is. She killed my entire family!"

"Your name Johnson?" the man behind George asked.

"Yes, Ezekiel Johnson…Uriah was my father."

"Good man, your dad. Hard worker and quiet," the man replied. "I used to work with him in the factory." He stepped from behind George and I noticed the man's left arm was amputated at the elbow. "I lost my arm in that factory. Would've lost my life had it not been for your daddy." He rubbed the stump and grimaced. Some memories carry fresh pain.

"Listen, guys…we might've gotten off on the wrong foot here. I'm trying to get out of Cypress Point, but all the roads lead right back into town! Can anyone tell me how to get to Pulaski and Tilden?" I asked. I wanted to get home; maybe my family's things were still there. Besides, I needed to relax, shower, and maybe get a few minutes worth of rest before Patrick arrived.

"You mean Uriah and Eliza's old place, don't you?" George asked.

"Yeah!"

"It's about three miles west of here. How come you don't remember where you live? You slow?"

It wasn't an insult. A lot of people in Cypress suffered from Alzheimer's-like symptoms.

"No, George. I'm not slow. I'm from New York and I've forgotten my way around. Look, if one of you can help me I can pay you."

"No need for that," the guy with half an arm missing said. "I'm more than happy to help out Uriah's kin."

"George, I didn't mean to come off like I wanted trouble. You understand, don't you?"

"No harm done, son. If you want some coffee with your pie I just brewed a pot."

"That sounds good. We'll eat and afterwards this gentleman—"

"My name's Eddie, but just call me One-Leg; everybody does." He held the stump of his arm and grinned. "Hell, it was your daddy that gave me that name—one night in this very diner! Ain't that right, George?"

"Yeah, Uriah was a funny one alright. Had a good sense of humor, loved to laugh."

Out of all the things I'd ever heard said about my father, this was the first time I ever heard anyone refer to him as funny. I don't think I saw the man smile a dozen times and as for telling a joke—well they *couldn't* be talking about *my* dad.

"You sure we're talking about the same person? Uriah Johnson?" I asked.

"Didn't know that side of him, did you? Well, it's true. Your daddy was a good man, loved to laugh and he loved to hear others laugh. Won't a mean bone in his body," George said, pouring the coffee.

Hearing them speak so fondly about my father made me miss him all the more. I remembered the night he had the first stroke and he was admitted to Cypress General's ICU ward. My brothers all told me to make sure I didn't break down and start crying when I saw him. They made me promise on everything holy that I wouldn't cry. They threatened to beat me so bad that I'd be in the bed next to him if I started bawling. The nurse let us into the room and I trembled when I saw this giant of a man so frail looking with tubes in his nose and being fed through an IV.

We were all standing around his bed in the order of our births. His skin was so dry that it cracked and bled whenever he moved. His once mighty sinews were now reduced to flaccid flesh. No one spoke as we stood there. I could tell from the looks on my brothers' faces that they were all one step from breaking down. My dad looked up at me and smiled, "Hey there, Ezekiel! Made it to see the old man!"

"*Oh, Daddy!*" I mumbled and threw my arms around him. My face betrayed me and I couldn't help crying. In that moment I didn't care what my brothers thought about me, or what they threatened to do to me. My tears flowed freely and I was proud of each and every one of them that fell.

Because I love my father.

I looked up, half expecting to see my brothers ready to drag me out of there and beat me into oblivion, but they were crying too—all of them. Weeping and blubbering all over the place, they all ran to him and the seven of us held dad tightly. It was the very first time I had ever received any physical affection from my brothers. I remembered how fiercely proud I was at that moment. I remember thinking that no one, not the Evangelist or even Lukie could beat all of us together.

"You okay, son?" One-Leg asked me.

"I'm fine, sir. Just a little sad thinking about my family. Hearing you guys speak about my dad like that brought back memories."

"Well, I reckon you have plenty of memories bout your brothers. I remember one time Mookie and Petey-Wheaty tried to rob ole man Hollands for his insurance check and your dad tore bout six inches of hide off both a them!" George chortled.

"Not true!" a voice shouted from across the room. "Uriah's sons were a lot of things, but none of them were thieves." I looked up and saw an old silver haired man, sipping coffee. "I knowed all Uriah's kin—'cept maybe you, Ezekiel. Don't think I rightly made your acquaintance! Which is more than a bit odd, seeing as how I lived in Cypress all my life plus nine months!"

Everyone in the diner chuckled at the old man, including me. I moved closer to him, somehow drawn by his warm manner and wrinkled old smile.

"How did you know my brothers and not know me?" I asked.

"I used to be the guidance counselor when they were in Elementary School. They were all very bright boys—a bit high strung and easily agitated, but very bright. My name is Franklin Earl Aloysius Roberts, and it's a pleasure to meet you."

He stuck out his hand and I shook it firmly. The man's hand was warm and moist—sweaty. His touch made my teeth grind, but I couldn't let his hand go. My mouth puckered, like I had just sucked a lemon. George and One-Leg were now behind me, looking at the old man oddly.

"I don't recollect seeing you in here before, ole timer."

"Before what, George?" Franklin answered, smiling widely. Suddenly he didn't seem as jovial as a moment ago. He somehow reminded me of an old poster I once saw of Santa Claus holding a bottle of Coca–Cola. The picture was supposed to express Santa's love for the beverage, but Saint Nick's rosy–red cheeks and wide grimace coupled with those sneering eyes somehow gave off a malevolent glare and scared the hell out of me.

Franklin's smile suddenly had the same effect. My hand itched where he held it. The skin blistered and welted as if I had grabbed Poison Oak and my mouth flooded with saliva that burned my tongue.

"Before five minutes ago!" George spat. "I ain't stupid, mista! You won't here when I came outta the kitchen!"

"And I been here since the place opened and didn't see you come in. Sides, Cypress Elementary School ain't had no guidance counselor till lately! An it's a woman sent from Elgin!" One–Leg chipped in, eying the old man suspiciously.

"Well now! Ain't you two bout the smart ones—"

"Smart enough to see a haint! *Smart enough to see a haint*!" George screamed. I think that's when it happened. The next few seconds seemed to take place in slow motion. The air became razor sharp, like breathing cold glass. The old man slowly rose from the table—that grin still plastered wide across his face; One–Leg reached to grab him with his one good arm and the old man's face warped and shimmered to reveal a horrible caricature of a person. His features more resembled a wolf than a man's did, but the eyes were most definitely human. The body was all wrong though—even for a wolf. The front and hind legs were set too close together and the fur was too long. It reminded me too much of human hair.

"Shoot it! Shoot it and don't look in its eyes!" George ordered. I could barely hear him, the wolf–thing had me mesmerized. Those eyes—those incredibly cold blue steel eyes had me paralyzed.

I stared deep into those frozen orbs, my thoughts kept repeating the Evangelist's words: *I'm going to teach you about pain, Ezekiel. I'm going to teach you about fear.*

The lesson was just beginning.

"I have a message from her holiness, The Evangelist," the thing said. Its voice was so heinous I became nauseous. It reeked of disgusting, perverted things. *"Anyone who gives succor to the last of Uriah and Eliza's spawn shall suffer a fate worse than Slim Ron's. This man has been marked. His last breath is scheduled for March 15th at exactly noon. So orders the Evangelist, the true owner of the Wheel!"*

George scurried into the kitchen and returned with a pump shotgun. One–Leg grabbed a meat cleaver and a few of the other patrons picked up chairs. I stood there, petrified with fear. I don't think my heart beat the entire time that thing spoke, but I marveled at the courage of the people around me. Here was something more terrible than any creature ever written about; here was something that slipped out of hell's sub–basement and people were willing to stand up to it like it was nothing more than a common thief.

"You go back to hell, where you belong! No haint ever ran George and I'll be good and *goddamned* if'n you gone be the first!"

George pulled the trigger and the blast of the shotgun ripped through tables and chairs like wet paper, but the wolf–thing just laughed. Its mouth stretched open and I saw the sharp fangs of its teeth. It howled and yelped wildly—not in pain, but in amusement.

I stood there watching this, but I felt detached from it. It was like watching a movie; my mind would not let me accept what I was seeing as reality.

"You're steppin on my shadow, Georgie! Now I gotta fix it so you shit in reverse!" the thing barked.

Tamara screamed so loud my head shook. Someone behind me threw a chair at the thing and a few people ran out along with the waitress. I had unconsciously backed away and moved over to the table where Tamara was sitting. The poor girl had an expression on her face that defied description. As for me, I don't think I could have been anymore afraid than I was at that moment.

How wrong I was.

The wolf–thing stood up, still laughing maniacally, walking toward George and One–Leg. George kept firing the shotgun in futility until the air reeked of gunpowder and strangely enough—Boston Crème Pie. The bullets didn't harm the thing at all. By now the diner was filled with the screams, that thing's crazy laugh and the blast of George's shotgun. The sound was deafening but I tuned it out. My mind shut down allowing the smallest amount of sensory input possible.

"Do something!" One–Leg screamed. "It's gonna get George!"

Instinctively I grabbed the glass pie top and flung it like a Frisbee. I watched as it sailed across the room and hit the wolf thing in the head. Its head snapped back as the glass shattered its skull. The cover cut its head so deep a flap of flesh hung off its eye. Blood gushed as if from a punctured artery, spraying the diner with stygian fluid so dark it looked like ink.

"No fair!" the wolf said in pain. "You cheated! You cheated and it's not fair! I had him! I had him!" It turned toward me, its one good eye glaring in hatred. "Maybe I can't kill you, Ezekiel! *But I can hurt you reeeeeeeeeal bad.* I hurt your brother, Mookie once. I had him crying like a baby! Made him get down on all fours and moan like a whore in heat! Made him moan, I did!" The thing grabbed its hind leg and pulled it, imitating a man masturbating.

The sound of its voice made my body quake. It sounded like it had gargled dirty mop water. It was coming closer now, leering at me. With all of my might, I grabbed the pie case and swung it, viciously connecting across its spine. It howled again and collapsed. George ran up to it and pushed the shotgun deep into its ear.

"*Tell that old tart to lissen close to this*! Cause there's another one wit her name on it!" He pulled the trigger and the wolf's head exploded, spattering the diner with chunk size pieces of potted flesh and fur.

The only sound was the echo of the shotgun blast. The diner was emptied except for George, One–Leg, Tamara and myself. I gripped the pie case so tightly my hands ached.

"Is everyone okay?" I heard myself ask.

"I—I think so. Why did that glass hurt it, when buckshot wouldn't?" One–Leg asked.

"*Fuggin haints! Gotdamn fuggin haints! Look at my bidness now! What I got now, huh? What I got now?*" George's lips quivered. My heart went out to him. It seemed that wherever I went, death and destruction followed. I was so tired, so very tired. At that moment, I wanted nothing more than to just lie down and die. To give up and admit I was in so far over my head I couldn't see daylight.

"This is all my fault, George. I should've never came in here—"

"If'n your daddy heard you talk like that he'd have a fit! Don't you ever blame yourself for the actions of another! It wasn't no more your fault than it was mine! It was that hussy and her cronies from hell! Well, if she think she can scare ole George with a hairy haint-bitch, she better think again!"

"I...I really appreciate you saying that, George. But I still feel somewhat responsible. Let me pay to get this place fixed up!" I pulled out my wallet and found an ATM card.

"Where's the nearest ATM machine?"

"*Where's a Eighty what?*"

"Forget it," I said counting what cash I had left. Only in Cypress Point would a business owner not know what an ATM machine was. "Here's four–hundred dollars. That should help cover a little of the damage."

George pocketed the money without counting it. "I'm gonna tell you sumpthin, boy. You lissen close to this, cause ole George's been around and I know a few things. Your daddy was a good man; helped me out many a day, so in a way I feel like I owe his kin this much. Cypress is a dangerous place. It's fulla spooks and haints and gawd onliest know what else. You git outta Cypress as fast as it'll take you. *You unnerstand?*"

"Tamara and I have tried to get out of here ever since we left Lady Ophelia's place! We—"

"Why didn't the bullets hurt this thing? Why did the glass kill it and the bullets didn't?" One–Leg asked again.

"One–Leg, I don't mean to be salty, but shut the fuck up! Any jackass could see what happened! The haint ducked the bullets, but this boy here bashed its ugly craw open with that glass and knocked it down. Then I stuck the peace–maker here in its ear and sent it back to hell! Man, you slow!"

"I ain't slow, George! The bullets didn't hurt the haint; it was hurt by the glass pie case! You shot it more times than I can count and it kept walkin, George! It kept walkin!"

One–Leg was right; bullets didn't hurt it, but my mother's glass pie case did. I wiped thick gooey gray matter off it and ran my fingers across the inscription.

To Eliza and Uriah...

"I don't think it was a haint. It was flesh all right. It wasn't a human or an animal, but something in between. Something that she sent to try to scare me," I mumbled. If Clara had demons like this at her disposal what chance did I have to defeat her?

"I could've sworn it was a man. I mean I could've bet real money that it was man, just an old man sitting in a diner. *What...what did it say its name was?*" Tamara asked. She sat staring at the spot where the seemingly old man just materialized. She was trembling, her eyes glassy and unfocused.

"It said its name was...Franklin... *Franklin Earl Aloysius Roberts*. Fear. And One–Leg is right; it wasn't afraid of the shotgun. My mother once told me the only way to stop a haint is to hit it with something you love. This pie case belonged to my parents; it was a wedding gift from Ophelia."

"Ezekiel," Tamara said, her voice was so strained that I barely understood her. "Let's get out of here. I mean, let's try to leave again. Maybe we can get out now."

"What's she talkin about?" George asked, looking at Tamara suspiciously.

"It's like I told you, George. We tried to get out of here but we couldn't. The road that leads out of Cypress is missing."

"What? What're you sayin? How can the road be missin?"

I told George the entire story, leaving out nothing. I told him of the telegram and my trip back to Cypress Point. I told him how I met Tamara and the red–neck diner we stopped in. I told him how we wound up in Cypress during one of my memory spells. I told him of the trip to the bar and Slim Ron's murder. I told him of my meeting with Lady Ophelia and how she's not crazy and dirty and she doesn't really stink.

Finally, I broke down crying and I told him how scared I was and that I didn't want to die on March 15th or any other day for that matter. I half expected George to slap the taste out of my mouth and give me a lecture on how a Cypress man never cries, but instead he put his arm around me and I was surprised to see him wiping away tears of his own.

"Slim Ron was my brother—"

Fwap...Fwap...Fwap!

"—We never got along, his drinkin and all—"

Fwap...Fwap...Fwap!

"He never held a honest job. Always beggin and tryin to get over, but I made a vow that I'd avenge his death. That's why you gotta take back this money—"

Fwap...Fwap...Fwap!

"It ain't yo fault the Evangelist sent the haint! She know I'm gonna—"

Fwap...Fwap...Fwap!

"George, what is that noise?" I asked, staring at the double doors that led to the kitchen.

"Wha—"

Fwap...Fwap...Fwap!

"It's coming from the kitchen! It's another haint!" One–Leg shouted.

"No—I don't think it's a haint. It's something else," I whispered. There was something eerily familiar about that sound. Something I couldn't place just then.

"Somethin else, huh?" George said, aiming the shotgun at the kitchen doors. "It's somethin else, awright! *It's sumpthin that's bout to get its fuggin haid blown clean off!*"

Fwap...Fwap...Fwap!

"*No!*" I said, walking cautiously toward the kitchen. I pushed the barrel of George's shotgun away from the doors. There was something familiar about that sound, something that somehow both scared and excited me. I had an odd feeling that I should have automatically recognized it—

Fwap...Fwap...Fwap!

That it was a sound that I'd heard hundreds of times—

Fwap...Fwap...Fwap!

Slowly I stepped to the kitchen doors listening, as the sound grew louder.

"Boy! Stand way from the fuggin door! Don't open it!"

"*I have to! Something is forcing me!*" I cried and it was true. I tried to pull myself away from the door; the sound behind it grew monstrously louder and more violent. My hands still burned where that creature had touched me, but when I placed them on the kitchen door the burning ceased.

"Don't open that door, Ezekiel! Are you crazy?" Tamara shrieked.

"Move, boy! I ain't got a good shot wit you standin there!"

I could feel my heart thumping in my chest. My head throbbed in rhythm with my heartbeat. Something beyond that door wanted me and oddly enough, I was more intrigued by it than scared.

Fwap— Fwap— Fwap!

The sound was right behind the door now, I could see the doorframe bulge as something behind it pulsed and threatened to explode. There was an incredible energy behind that door.

A power.

"*Ezekiel, get back! Get back here!*" Tamara cried and this time I listened to her. Instinct made me draw back to where she sat. George aimed and cocked the shotgun at the doors but before he could squeeze the trigger the doors flew off the hinges with a massive wind. I covered my face, thinking that someone had detonated a bomb in George's kitchen. The wind created an eddy in the diner; I had to grip the table to keep from being blown away, carefully cradling my mother's crystal close to my body.

"*What is it? What is it?*" One–Leg screamed. The wind howled and whipped through the small diner. I closed my eyes tight and tried to shut out the sound, but it was no use. The Evangelist's words kept playing over and over in my mind: *I'm going to kill you...*

Just then, the wind died down and everything became as silent as a grave.

FWAP... FWAP...FWAP...

The sound came closer. I opened my eyes and looked at what caused all this commotion.

A baseball.

A ripped and tattered baseball.

The same baseball that Petey–Wheaty knocked into Evangelist Washington's yard all those years ago. I screamed so loud my head shook.

I'm going to teach you about fear, Ezekiel...

Chapter VI: *That Ole Jew's Gold...*

I don't know how long I stared at that baseball before George picked it up. I couldn't take my eyes off it. Fragmented pieces of memories flashed and flickered in my mind. Something horrible happened to me while I was in Evangelist Washington's yard, and the part of me that was real smart wouldn't let me remember it.

All of those memories will surface soon, Ezekiel. The prophecy will be fulfilled...

I could hear Lady Ophelia's words ringing in my ears.

"There's...there's some writing on it," George mumbled, looking at me worriedly.

"I already know what it says," I said. "'*To Petey, knock them out the park.*' It's from my dad. A Christmas present to my brother." I took the old ball and held it. "The last time I saw this ball I was in her yard. I believe I fell through the cellar floor and passed out. I don't know what happened to me after that. I guess this is her way of torturing me before she kills me the way she did Slim Ron."

"Not so!" One–Leg yelled. "I don't think this is her doing at all! I mean, that haint was sure nuff her doing, but not the pie case and not this baseball! *I think your family is trying to protect you!*"

"What help can they give me from the grave, One–Leg? The dead are never known to return—"

"Then what do you call that thing George shot?"

Tamara put her hand on my shoulder and One–Leg covered the ball in my hand with his, curling my fingers around it in a tight fist.

"Be of strong courage, young Ezekiel. There are forces in your favor," One–leg whispered. I looked at him, trying to draw strength from his words. Here was a man with half of a limb missing, probably never finished Junior High School— what I spent on entertainment in a month he probably didn't see in a year and yet in that moment One–Leg was the wisest, richest man in the world.

I put the baseball in my suit jacket pocket.

"What...what do you suggest I do?"

"Well, first of all, let's get you home."

George managed to padlock the iron security gate as we left the diner. My heart went out to him as I viewed the damage that thing left. The diner was ruined. I climbed into the Mercedes. Tamara sat upfront, George and One-Leg sat in the back.

"Nice car," One-Leg mumbled.

"Thanks—"

"—His other car is a Mercedes, too. Different color," Tamara interjected, smiling.

"Say, Ezekiel…you ever call or write while you were gone? I mean it seem a bit odd that you get back here not knowin' nuthin bout your peoples."

"You're right, One-Leg," I mumbled. "It was like the moment I left Cypress I forgot all about this place. I would send a card home every once in a while, but I wouldn't give much thought to it. Weird, huh?"

"Not weird as you might think," George whispered. "They rumors that a man can't leave CYP-Press without the Evangelist's permission. Damn shame the way she controls our lives. Not mine, of course. Nobody controls ole Georgie! When came time for me to open my diner I didn't axe her nuthin! I jest went an did it. People tole me that I wouldn't mount to nuthin, but I proved them wrong—didn't I One-Leg?"

"That you did, George. That you did."

"Now lookit my bidness."

From the rear-view mirror, I could see tears welling up in George's eyes. My father once told me that a man has to always have something to hold on to. Something that he could claim was his and only his. Sometimes it's a woman, sometimes his children, sometimes a car, a house or a business. But it's always something. A man has to have something to hold on to— something to keep his sanity together. For my dad, it was his wife, my mother. He adored her—worshipped her. For my brothers it was their street smarts and neighborhood status. Radar's was his basketball. George's Something was his diner.

And now, thanks to something that crawled out of the back of hell's slimy sewer, it was gone.

"Tell me, George. Tell me how you managed to put together such a beautiful diner," I said.

George discreetly wiped his eyes with his shirtsleeve and formed a weak half-smile. He enjoyed talking about that diner the way a parent would enjoy talking about little junior's achievements.

"You axed me the right question, didn't he One-Leg?"

"That he did, Georgie. That he did, go on an tell him. Tell him how you done it."

"I came into some money—"

"Nah, George!" One-Leg interrupted. "Tell him how you done it! Tell him the whole thing!"

George frowned, he looked at One-Leg sternly and then back to me. He closed his eyes and began the tale.

"I was what you would call a hardhead as a kid. Always gettin into trouble an lookin for sumpthin to steal. I won't mo than 'leben—twelbe the most. These two real nice Jewish ladies took a fancy to me. What happened was I tried to rob one a them an they caught me an instead of turnin me in, they tole me to come by they house and helps them to clean it and run a few errands for the money. They tole me I'd feel much better bout myself workin for it than stealin it. At first I thought they was crazy, but they gave me the money and tole me to promise that I'd come by.

"Well I got home wit that four or five dollars and I felt so bad that I went over they house and tole them to take it back! That's right I did! They was twins! Adina and Adira was they name. They was school teachers in what they called *the Old Country*. I started workin for them, Ezekiel. They'd give me maybe five maybe six dollars a week, but truth to tell I woulda worked for them for free. I never met two more decent people. They won't rich, but they was *clean*." George bit his knuckle and I could see his eyes misting.

"They taught me so much about the world, Ezekiel. When I tell you that God never set two finer women on this earth, I mean it! That goes for my mother an yours too! They won't rich, but they was clean! They kept a tidy house and they kept everything anyone ever gave them! It was almost like a library there, but like a fun library—you know? I would grab a photo album down sometimes and sit between them and they'd tell me of the Old Country and the Old Ways. I just loved hearing them talk sometimes; they could make me almost see it! An man they could remember everything! You axed them anything and they could quote it like a book!

"Well I looked after them till I was around fourteen. Then people on they block started axin a lot of stupid questions, like what I was doin wit two ole women and such. They'd never say it to my face, though. Won't too many people that could beat me in a fair fight, an even fewer in a cheatin one—ain't that right, One-Leg?"

"Still is, George."

"You hot damn right! So one day I'se comin out the house an I'm countin my twos and fews an here come Boochie Castor, givin me the eye like he wants to rob me. Well, I folded my money twice an set it deep in my pocket. I let Boochie know right then an there if he wanted my money he'd better pack a lunch! Cause Georgie ain't nobody's bitch! Boochie run up on me and start hollerin that I'm makin it wit the two ole ladies an that's why they pay me. I punched him three times in the face an I started to beat him into next year sometime when Miss Adira grabbed me and tole me to behave like a gentleman. I let Boochie go an you know he had the nerve to spit at Miss Adira? I beat that boy ass for about a hour! I beat him till I was tired! Beat him like he stole sumpthin! I would a kilt him if'n Miss Adira and Miss Adina didn't pull me off his sorry ass. Lousy cock-sucker!

"Anyway, one mornin' I goes to they house just like usual and nobody opens the doe. I don't think much of it, they was gettin on in years an all. Sometimes they just wouldn't hear the bell. So I use my special key they made for me, and I went in an hollered for them like I do. Just in case they won't dressed. I comes in an the first thing I notice is they clothes laid all over. Miss Adina and Miss Adira were very *meticulous* about they clothes. They taught me that word; it means fussy. Anyway, I called after them an there was no answer so I went to they bedroom and I gently knocked and called they name. Still no answer. So I takes it on myself to peep in an I see they still in bed sleep. So I picks up they clothes and go bout straight'nen after them like I'm used to when it dawned on me sumpthin was wrong. I went back to the door and I didn't bother to knock this time. I opened it wide and ran in. They'd was both laying in bed holdin each other. They had died in they sleep, Gawd blessum. Just like they always prayed to.

"It won't the dead bodies in the bed that scared me; the both of them looked as peaceful as angels. It was the cloud over the bed that scared me, Ezekiel. It was the cloud of death hovering over them! Miss Adira and Miss Adina tole me plenty of times what to do if death came in. Sometimes it'll come in an it can't get out, they'd say. I held my breath an opened the window to let that cloud out.

"See, they taught me that before we born an angel—I fo'get his name, but he suppose to be the angel of death—he tells us all the secrets of life and death. He tell us how long we live and who we marry and if we rich or po' and he touch us right here—"

He touched his top lip in the center, the part we call the Cupid's Bow.

"And he say, '*Shhh.*' We fo'get all it when we come into the world, that's why we cry! Cause the knowledge leave us! Ezekiel, I seened him! I seened the angel of death! That what the cloud was in they room! It won't my time to go, but I seened him just the same! He flew out the window like a bird of made of smoke.

"I stuck my head out the window an I called up the block telling the people that Miss Adira and Miss Adina was dead an for them to get help. Well, don't you know that ole ig'nant ass Boochie starts hollerin bout how much money they got and how much gold they got. 'That ole *good* gold! *That old Jew's gold*!' he said. He just kept hollerin that stupid shit till enough people started listenin. Dope heads and winos start gatherin lookin up at me in the window tellin me to let 'em in. I tole them they'd had to come through me first an I aims to kill the first man that tried! '*That ole gold! That ole Jew's gold*!' Boochie kept screamin. I tried to tell them fools that the ole ladies ain't have no money. Not no real money. They was just as broke as anybody else in Cypress Point, but they carried theyselves like they had money, Ezekiel. Not like they was better, but like they was better! I don't know if I'm explainin it right—"

"I understand, George. Continue," I managed to say, wondering what the hell this had to do with his diner.

"I guess you do, being Uriah's seventh. They got a beam an busted in the doe downstairs. I ran and braced the couch and everything else I could find against the front doe, mad as hell that I didn't have a gun on me! I got a few knives from the kitchen and I was ready to cut somebody's ass too short to shit!

"Boochie kept screamin, '*That ole GOOD gold*! *That ole Jew's gold*!' whipping them dope heads to a frenzy. I hollered till I was hoarse that they ain't had no money and they ain't had no gold, but they kept poundin on the doe. I could see the hinges buckle in the frame.

"They busted in and I started swingin. I caught Boochie across the cheek, cut a smile in the side of his face! I could see his teeth sideways! An then a bunch a them grabbed me. Boochie wailed on me tryin ta make me tell where the money was. They tore the place up! Ripped up all they nice things: books, letters, pictures. They even tore up Miss Adira's little music box that she said her uncle gave her on her tenth birthday. Man, I cried and hollered at them fools but they wouldn't lissen.

"They kept screamin at me, 'Where the money? Where the gold? That ole Jew's gold!' I tole them there was no money an no gold! Boochie's sick ig'nant ass yelled that the money must be in the mattress. Ezekiel, what happened next is too horrible to even remember. Them fools threw Miss Adira and Miss Adina out the bed! Tossed them aside like they was dirty sheets! I saw they bodies land on the flo' like a heap a trash. Well that jest bout did it for me. I went berserk swingin' and fightin'. They tied me up to the bedpost and made me watch! They ripped the bed apart and the box spring! Boochie monkey ass kept laughin the whole time.

"Then Boochie said that sometimes ole people keep money in they drawers. They stripped the bodies naked, Ezekiel. Boochie fingered both a them! That sick fuggin tripe eater! No respect or shame for the dead. They tore up the floorboards and ripped holes in the walls. Tore the place up! Then when the dumb asses figured there won't nothin worth stealin they left me tied up there wit the bodies. Ezekiel I cried and cried for hours before I managed to get myself free. Anyway, I tried to straighten out as much as I could. I placed them back on the bed an I dressed them, mindful of them being females an all. I got hold of the sheriff an he called the morgue.

"I found out bout a week later that the two ole ladies did have money! They owned they house and they had between them twenty thousand dollars in insurance money! They left everything to me, Gawd bless em.

"I used the money to fix up the house and rent it out and I opened the little diner. I designed the place myself. I found an ole recipe book that been in my fambly for *years*. Learned how to cook and I made sumthin a myself. *Now whut I got... 'cept a heart fulla anger*. Guess I jest axed fer too much."

"It won't too much, Georgie. It won't too much," One-Leg said consolingly.

George's face quivered and trembled, tears streamed out of hard bloodshot eyes. He scrunched up his face and cleared his throat. "The hell of it is, I never got a chance to pay Boochie back whut I owe him. That no good evangelist bitch made him sheriff, but I swore on those two ole ladies' graves that I would pay Boochie back for what he did. And two things I never did is break a promise or shit on myself."

I turned my gaze from him to the road. I'd come to a fork in the street. I hadn't a clue as to which way to go.

"Which way should I turn?" I asked, glad that such a horrific story was over. It was a grim but accurate testament of just how sick the people were in this town.

"You're gonna go about three blocks to the left and turn left at Mittle's Place," One-Leg answered.

"Mittle's Place? Are you sure? We didn't live anywhere near Mittle's Place—"

"No, Ezekiel. Mittle's Place is your block!" George looked at me as if I had fell and hit my head.

"I'm going to try to absorb this as best as I can, George. You see I grew up on Tilden and Pulaski. Five-twenty-seven Pulaski street, between Tilden and Lorthing. Now, I'll be the first to admit that I've been away from Cypress for a while, but a man just doesn't forget his address. Especially since I lived there over eighteen years!"

"Calm down, son. From the time I saw you enter George's Diner I knew you weren't quite in your right mind. I don't mind telling you that you spooked me something good just listening to you. Now, I'll admit that every now and sooner I like a bit more than a swallow of strong liquor, but unless I'm as crazy as a outhouse mouse, Uriah and Eliza always lived on Mittle's Place. Now you can take my word on that and George right here will tell you that I'm not lying. I'll bet my shadow on it."

"Leave-em be, One-Leg. He's a little slow," George said, squeezing my shoulder as a suggestion that I interpreted not press it further.

I remained quiet, trying not to let my fear show. Mittle's Place was the graveyard. Everyone in Cypress knew that. The Cypress Point Cemetery ran the length of Mittle's place. There were no houses, stores, or anything other than headstones.

I glanced back at George and One-Leg, wondering if they were being totally honest with me. It would be just like the Evangelist to send these two to trick me, just like her.

I'm going to teach you about fear, Ezekiel.

A lesson I was learning very rapidly.

I cut on the CD player, letting Sade remind me how mine was no ordinary love. I turned the rear speakers up high, so One-Leg and George couldn't hear me.

"Tamara?" I asked in a faint whisper, clearing my throat.

"Yes?"

"What do you remember about Mittle's Place?"

"Mittle's place?" she squirmed. "Um, well, I don't know—"

I pulled the car over so hard the tires screeched. George and One-leg slammed into each other.

"Now all of you listen to me," I seethed. "I've seen and heard a lot since I've been back. I've been threatened by rednecks, saw a man mutilated and crucified, and I'm still not sure what the hell just happened back there at that diner. But, and I mean this with all my soul, nobody is going to tell me that I grew up on Mittle's Place! That's the graveyard!"

"Ezekiel, I want you to calm down and drive to Mittle's Place. I am telling you as a man and as a friend of your father's that your parents and your brothers and *you* grew up on Mittle's Place. The graveyard starts on Pulaski and runs clear down to Lorthing. Now, I don't know what's happened to you, maybe you're confused or maybe it's just the shock of everything that got you actin so strange, but when a *CYP-Press* man tells you he'll bet his shadow you damned well believe him or challenge him!"

I stared in One-Leg eyes, searching for the smallest hint of betrayal but there was none. The look on his face was so stern, so resolute. If One-Leg was right then perhaps everything I knew to be true was a lie.

I'm going to teach you about fear…

Could Clara have somehow hypnotized me to have false memories? I know that unscrupulous therapists have been known to implant thoughts into people and then label those implants as *repressed memories,* but such a thing would require trust and many counseling sessions. Was it possible that she could have sown these seeds within my psyche without my knowledge?

After all that I had seen, anything was possible.

Reluctantly I pulled off and followed his directions to Mittle's Place. Let him be wrong, please. Just let him be wrong. Let him be wrong, because if he's right then everything I know to be true might be a lie.

"Go straight for three blocks and make a left. Mittle's will be the next block."

I did as I was told, noticing the familiarity of certain buildings, but the setting was wrong. Like someone had taken buildings from one block and planted them on another.

"This is the block here, Ezekiel. Your house is coming up. Any of this starting to look right to you now?"

I stared at the block hard trying to call up memories that just weren't there. It was my block, but it wasn't. Some of the houses were right, but most I had never seen before.

This can't be right. It just can't be! We grew up on Pulaski Street! Five-twenty-seven Pulaski street! I remembered my block, with its run down tenements and abandoned storefronts.

"I'm real confused, One-Leg. I didn't mean to snap at you back there, but there's something really weird happening. Part of this street looks like my block, but most of it is alien to me."

"Ezekiel," Tamara interrupted, "you admitted that you've been gone for an awfully long time, and that you really don't remember too much about Cypress. I just think that you're making more out of this than it really is. I mean with everything that's happened you don't need to add to it."

I thought about that, it certainly was possible. Hell, it was more than likely! But something just didn't sit right with me. A man may forget a lot of things, but there're certain things that are inculcated—*ingrained* within him. Like that memory with my brothers and I visiting my dad at the hospital. No one— and I mean *no one* could tell me that didn't happen, that I imagined it, or wasn't remembering it correctly.

"There's your house, Ezekiel!" One-Leg announced. We got out of the car and I examined the building closely. It did look like my building, but there were distinct differences. My building had an alley that connected the backyard of the building behind it, this building didn't. Never mind other little differences that could easily be explained by the time I was gone; alleys just don't up and disappear. But the hole from the chunk of brick that Petey knocked out of the building's front was there. He missed this guy's head by a fraction of an inch with his bat and hit the wall, knocking a good size piece of mortar loose from the doorway. There were other things, like where Tom-Tom had carved his initials into the molding.

"Now you remember it, right?" One-Leg asked, beaming.

I gave him a weak smile. This was my house, and yet...

George walked into the foyer and headed up the stairs. One-Leg and Tamara went in behind him.

"Well? You comin'? " Tamara asked.

"Yeah," I mumbled as I entered the doorway. The foyer was as I remembered it, but it was reversed, like looking into a mirror. *"God, wouldn't it be wonderful if I were just dreaming this!"* I whispered to Tamara.

"Well it's not. If it was I think one of us would have woke up by now."

One-Leg and George were at the top of the landing waiting for me. I trembled walking up the stairs. Would the old apartment be the same, or a mockery of the place I once called home? I took a deep breath and held it. Analyzed it. There was one thing that no one could recreate and that was the *smell* of my building. No one knew what the building smelled like *to* me, but *me*.

It was the smell of bad air. I could smell the mildewed Sheetrock, the dank cloying smell of despair, the subtle but unmistakable scent of defeat.

This was my building.

One-Leg, George and Tamara stood in front of the apartment door. One-Leg stabbed at the wooden door with his finger.

"This is Uriah and Eliza's place. I brought you home, Ezekiel. Just like I promised you I'd do. A *CYP-PRESS* man always keeps his word," One-Leg said with a fierce pride. I realized then that I had insulted him deeply while we were in the car.

A man has to always have something to hang on to.

One-Leg's Something was his word.

"Thank you, One-Leg. How are we supposed to get in?" I asked.

"Ezekiel," One-Leg replied, with more than just a hint of exasperation in his voice. "The key to the door is in your pants' pocket."

How in the hell could he know that? Hands trembling, I reached into my pants pocket and pulled out a set of worn and rusted keys. I looked up at the three of them with tears in my eyes. I knew I had not brought those keys with me. I didn't leave Cypress with keys so it was impossible for me to return with them.

It was a struggle getting the key into the lock with my hand shaking so badly. I took a deep breath and unlocked the door; silently praying for the strength to cross the threshold into the small apartment I grew up calling home.

"You guys coming in, right?" I asked.

"Cypress rules say a man enters his house first, Ezekiel. This is your house. You walk in and then tell us we can enter," One-Leg said stoically. His eyes were hard and firm. I looked into the apartment really not knowing what I expected to see; maybe my folks' things packed away in boxes, or maybe just empty rooms.

It was too dark to really see anything inside. The single, dim bulb that hung from the hall ceiling barely lit the stairway. I stepped into the apartment and felt an odd rush of steam hit me in the face. My hand searched the wall for the light switch and when I flicked it on—

"Just where have you been, young man! Petey's been home over an hour! You had me worried stiff!" my mother bellowed. She was standing in front of the stove with her hands balled into fists resting on her hips. I blinked wildly, trying to get my eyes to focus on what I was seeing. Petey stood sheepishly behind her with a look of fear painfully etched across his face.

"Well! Don't just stand there with your mouth hung open ready to catch flies! I've half-a-mind-ta- wail-da- tar-outta-you! Where were you?"

I ran and held her tightly. My arms wrapped around her waist with a fierce grip. I was overcome with a love and a grief so deep it took my breath away and left a hard lump wedged in my throat. Hot tears poured from my eyes, soaking her apron. I hugged her tighter, relishing the smell of her. A delicious mixture of wonderful things baking and Camay soap. I squeezed her so hard I could feel her back crack.

"Ezekiel," she said, pulling my arms from around her. "You have to be a man now. You know that, right? You're all we have left. You have to do it, E.J, because you're all we have left."

"I love you so much, Mommy! I love you so much!" Tears stung my eyes. Everything looked like a watery haze, like trying to see the world through a cascade.

"Ezekiel, you listen and you listen well! I love you more than the breath of life itself! We all do, but you hafta listen! Do. You. Hear. Me? You. Have. To. Listen!"

Each word was like a punch in my mind. She gripped my shoulders hard; I could feel her nails digging into my clavicles. She was young again! Her hair was black and full with lustrous curly locks. Her skin was smooth and clear as glass. Her eyes were focused, cold stern brown intense orbs of wisdom. I reached to hug her again, but she held me at arms' distance.

"I love you so much, Mommy! I'm so scared! I just want to stay here with you. I don't care if Petey and them pick on me forever I just want to stay here with you!" I thrashed and flung my arms in an attempt to get closer to her, but her grip on my shoulders was steady and strong.

"You can't stay here, Ezekiel. Not just yet anyway. Time'll come soon enough. I don't rightly know when, but I know Time won't run out before you're called. We'll be right here when you are, though. All of us."

I looked behind her and saw my father smiling. He was big and strong again. Nothing like the last time I saw him in the hospital. The sheen was back in his skin and his smile touched the corners of his eyes.

"Hey there, Ezekiel! Came to see the old man, huh?" he said with a wide grin.

"Dad!" I ran and jumped into his arms. I hugged him tightly, my tears giving his neck a good soaking.

"Hey, there! What's this! My little man bawlin like a baby!" He put me down and I marveled at how tall he and my mother seemed to me. They towered over me like giants. Either I had shrunk, or they had grown four feet in an instant.

"You hafta mind your mom now, Ezekiel. She tole you what you need to do. We hafta go now, but it's real good seein you again. Ezekiel, I don't rightly know if'n you unnerstan all that's occurin, but don't fret bout it. It'll all be clear after while."

"Daddy, don't go. Please let me stay with you. I just want to stay here with you and Mom. That's all I want."

"Ezekiel, remember when you left to go to New York?" my mother interrupted.

"Yes."

"That was when we knew you were the one. Your dad is right; we have to go now. But, Ezekiel…we're never far from you. All you have to do is think of us, and we're near you. All of us."

The apartment disappeared in thick clouds of white smoke and I watched my dad and mom turn and vanish into the dense fog.

"NO! Don't leave me again! Come back!" I ordered, trying to run into the cloud after them. I managed to snag my mother's apron strings. I wrapped it around my hand and used it as a guide into the fog.

"Ezekiel, no! You can't! You can't go! You can't go!" my mother screamed. I could hear the raw naked howl of terror in her voice. The fog grew thick and gray, bearing an uncanny resemblance to the morgue at Cypress General. Her voice was faint but no less intense. I ignored her pleas and continued to step into the gray smoke.

"EZEKIEL, NO!"

The force of her voice struck me like a hurricane. The apron string unwound itself from my hand. A wind forced me back out of the fog. I shut my eyes, groping for my mother, determined not to let her leave me. The wind continued to batter me backward but I would not relent in my pursuit.

"EZEKIEL, NO!" This time it was my father's voice. So deep I thought he had yelled into a hollow barrel. The bass of his voice rumbled through my chest. My heart skipped a beat and for a moment I was convinced that it would stop all together.

I opened my eyes and saw the gray fog slink away from me. Like someone had cut on a giant Hoover vacuum cleaner and sucked all of the smoke out of the room. I stood numb as I realized my parents were in that smoke. I looked down at my hand and saw where my mother's apron string had dug a deep groove into my palm.

Hot salty tears stung my face like small slaps. I furiously tried to wipe them away, but they lit upon my cheeks and lips like hard jabs—

"Ezekiel! My God, man! Are you back with me? Are you okay? Tell me you're okay!"

It was Tamara, leaning over me, slapping me awake.

"I'm okay. Don't hit me again." I struggled to get up. Tamara was crying and her tears fell right into my open eyes, blurring my vision. I wiped my face and saw the slate-gray ceiling above me.

"Oh my God, man! You scared me so bad! I thought you were dead! One minute you were talking to me and the next you just went blank, like you were sleeping with your eyes open! I really thought you were dead! You were talking to your mother and father, answering them like they were right here in the room! I was so scared. I didn't know what to do! I—"

"Calm down, I'm okay!" I massaged my temples to get the blood flowing back into my head. My wit slowly came back to me. Everything was still hazy, but a few things started to make sense. The gray ceiling accounted for that thick gray smoke I saw my parents walk off in. Tamara's tears were what kept stinging my eyes in the dream.

"I was so scared! I didn't know what I'd do if you had died or went into a coma. That's what I thought happened at first, you know! I thought you slipped right into a coma! You looked like a zombie! I mean your eyes were open the entire time!"

"Where's One-Leg and George?" I asked, standing unsteadily.

"Who?"

"You know—One-Leg and George! The guys from the diner! They showed us how to get here. Quit playing!"

"Ezekiel, baby, I know you're under a lot of stress. I mean all the time you were laying there talking to your parents I kept saying to myself that it only proves you're human—you know? I mean—you've taken all of this in like you were superman or something. But, I'm telling you that no one from that red-neck diner helped—"

"Quit playing! Not the *redneck* diner! The one we went into after we left Ophelia's! Come on—quit playing! The haint! The glass pie-case! One-leg and George!" By now there was panic in my voice. I searched Tamara's eyes for any hint that she knew what I was referring to. There was none.

"Ezekiel, I think you may have dreamt a lot more than just your parents while you were out like that. Why don't you tell me what you *think* happened."

So I told her everything that happened from the time we left Lady Ophelia's place.

"Well, you got it all right except a few little things like we never went into no diner after we left that crazy lady. We drove straight here! We didn't meet no One-Leg, no Hank, and no George. You dreamt that part. We came straight here and I made you coffee. You sat right there on the couch and said you wanted to take a nap, when I came out of the shower you were laying there with your eyes wide open hollering for your parents."

"Tamara, I couldn't have imagined all of that. I mean I couldn't! That thing in the diner—it all seemed so horribly real! If I imagined that then the Evangelist has won already, because I'm crazy! And I'm not talking regular Cypress crazy—I'm talking schizophrenic! Paranoid delusional! I'm talking stark raving lunatic crazy that they lock up in the G Building!" The G Building was the psychiatric wing of Brooklyn New York's Kings County Hospital. It was famous for housing Crack addicted kooks who picked Saturday night to howl at the moon.

"Ezekiel, you listen to me and you listen good!" she grabbed me by both shoulders and stared deep and hard into my eyes. "Dreams sometimes seem real, but they are just dreams! Now, you've been under a lot! I know it's hard hearing your momma died and all your brothers died, but that's the only part that's true. The rest is just a dream."

I wanted to believe her, but I couldn't. One-Leg and George were real. The experience in that diner was real. The baseball was real—

The baseball!

"Tamara, where's my suit jacket?"

"Hanging over one of the kitchen chairs, why?"

"I'm going to prove it to you!" I walked over to the jacket and felt the pockets. The ball was in there, just as I remembered.

"This baseball came from that diner—the one we've never been in! This is the same baseball that Petey hit into her yard! The same baseball I woke up screaming about on the plane! Explain that!" I held the ball out to her, proof that I wasn't crazy.

She crossed her arms and raised her eyebrow with skepticism. "Ezekiel, listen to yourself. Just listen to yourself! You were the one that swore up and down that there was nothing magical happening! Look at yourself! This worn out ball is supposed to prove what? You must have brought it with you from New York, or you picked it up when you came in and put it in your pocket! I really need you to pull it together, man! You're scarin me!"

Her words stung like a wasp's barb. Every logical bone in my body told me she was right, but I just couldn't accept it. The very core of my being screamed that One-Leg and George were *real*. That horrible experience in that diner was *real* and the baseball I held in my trembling hand was definitely real.

"Maybe—maybe this is another trick of hers! Maybe she somehow hypnotized you to believing that they don't exist! She probably has them strung up some place like she did Slim Ron!"

Armed with this new insight I ran to the front door in a desperate attempt to rescue George, One-Leg and my sanity. Tamara snatched me back with a strength that belied her stature.

"I really need for you to be strong now, Ezekiel. I need for you to sit down and pull your head together. I don't want to leave you here, but I will because you're scaring me and I've been scared enough in my life."

She gently but firmly pushed me toward the couch. "Just lie here and I'll make you some coffee. I think I saw a bottle of brandy in the cabinet; you could probably use a taste. *God knows I could.*"

I sat down and furiously rubbed my eyes trying to force myself to remember the truth. One-Leg and George couldn't have been mere figments of my imagination. I'm just not that creative. I remembered too many details. The way that waitress licked her lips, the smell and texture of that Boston Crème Pie, the awful sound that beast made when I clocked it with my mother's crystal pie holder. That was real. I know that was real.

The pain in George's voice as he told me about those three little girls—were they his nieces or daughters? I couldn't remember if he told me. But Lukie raped them. Yes, that much I remembered. And that horrible story about Miss Adira and Miss Adina. I couldn't have just made that up.

Could I?

Tamara brought me a mug of coffee generously laced with brandy. My hands were so shaky I couldn't get a grip on the cup. Tamara held it for me, guiding it to my lips. The coffee was bitter and strong, but the brandy soothed my frazzled nerves.

I gulped the coffee, wishing she had just given me the bottle of brandy. This was definitely no time to be sober. I looked into her eyes and wondered what was going on in her mind at that moment. How did I look to her?

"You must think I'm a total moron, don't you?"

"Shhh! I don't think no such thing. I think the sooner we get outta dodge the better, though. I'm not trying to let what's left of my sanity be tested like yours is. I know I couldn't handle it."

"It's amazing! The apartment looks the exact same way it did from when I was a kid!" I stood and looked around, marveling at how pristine the place looked. Everything was set so perfectly—maybe *too* perfectly. The apartment looked like it had recently been cleaned. The windows were sparkling clear and all of the furniture looked almost brand new.

"Something's wrong," I whispered.

"What?"

"That window—the one behind the couch, it was broken! Mookie broke it fighting with Tom-Tom over who'd get to watch the television—"

"So? Your mother had it fixed."

"No! You don't understand! Mookie broke that window because he wanted to watch Batman and Tom-Tom wanted to watch Spiderman! I remember that, I know this can't be the same window."

I walked over to the window and inspected it carefully. The pane was old and beaten but unbroken.

"It's not the same. I know it's not the same. Not only that," I moved around the apartment slowly, cautiously.

"The carpet under the coffee table is wrong! This *looks* like the same carpet but it's too new! My mother had that carpet forever it seemed like!"

"I don't understand—"

"Oh, it's close…real close! She even managed to figure out how to make the hallway smell! But she screwed up royally in here!" I ran to the kitchen and flung open the refrigerator, peeling back the rubber seal. "Look here! If this is the same fridge where's my initials that I carved into the door? It's a trick! A trick!"

"Ezekiel, calm down! You're not making any sense!"

"Don't you see? This isn't my mother's apartment! This isn't where I grew up! She's trying to mess with my head! She's trying to—"

The room spun like wooden horses on a merry-go-round creating a mad eddy of furniture. The walls blurred into a dull gray and sepia swirl. I reached for Tamara but she joined the whirlpool. Her form blended with the room, an indistinguishable smudge with the walls and furniture.

I was the only thing that wasn't spinning.

"It's not real! It's a trick of hers to break me! It's not real!"

I tried to shut my eyes but I couldn't even so much as blink. My head throbbed with every sadistic revolution. The room whirled faster and faster and I was forced to watch. My eyes darted from side to side in an involuntarily effort to keep up with the vortex.

Fear and anger bubbled deep within me. It wasn't enough that my entire family had been slaughtered and that memories that were long since dormant padlocked and buried had escaped and erupted with a vengeful fury. It wasn't enough that I came home to a nightmare of biblical proportions—no that wasn't nearly enough! She had to make sure I couldn't even so much as get a good night's sleep and a moment of peace before I died. I imagined having to endure this until March 15th. Just being a puppet at her beck and call. Nothing but a pawn on her profane chess board.

I'm going to break you, smart boy. I'm going to stretch the limits of your sanity and have you beg me for death.

"No you won't!" I screamed at the swirling room. "I'm better than you! I'm better than you!"

The room spun faster in disagreement with me. My eyes felt like they were being sucked out of my head. The noise had reached a deafening level and I could feel little pieces of my sanity floating away like frayed threads in a hurricane.

You be better than good at it! You hear me, E. J? You bout the only one with a real chance, so you be better than good at it!

J.B.'s words cut through the chaos. I could hear him just as clear as if he stood right next to me. It reaffirmed that all of this was a shoddy trick to scare me.

"It won't work! It's not real! None of it is real! *NONE OF IT IS REAL!*"

The room suddenly stopped swirling and I went down on one knee with dizziness. It was quiet and I looked around for Tamara, One-Leg and George, but I was alone. Was this still a dream?

I really need help now. I'm trying my best to fight her and to keep her from driving me crazy but I really need help now. If there's anybody out there to help me, I really need to know!

I half expected to see my parents and brothers come out of a shrouded mist and tell me to fight the good fight, but instead I saw her.

Clara: The-Goddamned-Evangelist.

"Ezekiel, my poor boy…if this little parlor trick of mine has you shaking like this, what will happen when the real fun begins!"

She was wearing the same white gown from the park that night she drove Radar crazy. Her voice was inside my head. Her lips never moved. The room smelled of the funeral home and I could feel that intangible thing called sanity slowly slipping away.

She sauntered over to me, chuckling under her breath— mocking me. "I want you to know that you are going to be the easiest one yet. Your brother Petey put up a little struggle at least. Problem with trying to drive someone out of their mind is that you have to assume they are in their right mind to begin with!" She threw her hands to her mouth to stifle her laugh. "Oh I am sorry, Ezekiel. It's just that for a moment that harlot bitch mother of yours actually had me worried that you were some how different. She actually had me scared that you had a

125

snowball's chance in hell of beating me!" She crossed the floor, standing right in front of me. Her eyes smiled with an evil that numbed my soul.

"I'm going to kill you, Ezekiel. My promise to the Wheel will be complete when I drench it with your blood." She wrapped her hand around my throat, fingers as long as tentacles squeezed the blood in my head.

"I hate you, Ezekiel. I hate you like the fox hates the hare that got away and left him hungry. You look too much like your dad to me!" She tossed me across the room like an old sack. I landed in a tumbled heap, crashing into a dresser that fell on top of me. Everything went quiet and all I could see was white.

"Don't worry, Ezekiel. I'm not going to kill you just yet. That would ruin the grand finale! It's real important that you die the same way your infidel brothers did—tied to the wheel as it siphoned the blood from their veins. With your blood your mother's power passes to me, and then I'll be strong enough to put that crazy wench Ophelia out of her misery!"

She threw the dresser across the room. It shattered with a terrific crash. I scrambled away from her on my hands and knees. Scared beyond all comprehension. Her voice had a razor sharp hatred to it. It grated and churned every nerve in my body.

"What did we ever do to you? What did I ever do to you? All I wanted was to get out of this town!" I didn't want to say that. It sounded weak. My brothers wouldn't have said it.

They would've died with dignity.

I remember Ritchie once told me a man has to die anyway, so he might as well do it with honor. That was one thing I truly envied about my brothers now. They loved life, but had absolutely no fear of death. I used to think it was foolish, but now I thought it was somewhat liberating. If a man is not afraid to die, what can he possibly be afraid of?

"I know Ophelia told you about the Wheel. It will avail you naught! I am the Evangelist! I and I alone! There is no other messenger but I, do you hear me! I am the one chosen by the Wheel!"

She was maniacal now, ranting and raving at the top of her lungs. Veins stood out in her neck and forehead. I secretly wished she would scream so loud she's bust a blood vessel and die right then and there—and then it hit me—I scared her. Something about me really scared her!

"You cheated my mother and Ophelia out of their share of the power! You cheated and now your conscious won't let you sleep! You say you hate me, but you really hate yourself! You claim you're from God, but you don't really serve Him! My daddy could've never loved you! He loved my mother and that's why you hate me, because no one loves you!"

I thought on Lady Ophelia's words: *She could've killed your daddy right then and there. I think in her own way she loved him...*

"My dad could've—"

With one fluid puissant motion she snatched me up on my feet and held me above her head. I could not believe the power in the small frame of this woman.

"You push me too far, boy. You're going to make me maim you so that the Wheel won't accept the sacrifice." She grabbed my crotch and squeezed hard. Her eyes never left mine and that sadistic sneer stayed plastered across her face. Pain filled my torso in sharp, hot pulsing stabs. My eyes watered and I couldn't tell if it was from the pain or the fear.

Like it made a difference.

"Beg, Ezekiel. Beg me for your life. Swear allegiance to me and I will not only let you live I will let you serve me. Beg me, on all fours like a dog—naked. It's the only way to save your life."

My head felt like an electric bubble about to pop. My eyes felt like they were being forcibly unscrewed from their sockets. My thoughts were a disjointed hazy film as her hand around my throat forced my heart to pound wildly. Her other hand was crushing my testicles.

I'm going to die, I thought. I'm going to die right now and I'll see my brothers! What will I tell them when I see them? No doubt they'll tease me and be angry for not avenging them— but maybe I could do something that could let us share a laugh in the afterlife...

I mustered up enough saliva to hock and spit in her face.

"Then kill me now! My brothers will be waiting for me with a bottle of beer and a good laugh!" I groaned.

She shrieked and released me. It was an inhuman noise; a wail of demented wrath that undulated and shook the air with a long piercing violent sound.

"You will die skinless! Do you hear me, Ezekiel? You will die with your manhood in a jar and skinless! I will gargle your blood over the Wheel and inherit your mother's power! *I have someone who wants to play with you, Ezekiel!*"

Suddenly, behind her, Lukie emerged. His shadow filled the room like water from a burst dam. The Evangelist stood in front of him, my spit dripping off her face. Her eyes hardened into two steel marbles.

"I could let Lukie show you where your prostate is located, Ezekiel. I could really let you suffer right before the end, by letting him stretch you—*jail style!*"

My insides melted as his face became visible. My stomach heaved and turned as my gorge threatened to rise.

"Do you know what a Colostomy Bag is, Ezekiel? It's when you have to push through your side because your asshole's been torn out! There's no rule saying you have to meet March 15th hale and hearty! You always did seem a little sissyish to me anyway! You just might like it!"

I wanted to stand—I did not want to die on my knees, but I couldn't move. I wanted to fight, to display the same degree of courage and bravado in the face of death that I imagined my brothers did. I thought of how J.B died, *fighting* back—not on his back.

I wanted to, but the sight of Lukie standing over me filled me with such a numbing fear I couldn't breathe. My limbs wouldn't obey me. I was literally petrified with fright.

If anyone is there I really need help now! I REALLY need help right now! I can't do this by myself, please if there is a God out there, please give me some help!

"Beg me, Ezekiel. Beg me and I can stop this right now. Swear your soul to me and I can stop this…I can stop this…I can stop this—"

"Stop this, Ezekiel! Stop this and wake up! Wake up!"

It was Tamara again, only this time One-Leg and George were behind her. I was on my knees and she was shaking me.

I thrashed out blindly, thinking Lukie was still there. One-Leg and George held me. Slowly I came around, like a person waking from a horrible nightmare it took me a minute to realize it was only a dream.

"You okay there?" One-Leg asked, helping me to my feet.

"Just tell me that this is real. I don't think I could take finding out she's messing with me again! Just tell me that this is real!"

"You jest sit a spell. Whatever fit you was havin done passed. We right here witcha," George said consolingly.

"What happened to you?" Tamara asked.

I told her.

"Damn! That's scary as hell! If she can mess with you like that she can fix it so you don't know what's real and what's not!"

"Yeah...like right now, I'm not sure if this is all a part of her trick!"

"This is real, Ezekiel. You walked in here and started having a fit. Talking to phantoms and haints. We stopped you," One-Leg added.

I sat on the couch and George brought a bottle of brandy from the cupboard. I was relieved that this was really my mother's apartment. For the moment the nightmare had passed and this was real.

I sipped the brandy and relished the warm glow of the liquid sliding down my throat. Tamara had brought her bags up from the car and asked if she could take a shower. I pointed to where the bathroom was. George said he'd take a run to the store and pick up a few groceries. Cooking is what he loved to do and after all that had occurred in the past few hours he needed to be in the kitchen rattling some pots and pans.

One-Leg took the bottle from me and took a good gulp of the brandy. He sat next to me and I could hear Tamara in the shower.

"I'm glad we got a few minutes to talk alone, Ezekiel. I know you went to see the Lady. I know you ciphered her message." He reached into his shirt and pulled out a medallion that was around his neck. Although one handed he managed this with the adroit touch of a professional pickpocket. He held it out to me.

"I want you to take this, Ezekiel and wear it always. I found it years ago and for some reason I think I am supposed to give it to you. May it protect you as it has done me."

I took it and held it in my hand. "One-Leg, I really don't believe in any of this nonsense. There are no such things as good luck charms. Let me explain something to you. When ancient man looked up in the sky and heard thunder he thought that the gods must've been angry with him. He was scared out of his wits because he had no idea of the science behind what made thunder and lightning. He invented things to sate his unnerving curiosity. Well after a time a few unscrupulous but very shrewd people caught on and labeled themselves priests and such. They convinced the masses that for a fee the gods' wrath could be appeased, usually with money but sometimes a blood sacrifice would do if there were someone that the priest wasn't particularly fond of. So now everyone feared the thunder and lightning, but loved the rain which brought life to the crops and—"

"Hush, Ezekiel. I know how you look at us. Like we the most backward people in the world. You went away and discovered fancy teachins an all. You learned that the earth is round and the face in the moon isn't really a face; but Cypress isn't as backwards as you think. Neither was ancient man. He learned to fear the thunder and respect the lighting. He saw what the lightning did to the trees and he knew enough to seek cover when it rained. And yes, Ezekiel, he learned to fear an unseen God. Now I know that the rainbow is jest the reflection of the light through water, but it *soothes* me to think that it's God's way of sayin it's time to stop the rain. I know the sun don't really rise an set—but you try to 'splain that to somebody that *seened* the sunrise and set. Until you come to the understandin of these simple things, I'm 'fraid the more complex things will keep escapin' you."

He closed his hand around mine in a gesture so natural it reminded me of a father talking to his son. A powerful shock went through me. This had happened before: the medallion in my hand and my hand in his. As intense as the feeling of Déjà vu was, it passed just that quickly.

"When I was a child," he said. "I thought as a child. I *understood* as a child. But when I became a man—"

"I put away childish things," I finished. "I know the quote."

"But you see faith is not a childish thing, Ezekiel. When we children we believe harder because the world seems new and magical. A lot of things fall out our heads when we older. We give up a lot of dreams, but faith isn't one of them. You—"

"One-Leg, I realize you mean well. I also realize that you're a lot older than I am and that it's hard to let go of some beliefs, but the Evangelist is not God. She's not a super person. She might know how to get in a person's head and really scramble them up but that's about it! She's a magician! Don't you see? That's all she is! A charlatan! A—"

"Then the Wheel isn't real?" he asked rhetorically.

"It may be! But don't you see? The Wheel could be a meteorite from outer space! It could be some sort of material that causes hallucinogenic delusions! Hell, it could be a hundred different things including—"

"Real?"

The look on his face was one of a teacher trying to convince the student on the simplicity of fire.

It burns.

"Ezekiel, everythin you jest said is true. The earth is round and it's not the center of the universe as once believed. We've learned how to predict the weather and even capture the sun's energy to make a bomb big enough to blow everythin away. But there are things that were here before man…an things that'll be here long after he gone. The Wheel is one of those things, Ezekiel. The sooner you come to accept that you didn't learn everythin in school the better it'll be for you. You hafta let go of all your schoolin, Ezekiel. You hafta lissen to what Lady Ophelia told you—"

"I can't do that, One-Leg. A man has to have something to hold on to. George's was his diner. My father's was his love for my mother. My brother Petey had his baseball bat. Mine is my education. To take that from me is to take *me* from me."

"Then…" he paused trying to choose his words carefully. "Then make this like it was part of schoolin, Ezekiel. Make this like it was one of those college tests, but remember that I told you. The Wheel is real."

The medallion tingled in my palm. It's warm, I thought. I couldn't tell if it was made from wood or metal. It was a flat disc with a mark carved in the center. It looked like it could have been gold, but when turned in the light it gave off a lustrous platinum color.

"I've never seen any metal like this. What is it?" I asked marveling at the weight of it.

"Do you really want to know?" he asked me coldly.

"Ye-yes," I stammered not sure if I really did.

"People think I'm jest a drunk who don't know much. George kind of takes care of me, letting me sweep his diner and run errands for him. See, something happened to me a long time ago. Something to do with this here medallion. I don't really remember too much about it, other than I woke up one day with it and I was in the Evangelist's yard. Something I saw that day scared me bad. I don't remember exactly what, but I think it was the Wheel. People say I'm crazy cause anybody that saw the Wheel is either dead or crazy, so you can guess what that makes me."

A heavy silence passed between us. I knew One-Leg was pissed that I doubted his word when he said he'd bring me to my mother's apartment. It hadn't helped matters that he thought I was showing off my education. I had come to Cypress with a poised arrogance, making sure my suit and car let people know that I was of a certain social status, but none of that mattered now. One-Leg was right. If I wanted to survive this deadly game, I'd better recognize the rules.

Namely, that there weren't any.

"What do you remember about your daddy's first stroke?" he asked me, rubbing his amputated arm.

"I...remember how sick he was. I remember being scared that he was going to die. I remember hating the Evangelist for working him so hard that he got that sick like that. Why?"

"Your dad and I were working in the factory late one night trying to make some overtime. You see what happened today, at George's diner? Well that won't the first time I saw a haint. It was cold that night. Colder than I ever remember it being. Brittle cold, Ezekiel. The kind of cold that set in a young man's bones and stays there till he dies. Your dad and I were alone that night in her factory. Normally it be so hot that a man liable to melt in there. See we worked in the wood processin part. Puttin the shine on the caskets. I knew somethin was wrong from that cold. Your dad knew it, too. We was scared, Ezekiel but we kept workin anyway."

He pulled a pint out of his pocket and unscrewed the top with his teeth. He spat the top on the table and took a long hard swig. I looked at him and saw beads of sweat line his forehead. The sharp smell of corn liquor danced on his breath as his hand shook so badly he almost dropped the bottle. I placed the cap back on it for him.

"Thanks, Ezekiel. We were scared because that night we seened a side to her that we never seened and we knew we was in trouble. She was in her office, chanting some madness—craziness, Ezekiel. The sounds she was makin won't part of no language made by man. It was like…it was like animal sounds, but I be hanged if'n I know an animal that sound like that."

He reached back for the bottle and I thought about the day I mistakenly walked into her office and saw her chanting. I wanted to join One-Leg with a hard swig of that moonshine, because I knew what scared him that night.

"Your dad, he told me to leave. He said he'd finish up and he'd clock me out with him. He…your dad tried to save me, Ezekiel. Nobody ever gave a rat's tail about me, but that day your dad tried to save me. He was the one who got me that job there. He was the one who tried to get me to stop drinkin so much and I really tried, Ezekiel. I tried for him cause he really cared about me. You see…after I found this medallion…I had woke up screamin and I took to drinkin like a fish takes to water. I had to. It was either drink or really go crazy." He stared at the bottle on the table, his eyes starting misting up.

The room was quiet except for the sound of Tamara in the shower, I could hear the water running. I unscrewed the bottle and passed it to him.

"Now, I'm gonna tell you this and you gonna tell me I'm just a one-armed drunk that swallowed too much rubbin alcohol, but I swear to you I am not lyin. She came out her office butt naked and her feet never touched the ground! She *floated down the steps at us!* Her eyes were all glazed an her skin was covered in some sort of thick gel. Looked like gray lotion.

"As cold as it was my nature got *hot seein her.* You know what I mean by that, don'tcha?"

"You were sexually excited," I said, remembering Lady Ophelia's story of how Clara tried to seduce my dad.

"Not just excited like a man would want a woman. I was…*hungry* for her. The way a animal would be hungry for food. I won't a man that night, Ezekiel. I was no better than a rabid dog.

"I remember your daddy pulling me off her an us runnin like the devil himself was after us. When I looked back at her she won't the Evangelist at all. It was somethin like what George shot. And it was comin at us hard an fast. We ran and ran through the factory, the basement and then through the cellar until we came through a set of doors that led to an old cave. Ezekiel, I could hear that thing yellin behind us. Tellin me to finish what I started. And a part of me wanted to! I was never so disgusted wit myself. Your dad...he kept me on my feet, runnin."

He took another swig of the corn liquor and passed it to me. I declined as politely as I could. The wisps of smoke that came out of that bottle smelled like pure alcohol. Anything flammable within twelve feet of One-Leg would have probably exploded.

"I don't rightly remember what happened that night, but I know when I woke up I was in the hospital with half an arm and your daddy was standin over me. He said that even though I was missin half an arm I was lucky to be alive. This medallion...I believe it saved me somehow. Ain't been a day I don't wake up screamin about that night. I had to go back to drinkin after that. I have to drink everyday to quiet the nightmares."

"I know a lot about nightmares," I whispered. "This whole town is a nightmare."

"There's some good in this town, Ezekiel. Jest take some diggin and an open mind."

The playing of Fur Elise broke the silence between us. One-Leg looked around in wonder and it took me a moment to realize where the music was coming from.

My cell phone.

I nervously grabbed it out of my jacket pocket, thinking it was another one of the Evangelist's tricks. "Hello!" I shouted angrily. I just knew it was the Evangelist playing with me again. I was ready and loaded for bear.

"Hello! Mr. Johnson! Where are you?"

The voice sounded muffled, filtered. I could barely hear through the static.

"Who is this?" I demanded.

"It's Patrick, sir! I'm here about the car. Where are you?"

"Where are *you*?" I asked, gasping. In all of the commotion, I had completely forgotten about Patrick! I was home free!

"I'm standing by the car, sir! Where are you?"

"I'll be down there in a second! I'm in the building the car is parked in front of!"

I closed the cell phone and ran out to let Patrick in.

—   —   —

Patrick stood in front of the car, his enormous girth blocked the entire cab of the Mercedes. His eyes swept up and down the block coolly. I stood looking at him. He appeared even larger than I remembered.

"Man, am I glad to see you! Where's the car you came in?" I grabbed his hand and pumped it vigorously. Patrick stared at me coldly, then he stepped aside and I saw that the Mercedes had been totaled. Stripped. The windshield and windows were gone, the seats, airbags, dashboard, music system, steering wheel, all gone. Removed as cleanly as if done with a surgeon's scalpel. All four tires and rims were gone. Even the hood ornament and trunk medallion.

I peered into the pristine cab wondering how anyone could have stripped a car so cleanly. No rips, no tears. Not even a thread hung from the roof of the interior. You would think the car came off the showroom floor in this condition.

"The car I came in is wrapped around a tree just before a sign that reads, '*Welcome to Cypress Point.*' I was hurled about sixty feet into the air and landed in a rough brush. If you can imagine a man of my girth traveling through the air like a circus acrobat shot out of a cannon then you'd begin to understand the shock I'm feeling now. And forgive my brusqueness, but just what in the name of sanity is going on around here? This automobile has been picked clean! Not to mention the fact that everyone I came across ran from me as if I were the devil himself!"

Foreigners aren't allowed in Cypress, Ezekiel...

We were stuck now. I had inadvertently led Patrick into a trap.

"Patrick, perhaps you should come upstairs, but I want you to check your commonsense and sanity at the door, because if I'm only partially right we both took a left turn into the Twilight Zone!"

You could be bringing that man here just to get him killed!

Thunder rumbled overhead as the wind picked up and somewhere in the deep dark distance, I could hear the Evangelist's maniacal laugh...

<u>Chapter VII</u>: Were there no graves in Egypt?

When Patrick walked through the door One-leg and George looked like they saw a ghost. Tamara drew away from him as if he was a leper. I was so embarrassed I could have died. Was it Patrick's size that forced this reaction?

"You have to excuse them—"

"Why them? This is the reaction that I've been getting since I arrived."

"*From whence comest thou*?" One-Leg gasped. There was a look of naked terror in his eyes. Patrick stared at him oddly. What was happening?

"What's wrong with you people? This man is here to help me! You guys are treating him like some sort of plague—"

"You chose the right word!" George blurted. "It's the fulfillment of her prophecy! We gotta get her help now! Don't we, One-Leg?"

"Who are they speaking about?" Patrick asked.

"I have no idea!"

George crossed himself and kept kissing his thumb and forefinger.

"Will somebody please tell me what the hell is going on?" I screamed.

"Ezekiel, you broke the first rule. You let a stranger in Cypress," One-Leg said solemnly.

Him got the looks of foreigner...

"And just what in the name of Voodoo Vera is that supposed to mean? I mean, forgive me if I seem a bit curt about this, One-Leg, but I don't give a damn about that! I want out of this town and this man—*whose name is* Patrick by the way—came here to help me get out. Now, let's all play nice like good little boys and girls and give our new guest a warm greeting. Shall we?"

"How did you get to Cypress Point, Patrick?" One Leg asked.

"I came by car, why?"

"And where's the car?" George asked.

"Well, it's like I told Mr. Johnson here. The car crashed and   I   had   to   walk   into   town."

They looked at each other, glancing back and forth,

grading his answer. Patrick stared at them with an odd look on his face. I was the only one that wasn't let in on the joke.

"Ezekiel, I told you it was a bad idea calling him in the first place! A lot of people probably saw him and now they know you're here!" Tamara scolded.

"Tamara, what the hell is wrong with you? What the hell is wrong with all of you? This man is going to help me get out of Cypress Point—PERIOD! Now I'm sorry if you guys can't understand that I am not interested in a knock down drag out fight with Clara and her gruesome henchman, but that's just too bad. Uriah and Eliza's baby boy is going home to good old New York City, back with the terrorists, gangbangers, thugs and muggers where it's safe!"

"Perhaps someone should tell me what's going on." Patrick crossed the room and unpacked the bags of groceries that George had brought. He picked each item up and inspected it carefully.

"Don't like the food, Patrick?" George asked. There was a trace of sarcasm in his voice.

"It's not that at all, sir. You can probably tell from my size that I'm a man with a more than a hearty appetite. It's just that everything in this bag is generic—"

"*Genawha?*"

"Generic. See? There's no company label on any of these cans." He held the cans up. "This one says, peas. This one here merely says, corn. Even the boxes don't have any information as to who processed the food or how old it is. It's just odd. Even generic items have some sort of information on the labels. Where the item was packaged, ingredients, stuff like that."

"So?" One-Leg asked. I walked over and helped Patrick empty the bag. He was right, the loaf of bread simply read, Bread. No clue as to when it was baked or by what company.

"What do you make of it?" I asked, wondering what it meant.

"Nothing, if it was just this, but coupled with the other things I've seen in this town I'm starting to wonder."

"Things? You haven't seen *things* yet, but if we don't get out of here I think you will!" I replied.

"Please tell me what's going on around here, Mr. Johnson!"

I told him everything, from the phone call to the moment he arrived. I told him the entire story, without embellishing or omitting anything. When I spoke of the Wheel George and One-Leg's eyebrows curled. I was treading on sacred secrets.

"Well, Patrick there you have it. My entire family is dead because of this woman and she means to kill me on March 15th. I have to get out of this town."

Patrick sat his massive frame on the couch deep in thought. No one spoke and the silence was deafening. We all just stared at him. I stared because I prayed that he would believe me. He represented someone from *my world*, the sane and normal part of existence.

"There is only one way for me to help you, Mr. Johnson. You have to face this woman and make her release her hold on you."

"Are you crazy? Have you heard a word that I've said? I brought you here to get me out of Cypress! Not to lead me into the jaws of death!"

"Were there no graves in Egypt?" Patrick asked.

"What?"

"Because there were no graves in Egypt, hast thou taken us away to die in the wilderness? It's from the Bible."

"Exodus, chapter fourteen verse eleven. I know where it's from! Why did you say it?"

"How do you propose we leave when we have no mode of transportation? The Mercedes is now an empty husk sitting on concrete blocks, remember?"

I stared at him, wondering what to say to that. Tamara was right: I probably brought him here just to get him killed.

"Patrick, listen to me carefully. There is no way I'm going up against her. She is the personification of everything evil. I want you to help Tamara and I get out of town! I know I told you a thousand dollars, well make it five thousand! Payable as soon as I'm beyond the city limits! I know I owe you a new car, and that's no problem! If the insurance won't cover it I'll pay it out of my own pocket! I—"

"Your money can't solve everything, Ezekiel!" One-Leg blurted, gulping the remainder of his liquor.

"Tell me again, about the dream you had on the plane. Tell me again," Patrick said.

"I told you! I was in her yard trying to get a baseball. The same one I picked up in George's diner. It's...it's a mystery. I can never remember how I got out of her yard. It's a nightmare that I have from time to time. Why?"

"Because it's the key, Mr. Johnson. Just tell me again."

"I *told* you! I can't remember what comes after that! I'll tell you what, let's get the hell out of here and we can talk about it on the way!"

"How?"

"We'll steal a car if we have to! Or we can walk out of town! We just walk in one direction until we hit the ocean! We—"

"No, sir. There is no leaving here until this is done. Have a seat."

He pointed to one of the kitchen chairs and politely but firmly ordered me to it. There was something about his presence, something gentle yet demanding, and it wasn't just his size—it was his demeanor. Here I was one step from a total mental meltdown and yet his calm insouciant attitude kept me from pressing the panic button. I sat in the chair as ordered.

"I want you trust me on this one. I've had experience dealing with survivors of mental and physical abuse. The mind is a wonderful and amazing instrument, Mr. Johnson. It has the ability to alter its perceptions in an attempt to heal itself. You've no doubt suppressed certain things deep within your psyche, but I think they're just bubbling below the surface. I'm going to give you a sort of mental antacid, we're going to burp this memory to the surface and take all of the mystery out of it. We're going to do this together, you and I. I'm going to be here with you every step of the way and I promise you, that you will be free from this nightmare forever."

There was a soothing, caressing tone to his voice. He placed his massive hands on my shoulders and I felt all of my pressures melt beneath his hot palms.

"Close your eyes, Mr. Johnson and just relax. I could tell from just looking at you that you probably hadn't had a good night's rest since before the plane ride."

I vigorously nodded yes, drifting off into a peaceful trance. I felt like I was on the beach watching the tides gently ebb and flow.

"I want you to focus on nothing else other than my voice and maintaining a feeling a peace and comfort. You deserve this, Mr. Johnson. This feeling is yours for the taking and no one is here to take it from you. Do you understand?"

"Yes…I deserve this."

"That's great, Mr. Johnson. You are totally relaxed right now. Nothing can or will interrupt how peaceful you feel right now. You are totally in control, Mr. Johnson. Totally in control."

"Totally in control," I whispered.

"Now, Mr. Johnson, we're going to watch a movie together. It's a movie that only you can see, so I'm going to need you to describe everything you're seeing to me, okay?"

"Okay."

"There's a little boy, going into a yard for a baseball—"

"No!"

"Yes, Mr. Johnson. It might be a scary movie, but that's all it is. A movie, okay?"

"O-Okay."

"Tell me what he's doing."

"He's climbing the fence, he's so scared."

"I know, but he's going to be okay. Trust me. I just need you to watch him and tell me what he does."

"He jumps half the fence instead of climbing the rest of the way down. He hurts his ankle but he doesn't know it just yet. He's too scared. His brother is yelling at him and he is so angry with his brother…but not just his brother…he's angry with God for making him the youngest. He's always being picked on and no one cares how he feels. He's weak and skinny and…and…"

"Go on, Mr. Johnson. Remember it's just a movie."

"And he wishes his brothers were dead—all of them. He wishes they were dead and that way no one could pick on him. He is so mad and he has so much anger in him, but he doesn't realize it because he is so afraid."

"I understand, but let's just concentrate on what he sees."

"He sees the baseball sitting in the grass and he hears his brother screaming at him to get the ball. He is scared beyond anything imaginable. There's…a smell…horrible…it's the hospital's emergency unit. He knows that smell from when his dad got really sick."

"It's just a movie. Just a movie."

"He walks over to the baseball...the ground is soft, fleshy. It's hot out, very hot. He is sweating and he keeps licking his lips because the sweat is so salty. He bends down to pick up the ball and...and..."

"Yes, go on. It's just a movie."

"Something grabs his foot—a hand reaches out of the ground and grabs his foot. Oh my God! Someone help him! Someone help him!"

"Calm down, Mr. Johnson! It's only a movie! Whatever is going to happen has already happened and I can tell you the little boy makes it home. You know that, don't you?"

"Yes."

"Good. Now tell me what happens next."

"He is pulled through the ground. He falls into a giant cave, his head and back hurt. A small light blinds him. The light...it's not natural. It's not real light—it's—"

"Just a movie."

"He stands and tries to gain his bearings. He screams for his brother, but no one comes to his aid. He is small and weak and scared senseless. He screams and screams but no one hears him. The light scares him. He thinks it's the light for dead. The light *speaks* to him. It consoles and agrees with him. He stops crying. The light now intrigues him. It is a small ray, but very powerful. He steps into the light."

"Yes, and what happens?"

"I can't see him anymore."

"Why?"

"The light has swallowed him."

"Look deeper, Mr. Johnson. Look deeper...tell me what the little boy sees."

Silence.

"Mr. Johnson, I want you to stop watching this movie now. I want you to remain feeling relaxed and very much at peace. Do you understand me?"

"Yes."

Patrick released my shoulders and I felt like someone had just woken me from a very deep sleep.

"Whereja learn how to do that to people?" George asked Patrick.

"It's just simple suggestion."

"Simpa suggestion my clean ass! I seen people work roots on people's minds and that's jest how it starts!" George spat. "Where you from, mista? How'd you get to Cypress?"

The chill in the room became evident from George's frosty tone. Patrick regarded it impassively. "Have a seat," he said, preparing a sandwich. "My story is best told on a full stomach."

George and One-Leg sat, their eyes never left him. Tamara glanced nervously out of the window. I was a more than a bit intrigued by Patrick. He just seemed to take all of this in stride. I wondered what it would take to make him lose his cool, break down and really panic. Unfortunately, I knew if he stayed in Cypress for any length of time I would find out.

"Before I tell you about me, there's just a few questions I have about you all. Has anyone other than Mr. Johnson seen this wheel?"

"I've never seen—"

"Yes you have, Mr. Johnson. The day you fell into her cellar chasing the baseball. That was the light you saw."

I stood silent as bits and pieces of a horrific memory swirled in my mind. What was that light? How did I get out of that cellar? What was *The Wheel?*

"No one has seen the Wheel. No one," One-Leg stated hotly. He gave me a look that I knew meant for me not to say anything about what we spoke of.

"Mr. Johnson saw it."

"No one saw it, 'cept for the Evangelist, Miss Eliza and Lady Ophelia. Many men tried to find it, but they all either went crazy or died."

"Well, if no one has seen this Wheel, how do you know it exists?" Patrick asked.

"Because the sun exists!" George shrieked. "Because there's proof of it in—"

"Hush, George! You speak of things beyond even your reckonin!" One-Leg rebuked. George remained silent and I stood there wondering what in the hell was going on. Patrick looked at me strangely, like I was missing something that was glaringly obvious.

"What's your point, Patrick? I mean I can tell you there's a lot of superstitious people in this town. As you can see this thing called *The Wheel* holds a religious type zeal with the local residents."

"Do you believe in this Wheel, Mr. Johnson?"

"I believe there's a logical explanation for whatever it may be."

"Define logic."

"Excuse me?"

"Define logic. Ever since I've arrived I've seen nothing here that remotely resembles logic. The Mercedes is sitting in front of this building picked so clean that only a group of master mechanics could have dissected it. I found you entirely by a combination of luck and sheer will power. This entire town defies the term. So I ask you, to define what you see as logical, because, Mr. Johnson, I believe what I have seen and what I have heard. The Wheel is real and this woman who calls herself an evangelist means to kill you. The way I see it you have very little choice in this matter. You have to face her and in my opinion it would be prudent not to wait until March 15th to do so."

There was a stony silence and then George spoke. "Boy, you talk fancier than a ten dollar whore, but a tree recognize a carpenter! You sayin what I think you sayin?"

"I'm saying that the best defense is a good offense. I'm sorry I don't have a wittier way to put it."

"So in other words, we take the heat to her! Yeah! We attack her instead of waiting for her to attack Ezekiel!" George was excited, like a wild cat that suddenly smelled prey.

"That's exactly what I mean."

I stared at Patrick angrily. He was supposed to be the voice of reason in this madness. He was supposed to represent the normal aspect of reality, a person from my world. He was supposed to pick me up and remove me from this hellhole. Instead, he now joined the same nightmare that I had hired him to rescue me from.

"Patrick, I want you to listen to me and listen to me well. I know you think this is just a hick town with very unsophisticated people, but I am telling you that all of your tenth grade psychology is useless. We will not attack the Evangelist. We will go downstairs and we will find a way out of Cypress Point together. That is the only way we can—"

"Did you love your brothers, sir?"

"What?"

"Your brothers. Did you love them? I listened to you tell me how much you hated them as a child, but did you learn to love them?"

"I...I don't want to talk about my brothers. You wouldn't understand."

"I think I understand more than you realize. You grew up thinking your brothers hated you. That they looked upon you as weak and timid. You wanted their love and their acceptance. Instead, you felt bullied and picked on. You despised being the youngest, the weakest. Your brothers were all muscular, *strong* men and you wondered why you didn't inherit your father's strength. But, Mr. Johnson, I think—*I know* you've inherited something far greater than physical strength."

"Does your crystal ball come with the directions out of this hellhole?"

"Yes. It does. I know you're being facetious, but the only way out of here is to face this woman and make her release you. Sometimes you have to face what scares you, Mr. Johnson. Facing your fears is the definition of bravery. Only the fool doesn't know fear."

"Then my brothers were fools, because there was nothing they were afraid of."

"I think they were more afraid than you can imagine. Can you envision being a part of such a homogonous family and yet an old woman seems to have the power to pick off your brothers one by one? And she starts at the top. With your eldest brother; the toughest member of your family. Jim Bruce. Now picture what Danny must have felt when the very next year, on the very same day Ritchie passed on. Coincidence? Perhaps, but now think of your brother Tom's reaction when Danny dies— also on March fifteenth. By now he, Henry and Peter are plotting revenge as it is undeniably obvious that the Evangelist is behind these heinous acts. But none of their plans mean anything. They can rant and rave, beat up as many people as they can, but it can't bring back their brothers. They are afraid, Ezekiel. Not for themselves, but each other. For the first time their strength and neighborhood toughness means nothing. Each one of them wants to achieve what the brother before them could not. To defeat the Evangelist. To stop your mother from mourning each year. To save the rest of Uriah Johnson's children. To save you."

"How do you know that? How do you know what my brothers felt?"

Patrick ignored me and walked from the kitchen to the coat closet and opened it. He walked around the apartment like he'd been there a million times before. All eyes followed him. No one said a word. He reached into the closet without looking in it and pulled out a rolled piece of canvas.

"Do you know what this is, Mr. Johnson?"

"No."

He unrolled the canvas to reveal a painting of a young boy staring out of a dirty window. The vivid colors and bold strokes were magnificent. I stared at the painting first wondering where in the hell it came from, then how in the hell did Patrick know it was in there. I couldn't take my eyes off that little boy; the painting was so *lifelike.* I could see the frown lines around his mouth, the detail of hopelessness etched in his face. It was the face of despair and defeat. I walked closer to the painting vaguely aware that Patrick's eyes were burning through me.

"What do you see in this picture, Mr. Johnson?"

"I...I see the children of Cypress Point."

"Any child in particular?"

"Excuse me?" I reached out and touched the painting, feeling the rough texture of the dried paint against the canvas. My eyes were glued to it. The longer I stared the more the painting told me. If a picture was worth a thousand words then this one was worth a million. The little boy was staring out of the window. He'd been crying, he was sad, but he was also proud, resolute. There was a glint in his eyes—a fierce, staunch, unwavering determination. He refused to accept defeat. That little boy represented the underdog in the righteous fight. No matter how great the odds you *had* to bet on him, because to bet against him was to believe that evil overcame good.

"Who painted this?"

"Your brother Ritchie painted it. This is his rendition of you. He painted it while you sat staring out of that window, crying and praying to an unseen God to get you out of Cypress. Your brothers loved you, Mr. Johnson. They loved you so much they died for you. One by one."

"*How do you know that? Who are you?*" I asked, shocked. I never knew that Ritchie had *any* artistic talent, forget painting a picture of this caliber. Besides, Ritchie always seemed so indifferent and withdrawn, like he never had any time for me at all.

"Is that important, Mr. Johnson? I mean — really, isn't it more important that your brothers loved you and wanted to see you leave this place safely? Who I am and how I know these things are irrelevant compared to that. Your brothers had talent. All of them. Jim Bruce was a mathematical genius—that's why he was nearly unbeatable at billiards, dice or cards. They called him J.B, the Gambler but he never played against the odds and that's why he won so often. He was also a marksman with weapons because he knew angles and trajectories without thinking about them—"

"How do you know that?" I repeated.

"Danny had the voice in the family," Patrick continued, ignoring me. "He loved singing although he hated when your mother insisted that he sung in church. Henry was the strongman, taking after your dad in physical strength. He was a body builder, blessed naturally with a flawless physique. Every muscle in his body honed and defined to perfection. Yet, on March fifteenth he met his end by being beaten to death on the same corner as his older brothers.

"How do you know that! How?" I screamed, tears leaking from my eyes.

"And lastly imagine, Petey. The last of Uriah's sons in Cypress Point...sitting and waiting for March Fifteenth. Confident that he would end this ferocious cycle. Imagine your mother's terror when that dreadful day came. Imagine Petey's false cockiness that this time things would be different. Petey died with his bat in his hand, Mr. Johnson. Your brothers loved you. That much I know for sure. Your brothers loved you."

I collapsed in the chair weeping over my brothers for the first time. I stared at the picture and thought on Patrick's words.

Who is this guy?

George walked over to the painting and touched it. "I knew Ritchie liked to draw, but I never saw anything like this from him! He was a graffiti artist! Marking up the walls and things! This is really good! Ain't it, One-Leg?"

"Yeah, it's got the real stuff. But I still wanna know who this man is. I don't like my whisky watered, Patrick."

"I'll tell you what, why don't we concentrate on the problem at hand and after it's been resolved I promise to tell you everything you want to know about me, deal?"

George, One-Leg and Tamara murmured among themselves that they agreed. I realized then that Patrick had shrewdly taken charge of us. His unassuming manner disguised a powerful skill for taking command.

Who is this guy?

"Okay, Patrick. What do we do first?" Tamara asked, combing her hair. She had changed into a pair of tight fitting jeans and a sleeveless shirt that plunged at the neckline.

"Well...Tamara, isn't it? Well, Tamara I suggest we form an alliance. This woman whom you referred to as the Lady—Ophelia, I believe you said her name was, seems to have knowledge about the Evangelist that may prove useful. I suggest we go see her as a group, maybe align ourselves with her and map out a plan of attack."

"A plan of—you mean attack the Evangelist?" I gasped.

"Who else? If I were a man who had his entire family wiped out by one person and she wasn't satisfied with that, but also vowed to kill me, I know I wouldn't just sit around waiting for the end!"

"I'm not sitting around waiting! I want out of here! I didn't come here to fight! You have no idea as to the evil that woman commands! It's like sending me to fight Mike Tyson with my hands tied behind my back and hot sauce on my ears!"

"Actually, I think it's worse than that."

"Look a here, I don't know about all this fancy teachins you and this guy spoutin, but I do know a good plan when I hear it! I say we round up some peace makers and blast that floozy to Kingdom Come!" George said.

"I don't want no part of this. I'll just stay here until yawl get back!" Tamara said. She no longer saw any reason to be refined by pouring the brandy in a glass, opting instead to just drink straight from the bottle. She and One-Leg shared it back and forth.

"The plan is, one go, we all go. First I propose we go and see this woman called Ophelia. She seems to be your most important ally, present company excluded. She'll be able to tell us the best plan of attack. I'm sorry, Mr. Johnson but there's really little choice."

"Don't tell me that! There is always a choice! We just start walking! We get a cab, a bus, anything! There has to be a way out of here!"

"Don't you think I would do that if it were possible? Whatever is keeping *you* here is also keeping *me* here!"

You could be bringing that man here just to get him killed!

I stared at him hard, feeling small again. Feeling afraid again. Feeling my wishes and wants didn't count—just like when I was younger.

"Okay, Patrick. I'm sorry I got you mixed up in all of this," I sighed accepting the inevitable. "You lead, I'll follow."

"The shit bout ta hit the fan!" George said excited.

And we all left to find Lady Ophelia.

Chapter VIII: The Attack.

George, One-Leg, Tamara, Patrick and I set out on foot.
I literally had no idea which way to turn, so I had to totally
depend on One-Leg's directions. The block had changed since
when we first arrived. Instead of the building being in the
middle of the block it now sat on the left hand corner of a cul-
de-sac. The other buildings on the block were either boarded up
or just empty shells. Picked as clean as the Mercedes. No one
else mentioned it or seemed to notice, so I decided to remain
quiet about it.

So many thoughts ran through my mind while walking,
but the first and most pressing was the obese enigma walking
next to me. Who was he? How did he know so much about my
brothers? Why was he so secretive?

My mother prided herself on being an excellent judge of
character. It was said she knew a man's soul just by being in the
same room with him. People have an aura, she'd say. A man's
aura can't lie. You can tell a good man from a bad man by his
aura, she'd say. A man's aura is his soul—and the soul can't
remain hidden.

But I couldn't read Patrick's aura.

"I'm glad the weather cleared up. Those hailstones really
stung," Patrick said to no one in particular.

"Wait—there was a hailstorm when you got here?" I
asked.

"That's what caused me to crash the car."

"I don't remember a hailstorm before you arrived. There
was one when I was at the airport, just before I made it into
Cypress. I thought the hail would crack the windshield but they
were hollow, slushy! Listen, did you pass a diner? A red-neck
diner that looked like even bacteria wouldn't eat there?"

"I passed a place that had been closed for what looked
like an eternity. I pulled up to it hoping for a bite," he rubbed his
massive stomach. "You can imagine my disappointment when I
found out it was closed. Condemned more than likely."

"I have a funny feeling that's where Tamara and I
stopped for coffee and pie. That's where I first saw my mother's
pie case."

"You got the clear sight, dontcha!" George asked
Patrick.

"Clear sight?"

"You know! The Gift! You can see things before they happen or you can tell things that already happened. That's how you knowed about the paintin and that Ritchie painted it. The clear sight!"

"I guess that's one way of putting it."

"Miss Adira and Miss Adina had it, didn't they, One-Leg?"

"Yes, they did, George."

"Sure they did! You got it, too. I knowed it when I seened you! That bout 'splains everything! I mean how you got into Cypress an all!"

"Yes, I guess it does."

George turned and gave One-Leg a knowing smile that One-leg barely returned. I knew then from that exchange that George had accepted Patrick, while One-leg still had reservations.

Meanwhile I was torn between the two positions. After all, I was the one that called Patrick and brought him into this nightmare, but his presence seemed to only add fuel to fire.

Who is this guy?

I saw a group of teenagers smoking reefer, passing a brown bag between them. They were about half a block away, sitting on the stoop of an abandoned building.

One of them turned and looked at me. He then scanned the group and when he saw Patrick the blood drained from his face. Like he was looking at death itself.

He reached into his waist and pulled out a pistol. The others turned, saw Patrick, had likewise expressions of shock. Soon we had a half dozen boys whose ages ranged from twelve to about sixteen pointing a variety of guns at us. Everything from a twenty-five to a Desert Eagle Magnum.

"Whoa! Whoa, guys it's okay! It's okay! I'm looking for Lady Ophelia! My name is—"

The guy holding the magnum fired one round up in the air. The report of the powerful handgun shattered the silence and boomed like thunder. The teen pointed it at me and motioned for us to keep moving.

"I just want to talk—"

Again he fired into the air, staring at Patrick with eyes that read terror on an unimaginable scale. It sounded like a cannon had gone off right by my ears. I turned and saw that George, One-Leg and Tamara had scurried for cover, but Patrick stood staring at the teens, almost daring them. Without a thought I approached the teen holding the Desert Eagle, my arms outstretched, palms open, pleading.

"We're moving, man. No need to waste anymore ammunition. I get the point."

"Git, then! Git fass and keep movin till you caint see us no'mo!" He pointed the gun at the ground and the rest did the same as we crossed the street and headed up the block. I looked back and saw they were spitting between the V of their fingers, the Cypress sign to ward off evil.

What was it about Patrick that evoked such a desperate response?

We came across a block where someone had demolished entire buildings and set the all rubble in the middle of the street, totally obscuring our view from the next block. This massive pile of bricks, concrete and stone towered over me. It had to have stood at least five stories high. We had to walk around the block instead of being able to continue straight. The debris was placed there purposely and recently.

"This is how she's trying to keep us here! You see this don't you, Patrick? She put this here because I'll bet you the path out of here is on the other side!"

Excited that the path out of Cypress was just over the mountain of rubbish I ran to it and tried to climb over the enormous pile of bricks and concrete. I managed to get at least six feet off the ground when the entire mound rumbled and shook violently. I cut my hands on the sharp outcropping of rocks and bricks and my feet lost purchase as I almost caused an avalanche of wreckage to come crashing down on top of me. The mound shook me off it and I landed on the ground in a heap. Patrick helped me to my feet.

"I don't think it would be wise to try that again, Mr. Johnson."

"Me either. It's like that pile of rocks is alive, Patrick!" I said brushing myself off. My hands were scrapped pretty good from those bricks. "She really is keeping us here!" It was really dawning on me that there was a good chance I would never see my home again. That I would die in this godforsaken place just as my brothers did.

On March fifteenth.

I thought of two old Greek myths that I had read as a child. Tantalus and Sisyphus. Tantalus was cursed by the gods to starve while food was right in front of him. The moment he reached for it, the food would move out of range. Sisyphus was condemned to roll a massive boulder to the top of an incredibly steep hill—only to watch it roll back to the bottom and start again.

Standing there in front of that colossal pile of detritus, knowing that the exit was just over that ridge, I realized how those two felt. It was like being imprisoned and having to watch through barred windows the world go on without you.

It was then that her power really scared me. Maybe she really was the Evangelist. The chosen messenger of God and maybe the Wheel was some sort of powerful entity from another realm of existence, and maybe…just maybe I was an educated asshole who deserved to die because I wasn't strong enough to defend my family's name and honor.

"Man can't escape his destiny, Mr. Johnson. Let's hurry to this woman named Ophelia. I'm sure she can—"

"Can what, Patrick? Can she move all of this out of the way and show us the way out of here? Can she assure me that I won't die on the fifteenth like my brothers did? Can anyone of you assure me that all of the bedtime stories my mother told me when I was young about good being its own virtue and the righteous always wins in the end are true? Can you?" I screamed shaking in a mixture of so many bottled emotions I couldn't truly say what I felt. I know I just felt impotent. Helpless.

Little.

"Now you cut this out and lissen to me, E.J.!" One-Leg scolded, holding me by my shoulder with his right hand. The strength in his one hand was incredible. It reminded me of my father's powerful right hand. A hand strong enough to crush stone into powder, but not strong enough to hold a little boy's dreams in its massive palm and protect them. A hand strong enough to knock the soup out of a man, but not strong enough to shoo away the cramps of hunger.

"You are alive and here and looking into God's beautiful sun. Your daddy once told me a man caint know too much bout his tomorrows. That's what makes a man a man. He gotta deal wit today, Ezekiel. You here an you alive. You alive, so live an quit playin dead."

He pulled me to my feet and I felt an overwhelming sense of embarrassment. None of my brothers would have reacted this way. I wondered then how One-Leg, George and Tamara looked at me. Did they think I was a fitting heir to Uriah?

I brushed myself off, mindful that my suit was ruined. I must have looked like a homeless derelict. "Let's just get to Lady Ophelia's place as quick as we can. Do you know the way One-Leg?" I asked him.

"I...well, I..." He looked around, rubbing his chin nervously. "I mean, I think we—"

"What he means is, we lost. I've been in Cypress Point all my life an I never seen this block before today. I should've said somthin bout it back when we left the house," George said, "but I thought maybe my mind was jest messin wit me."

"That's just great! Oh, this just keeps getting better and better!" I shouted, on the verge of panicking. "What about those guys back there that shot at us? Did anyone know them?"

"Never seen them before today. I never seen that block before today," One-Leg said.

"So what do we do now?" Tamara asked. She was chewing her nails and trying hard not to fall to pieces. If the Evangelist was powerful enough to *rearrange* entire blocks of a town this old, what couldn't she do?

"I propose we continue the path and see where it leads. It's obvious someone or something is guiding us. That's why we can't go straight, but we can continue up this block here," Patrick said, pointing to the only avenue not blocked by debris.

"I guess that sounds as good a plan as any," One-Leg murmured. Everyone seemed to agree with him, so we quietly continued up the only path available to us.

"Patrick, how do you think this is possible?" I asked. "I mean that she can change whole blocks like this at a moment's notice?"

"She certainly seems to be very powerful, Mr. Johnson. Very powerful. But I've run across witches like this before. I am telling you to listen to me and we shall prevail."

If that was supposed to reassure me, it didn't. Patrick's cryptic and enigmatic manner only served to further unnerve me. For such a huge man he moved very quickly, his gait brisk and spry. He carried his weight effortlessly. He had a way of commanding just with his presence, but not because of his size—his obesity was not the cause of his intimidating carriage. There was a certain air about him.

Alien, yet hauntingly familiar.

Finally, after so many turns and detoured blocks and roads, we came to the Molina houses.

"We gonna be okay now! I know where we at!" One-Leg said wiping his mouth nervously. He looked like a man badly in need of a drink.

The streets were unusually quiet. A few people gawked at Patrick, but most were apathetic. I was relieved that no one tried to shoot at us again.

"It's a little tricky from here," I said. "We go into this building but the floor—"

Patrick walked past me without listening. He entered the building with a confidence that made me think he'd been here before. George, One-Leg and Tamara followed silently behind him.

Even in daylight the building was dark. Although not the pitch-black darkness Tamara and I encountered earlier. At least now you could see your hand in front of your face if you squinted hard enough. Patrick maneuvered the narrow halls with the agility of a much smaller man.

"I see that what Mr. Johnson was talking about. The floor in this building isn't whole. We should stay to the left."

"What do you make of these symbols on the doors, Patrick?" I asked.

"Some strange hieroglyphics. Looks to be a combination of different ancient languages."

We stood in front of the door that we last saw Lady Ophelia in. Tamara held my hand tightly.

"I guess from the look on your face that this is the room." Patrick pushed the door and it opened with a loud creak. He entered with the swagger of a man walking into his livingroom.

"*How does this guy know all of this*?" Tamara whispered to me.

"*I have no idea*!"

George and One-Leg walked in behind him. Tamara gave me a slight nudge and I followed. The room was as silent as a tomb and pitch black, but I could feel that we were not alone. Although the unearthly darkness and hollow feeling of the room was gone, there was still something not quite right about it.

"Lady Ophelia, show yourself," Patrick commanded. At once the lights came on, blinding me. I squinted and saw George, One-Leg and Tamara all covering their eyes, but not Patrick. The light didn't seem to affect him at all.

"I am here, Patrick!" Ophelia answered. "I see you've come back, Ezekiel. And you brought company!"

"Yes! I brought George and One-Leg, they were friends of my father and this man is—"

"Not supposed to be here."

She was sitting in her chair with Buford and a couple of other very large men standing by her. Around the chair, lined on both sides of us were dozens of people kneeling and praying. The crazy lady ruse was gone; she looked even more graceful than last time.

"I...I called him here thinking he—"

"Could help you escape."

"Yes."

"But now you realize that can't happen."

"Yes."

"And—"

"And he wants to challenge this so called Evangelist so that he could break whatever ungodly hold she has on him and release him from this place," Patrick finished.

All eyes turned coldly to Patrick when he said that. He had disrespected Ophelia by interrupting.

"Ezekiel, tell your guest that it is not polite to enter the home of a stranger without first consulting on the ways of the household."

"I—"

"I apologize Lady Ophelia if my tone seems a bit curt, or my manners brusque, but we are dealing with life and death and a strict timetable for both."

"You meddle in ways that you cannot begin to fathom! You—"

"Have no time for such trifles."

Ophelia stood, her jaw locked, her fist clenched tight. "There is a mark on the door you entered. Cipher it!"

"It means sanctuary."

There was a murmur throughout the room. Ophelia raised her hand and all became silent.

"Lady Ophelia," George said humbly, "He's got the clear sight."

"Any fool can see that, George! Lady Ophelia don't need nobody tellin her nuthin!" Buford reprimanded. Patrick stood tall, his massive frame defiant. The crowd regarded Patrick with a look of awe. Not just at the fact that he correctly answered Ophelia's question, but his mere presence in Cypress seemed strangely upsetting to everyone.

Him got looks of Foreigner!

"Ask what you will, Patrick. It seems my time is just about done," Ophelia said. There was a hint of defeat in her tone. With that statement she abdicated her power and authority to Patrick.

Who is this guy?

"We need to have total access to The Wheel. Also I need to know how many followers the Evangelist has. It is my intention to attack her on multiple fronts simultaneously, increasing the odds of success."

"You realize the odds of surviving such an attack?"

"I do. But I have little choice in the matter. Mr. Johnson called me here and I mean to help him."

"Why did you call him, Ezekiel? Why didn't you just believe in what I told you? I could have helped you fulfill the prophecy, now you have introduced a huge random element into this. I can no longer see what will happen!"

"If you couldn't foresee my coming then perhaps neither could she! This random element as you call it may be our Ace-in-the-hole so to speak!" Patrick said.

"Mayhap you're right, but by now she knows you're here and—"

"And we need to hurry! March 15th is rapidly approaching!"

There was a thorny silence between them. Their eyes bore into each other as a drill bit bores into wood. In the end Ophelia turned her head and acknowledged that Patrick was right. I felt like I was a patient with two preeminent doctors arguing which treatment was best.

"I'll need all of your people, along with any weapons they can muster up. I'll also need a map of the funeral home, especially detailing any underground tunnels or caves. And I'll need intelligence on how many of her followers are with her at a given point in time. Naturally, we'd want to attack when she's with the least amount of people."

"Excuse me, Mr. Bond, but don't I get a say-so in this?" I asked hotly.

"No. Now as I said, I need for one person to take account of what weapons and ammunition we have, another group will do reconnaissance and report back here to headquarters—do we have any walkie-talkies?"

The throng gathered around Patrick as he handed out orders like a born general. Tamara pulled me away from the crowd into a secluded corner of the room.

"What are we doing? Huh? What are we doing? He's talking about attacking the Evangelist! It's suicide! Suicide! Who is he? How does he know everything about this place? Even Lady Ophelia doesn't trust him! One-Leg doesn't like him and neither do I!"

"Calm down! I know what you're saying, but in a lot of ways he's right! We can't get out of here and the only way out is to fight. I don't want to, but at least I won't have to do it alone! I mean...*I'm scared, okay*? I'm not the tough guy my brothers were, and I'm really scared!"

"I know...I know, but to attack her? That's like playing with dynamite!"

"Actually," I said, remembering Patrick's answer. "I think it's worse than that!"

"Remember your promise to me. Nothing will happen to us!" She reached to kiss my cheek but I turned my head and caught her fully on the lips. Passion exploded within me and I grabbed her tightly, my tongue explored her mouth and neck. She responded with a low throaty moan. I don't know what came over me. Nothing else in the world existed in that moment. I wanted her so bad that nothing short of taking her would sate my libido.

She pulled back, her face red and flushed.

"No, Ezekiel. Believe me, you don't want a girl like me...you deserve much better."

"Why do you say that?" I panted hard.

"I—I'm not the girl for Uriah's youngest."

"What's that supposed to—"

A loud crash came from just outside the door. It sounded like someone had detonated a grenade right outside the room.

"What the hell was that?" I screamed. All eyes turned to the door.

"This is the Sheriff! We know you have a murderer in there! Come out with your hands up!"

"You've got to be kidding me!" I screamed.

"They talkin 'bout Patrick! They blame him for Slim Ron!" Ophelia explained.

"That's ridiculous!" I said. "He wasn't even in Cypress when Slim Ron was killed!"

"That ain't nobody but Boochie Castor Ig'nant ass!" George said. "We got any weapons up in here, Buford?"

"George," Buford grinned, "We got a shit load a weapons!"

He went to a closet and pulled out a duffel bag. He dumped the contents on the floor. Out spilled weapons of every caliber and variety. George grabbed a Mossberg shotgun. One-Leg grabbed a Desert Eagle .357. Buford chose an AK47 for himself. "For those special moments," he whispered. Most of the people in the room scurried out the back door, but a handful stayed and loaded up pistols and rifles.

I saw myself grab a nine-millimeter and check the clip. It was like I was moving in a dream. J.B. taught me how to shoot and handle firearms, so it wasn't holding the weapon that frightened me.

It was the fact that I would probably really have to kill someone.

I stood looking into the faces of those around me. George and One-Leg looked like this type of thing happened everyday. They didn't seemed phased by it at all. Patrick walked up to me with two magnums in his hands. He looked like a cross between Dirty Harry and Ralph Kramden.

"This isn't how I had it planned, Mr. Johnson. But you know what they say, *the best laid plans...*"

The banging on the door grew louder and more violent. The hinges bulged with every thrust, but held. Ophelia held her hands up, somehow I knew she was keeping the door closed.

"I can't keep them back much longer, Ezekiel," Lady Ophelia rushed. Her voice strained from holding the door shut. "Already I can feel the door's protective symbol about to give way. Buford, get those guns loaded! If we're to make a stand now is the time! Ezekiel, you put into motion a wheel that turns on its own. Not even I can see what will happen next!"

"Don't you fret none about it, Lady Ophelia!" Buford boasted. "Me an these boys here gonna send these fools to the dark place! You jest git to safety before things get real hot and stink!"

She backed away from the door, her hands still outstretched, pushing at the empty air. A few people followed behind her. Buford pulled me down and told me to stay low. He passed me two plastic bags of bullets and told me when the shooting started to aim for the spaces between the slats. The windows were all boarded up, shuttered. The space that Buford referred to was less than a quarter inch wide.

"You guys got all of about five seconds to come out with your pants down and your hands up! Or else I'm a comin in blazin!" a voice shouted through the door.

"Give us more time than that, Boochie!" George retorted, firing out of the slatted window. "One-Leg here has your momma on all fours an she jest got all his dick in her mouf!"

"George, you ole lady diddlin sissy! When I drag your chicken-fried ass outta there butt naked we gonna have a parade up and down Cypress!" Boochie replied, firing back.

"Aw, have a heart, Boochie!" George pleaded, firing two shots. "Your mamma suckin One-Leg off like she hungry! Hey, when was the last time you fed this nasty heifer?"

Buford and One-Leg aimed and fired through the boarded up windows. Bullets rained on the walls and doors and I could see the wood dimpling from the impact. George and Boochie continued to insult each others' mothers, fathers, penis size and anything else they could come up with. The way they carried on, you'd think they were two guys in a bar entertaining the pub with their best quips and ranks instead of two guys literally trying to kill each other.

"Hey, One-Leg! You in there, you old crippled shit hose? How in the hell you hold a gun? Come on out before you shoot yourself, you old drunk! Hey, come on out an I'll buy you a fifth of rubbin alcohol! The wintergreen kind you like so much!" Boochie yelled.

"Yeah," One-Leg answered. "I'll come out! I'll be right out! Jest as soon as I finish here! Me an George here an we takin turns on your momma! George had ta tie a board to his back ta keep from fallin in. Normally I wouldn't do a chick this ugly, but you know how it is wit us drunks, any port inna storm! You make sure you got that fifth, you hear! Cause I'm gonna pour it over your grave!"

More bullets. The air hung heavy with the smell of gun smoke and scorched wood. I had yet to hear anyone fall. As far as I knew, neither we or they had yet to take a casualty.

"Hey, Buford! C'mon out an I won't tell them how you helped us set up Slim Ron!" Boochie yelled.

"Fuck you!" Buford screamed firing out of the window. "You and the horse you rode in on!"

"That wasn't a horse, Buford!" George said. "That was his hairy ass momma!"

"Oh! I'm sorry, Boochie! I thought that was a horse! Then again I never seened a horse that damned ugly befoe!"

"Hey, Boochie! Your momma said she miss you!" George hollered. "Least that's what I think she said in between slurps! By the way, I saw your daddy this mornin! He came by an tore my place *up*! Least I think it was your dad. He had a real hairy ass jest like you! Coulda been your aunt though! Hairy asses run in your family like hot water down a drainpipe!" He shot three times out of the window and then turned to me. "Ain't you gotta dog in this fight, boy? Pistol too heavy for ya?"

I reluctantly went over to him. I crouched by the window and stuck my gun through the lowest slat and pulled the trigger. The recoil was deafening. The echo seemed to oscillate through everything. At the end I heard a man scream in pain and then a body drop.

I drew first blood.

"Oh no!" someone outside yelled. "He shot Hollands Junior square in the back! No good bastards! Shot that boy in the back and he won't but sixteen!" I almost dropped my gun and I would have too, but just then so many bullets hit the walls and door that the apartment shook like thunder were released in the room. The planks began to chip and give way and soon the gunfight began in earnest. Bodies dropped on both sides and I had to stay low to avoid being shot. One-Leg and George no longer had remarks about Boochie's momma. The only speaking now was the reports of pistols and rifles mingling with the screams of those shot and the thuds of bodies landing.

The plaster crumbled away from the walls, revealing the splintered lattice board beneath. The room drowned in the thick fog of gun smoke. I stayed low and continued to fire out of what was now a totally opened window. Tamara was near me, loading bullets into clips.

"We can't stay here!" Patrick shouted. "They're bringing in reinforcements and we're stuck with a finite amount of weapons and ammunition. They'll let us shoot until we'll out of ammunition and then they will come in and finish us. We have to get out!"

Someone mentioned that they had the back way covered. We had divided our forces now, half of us shooting out the front door, the other half out the back.

"God in heaven, just let me hit him one time! Jest one!" George spat, firing wildly. Buford kept unloading the AK47 and reloading with a banana clip. He motioned for us to get to the back wall.

We all backed up, trying to reach the wall he pointed to. The door buckled badly. Bullet holes ranged from the size of bottle tops to small oranges. I duck walked across the room, choking on the acrid smell of gunpowder. A chip of wood hit me in the face and at first I thought I'd been shot, but One-leg shoved me with the nub of his arm and I kept moving. My face stung like hell, and I could feel my cheek swelling, but there was no time to think about that now.

The door had flown off the hinges, the protective shield gone.

A dozen men came in with guns blazing from both, the front and back doors. Patrick stood and methodically aimed both pistols, firing with the cool precision of a skilled ambidextrous killer. He must've had marksman training. He scored nothing but headshots, killing at least nine out of the dozen. The remainders ran back through the doors, using what was left of the walls for cover.

"If there's another way out now would be a judicious time to use it!" he screamed. "I can't hold them off for much longer!"

Buford searched the wall and pressed a lever that slid open to reveal a secret hall. He rushed in, with George, One-Leg, and Tamara behind him. There was no way that Patrick could fit in that hall. It was too narrow.

"I'm not leaving Patrick! It wouldn't be right!"

"I'll be right behind you, Mr. Johnson! I've squeezed into tighter places than this!"

Buford struck a match on the wall and ran into the narrow passageway, urging us to follow.

They came in just as the door to the hall slid closed. The men shouted and banged on the walls, cursing. The hall shook as one of the men let off a shotgun, trying to blast through the wall. The sound echoed throughout the hall and reminded me just how close to death we all were.

Did the Evangelist order all those people killed just to get to Patrick? By calling him, had I unwittingly placed myself in even deeper danger? How did Lady Ophelia know him? Had he been to Cypress before, or did *The Wheel* tell her?

What did she mean by saying his presence introduced a huge *random element*?

The hall was so narrow there was barely room to turn your head side to side. I was amazed that Patrick managed to maneuver the hall with ease. In the distance, I could hear screams and the staccato bursts of gunfire. There were six of us in the hall: Buford, One-Leg, George, Tamara, Patrick, and myself. The air was thick with dust and it seemed the farther we went the narrower the tunnel became.

"How much farther?" I asked.

"Shh! You'll let them know where we are! If they figure out how to open that doorway one bullet'll rip us all apart!" Buford whispered.

Being in that tunnel was like sealing a live man in a casket. Suppose Patrick got stuck? We could all suffocate. Buried alive, sandwiched between two walls in a vault of stone. I fought against these thoughts, but it was hard.

The sound of gunfire ceased and my thoughts turned to Ophelia. Why did she so generously abdicate her authority to Patrick? For that matter, who was Patrick? He had proven to be as much of an enigma as *The Wheel*.

"Watchya step! We goin down deep!" Buford whispered. The ground took a steep drop, one careless move and a broken limb was assured. We were in total darkness now; the last match had finally burned out.

"One Leg, hold on to me tight! These rocks ain't sturdy!" George said. Tamara squeezed my hand tightly and I could feel her pulse pounding through her fingers. The tunnel had gotten smaller. The sides of the stone wall had now begun to scrape my face.

"The walls are pressing in! We're stuck!" Tamara shrieked.

"No! You're just getting claustrophobic! Keep going!" Patrick said.

"No! The walls are really closing in!" I gasped. I tried to wiggle and squirm through, but it was no use. I could not move. It was like trying to force a four inch square peg into a three inch round hole.

"I'm stuck! Stuck! We have to try to go back! Hurry!" George shouted.

"Don't worry! When I give the word push with everything you got! We hafta throw this wall back off us!" Buford ordered.

"Throw the—is everyone in this godforsaken place insane? We're talking about solid rock!"

"Never you mind, Ezekiel! You jest lissen and do what I say! When I count to three we all shove this rock back, it'll go— believe me! It'll go!"

I scraped my arm and ripped my jacket and shirtsleeve to shreds trying to get enough leverage to get my hands in front of me. Buford counted to three and we all pushed. I could feel my back crack from the exertion, but the wall did move ever so slightly.

"Push hard! It ain't gonna go nicely! Push hard!" Buford barked and I doubled my efforts. The wall gave way and toppled over. A smell like breath from a bad tooth hit me. There was some light now, barely enough to form silhouettes. The light came from above us. Splintered beams pierced small pinpoint holes in the rock. I took it as a good sign. We were close to the surface.

"*Keep up! We got mo' to go!*" he whispered.

I remembered Mookie once told me that tunnels and passageways laced Cypress's underground into one huge labyrinth. He said you could wander down here forever and no one would ever find you. He said no one knew for sure who built it, but after Lady Ophelia's story I figured it was the Native Americans.

The passageway was a lot wider now and although the air reeked of decay and spoil, I was happy for it. The steady air flow, no matter how stink suggested a way out.

"We almost there! Keep on!" Buford ordered. "You caused this, Ezekiel when you brought a foreigner to Cypress. Whut dahell was you thinkin?" Buford scolded.

"I just want to get out of Cypress and forget that this place even exists."

"You too soft, Ezekiel. If'n you gone fight the 'Vangelist you best get CYPRESS TOUGH!" he sneered.

"Where are we going? Are we going to The Wheel?" I asked. No one answered. I decided to keep quiet after that, remembering that a CYP-Press man doesn't talk much. The bad tooth smell grew stronger overwhelming me. It was a sickly sweet syrupy smell. Rancid. Decaying. My stomach rolled and heaved.

"Do any of you smell that?" Patrick asked.

"Yes! I do! It smells like something that died with perfume on!" I said, trying not to inhale too deeply.

"We keep movin! Never mine the smell," Buford murmured.

"No! That's the smell of flesh! Decomposed flesh!" I screamed. That reeking scent brought to mind Radar's body. I shuddered in waves of disgust as my stomach threatened to erupt.

Buford picked up two rocks and struck them together making sparks. He then got the sparks to catch a stick and got a fire going. The fire illuminated the cave like a halogen lamp. "I think it's comin from over there." He pointed to an area about twenty feet away from us, just above where the slab landed.

I saw what he pointed to, but my eyes refused to accept what they were seeing. There were bodies—badly decomposed bodies.

I want to see their graves. I want to know exactly what happened to them.

It was my brothers! Piled into the dirt like so much refuse! No caskets, just bodies strewn about like garbage!

In the light, I could see that Mookie's body was the closest. His clothes were torn and tattered rags. Bugs crawled out of his mouth and eye sockets and there were so many maggots in his hair it looked like a white wig.

Stacked next to him were Tom-Tom, Petey, Ritchie and Danny-Boy. About a foot away from them was a corpse so badly decayed that it would have been unrecognizable if not for the suit.

It was J.B.—my oldest brother. He looked like someone filled his clothes with flour.

I want to see their graves...
You will see and you will know, Ezekiel.
This was beyond disrespect.
Beyond hatred.
Beyond revenge.
This was blasphemy.

I was taught that death was a sacred and solemn event. The only way to truly venerate life was to acknowledge its frail but indefatigable resilience. The rituals of the wake, funeral and burial were necessary steps in the healing process. Seeing my brothers piled up like discarded beer cans in the corner of some godforsaken cavern kindled a rage within me. Inhaling the stench of their rotting bodies made my head swoon with nausea and anger. Feeling frustrated and totally helpless, I burst into tears. I reached to grab their bodies, but Patrick stopped me.

"Mr. Johnson, I know this is a terrible thing to see, but you have to remember that we're dealing with a woman—a *creature* who thinks that this is a joke. Let's get out of here. Don't look anymore. We need for you to be strong now, Mr. Johnson. Whatever anger and pain you're feeling let it turn into something else. We'll get her. I promise you that. We'll get her."

George squeezed my hands and looked deep and hard into my eyes. "You see you can't run from this kind of evil, dontcha? You see that this kinda evil has to be dealt wit up front. Your brothers died fightin this evil—but that don't mean you gotta die like this, Ezekiel! They tried to fight fire wit gasoline! You gonna fight fire wit water!"

I nodded meekly and allowed them to pull me away. About fifty feet deeper the tunnel opened into a wide cavern. The smell of death was replaced with the stench of the sewer.

"We jest bout here! A little farther an we come out the manhole," Buford mumbled. I could hear the sound of water running and the faint hum of machinery. We were under the streets of Cypress now. Walking beneath her like so many sewer rats.

"Why weren't my brothers properly interred? Didn't anyone at the funeral make sure they were decently buried?" I asked. My voice was hoarse from screaming.

"Ezekiel, you hafta remember that in this town all morgue things are handled by the Evangelist. I went to *all* of your brothers' funerals and I'm telling you as a man and as a friend of your father's that they were buried properly. This is the work of grave robbers!" One-Leg said.

"Yeah, grave robbers named Lukie and Clara!" George hissed. "She wanted the town to think that she had nothing to do with your family's deaths. She wanted people to believe that Uriah and Eliza was cursed, but there's a few of us that don't believe that, Ezekiel. Not many, but a few."

"If she did this to them, where's my mother? Where's my father's body? Suppose it's thrown around in some place like this—"

"That's not whut happened," Buford interrupted. "Lady Ophelia made sure that she couldn't get near Mrs. Johnson's body. Me and a few others got your father's remains and turned them over to Lady Ophelia. She said she burned them together. She said they would've wanted it that way. Bound in life. Bound in death."

"Can...*can* you tell me how the rest of my brothers died? I mean I saw J.B, but what happened to the rest of them? How did they not *know* about the curse? It's inconceivable that they wouldn't try to escape Cypress!"

"This is what I meant by fightin fire with gasoline," George said. "Each one of your brothers swore they'd succeed where the one 'fore them failed. That's how she got them. Through they pride."

You're a strong but stupid man, Uriah...

"I seened Danny when he passed. I...I tried to warn him, but he was buck wild and won't lissen. He died from a stray bullet. He won't even involved in the ruckus, Ezekiel. He was standin on the death—uh—*the corner* when the shootin started. Two guys across the street was in an argument bout somethin or the other. Ain't had nuthin to do with Danny." George stopped and grabbed me by my shoulders. His jaw was set and his eyes were sharp. "They tried to say he died from a stray bullet, Ezekiel. But I seened it. That bullet won't stray, Ezekiel. It hit the wall, ricocheted three times and had to of made a U-turn in mid air to hit Danny! It was impossible! No bullet could've done that! I been shootin guns since I was knee-high to the duck's tail and I never seened a bullet do that! I tole your mamma bout it, but she already knew.

"You see, Ezekiel? Clara makes it look like it was somethin expected. Somethin *natural* but won't nuthin natural bout it. They learn you bout this town? Lady Ophelia I mean. Did she tell you bout the hiss-tree?"

"The hiss-tree? *You mean the history!* Yes, she told me about Cypress being founded after the Civil war. That's when she told me about the Wheel and Clara Washington wiping out my family because she couldn't have my daddy."

"That's not the hiss-tree I mean—"

"Hush, George! You still flippin your lips before your brain in gear!" One-Leg admonished. Buford and One-Leg shot George a glare that could've melted titanium. Patrick stared back and forth at the three men coldly. In a flash he grabbed George in his collar and held him over his head.

"Well, it seems that now is as good a time as any to reveal this *hiss-tree*, George. Any information that *any of you have* may prove to be pertinent. Pertinent—that means relevant, important—you understand that word don't you, George? Pertinent?"

"Yes! Yes!" George stammered. I fell back in shock at the sudden change that came over Patrick. He spoke with such a cold-blooded calmness. I shuddered remembering how easily he shot those men. Patrick slowly sat George down and unruffled his frayed collar.

"Now why don't you tell Mr. Johnson and I about this *hiss-tree*."

George glanced nervously between Buford and One-Leg, his eyes twitched erratically and he wrung his hands vigorously. This man who stood toe-to-toe against a creature from the depths of hell without blinking was now completely unnerved by Patrick. This man who was *anxious* to go up against the Evangelist, who wasn't scared of anything was now reduced to a wimp—because of Patrick!

"Speak, George. The time for secrets passed when we entered this tunnel," Patrick said calm but firmly.

"May-may-maybe some-some-someone else should tell it. I-I-I'll jest mess it up. I'm a little—"

"Oh whut the hell! I'll tell it! George, you always had a big mouf, jest like your brother!" Buford spat. "The Lady only tole you half the story. She was gonna tell the rest, but you came back with the Foreigner. Anyway, I guess it's jest as well. Slim Ron gave his life trynta jump the gun, but it's too late now."

"Too late for what?" I asked. "I don't like the idea of everyone knowing something that I don't. Not when we were supposed to be partners in this."

"Ezekiel, if there's one thing you better learn and learn *quick* is that you have no partners in this town. The Evangelist won't rest until your body is dead over the Wheel! *She'll kill anybody to get to you*! The prophecy says that you bout the only one that can stop whut's happenin in this town."

"The Lady tried to tell you, Ezekiel," One-Leg broke in. "But you and your high-flyin education wouldn't lissen! I tole you, *the Wheel is real!* Why do you think you couldn't find your house? Why do you think the streets are all twisted up? Bet they didn't teach you that one in your *fancy school*, did they? No! I knowed they didn't! The Wheel turns the town! The Wheel controls the Evangelist just as she controls the town!"

"Look! I'm sick of this! What are talking about here? Is this like a flying saucer or something?" I asked.

"You 'posed to be the smart one. They died to let you get out to get an education and you come back dumb as One-Leg's stump! A flyin saucer! Boy, you better sit down! The Lady tole me you wouldn't be able to handle the whole story, but you and this walkin wall here better git smart quick!" Buford thundered. Patrick stared at him coldly.

"Watch your eyes, fat man. I ain't George—"

"Just tell your story, Buford. I'll determine who and what you are."

Buford shook his head slowly. A wry smile curled his lips.

"Ezekiel, you have no idea whut you stepped into."

<u>Chapter IX:</u> **The Truth**

"The Lady tole you the truth—up to a point. She left out bout fifty years of *hiss-tree*. Your mother and Lady Ophelia ain't blameless in this town's mess. They help contribute jest as much as the Evangelist. Only difference is your mother fell in love and Lady Ophelia spent a spell on the wrong side of sanity. The three of them terrorized this town fer *years*!

"You look like you don't think my liquor's *proof.* Well, you jest best believe me, cause Buford Thillton may be a lot of things, but he's no liar! I heard men say tell that the three of them could walk pass a man and cripple him with a look! They were witches, evil bitches bred in the stove of hell—"

"You shut your mouth! You shut up about my mother or I'll kill you!" I lunged determined to grab Buford, but Patrick held me firmly. I struggled to reach him but it was no use. Patrick held me immobile.

"Watch your tone and your descriptions, Buford. That's still Ezekiel's mother you're referring to," Patrick warned. "Continue."

Buford gave me the same look he gave Slim Ron in that bar when he offered to reveal the truth about my brothers' deaths. He looked at Patrick and a hard moment passed between them. Buford lowered his gaze and muttered an apology.

"Continue," I said, my curiosity overpowered my anger. Patrick released me.

"I'm saying that back then they were...*drunk* with the Wheel's power. Many men tried to escape this town. They tried to warn others not to venture here. To come to Cypress Point was to enter hell, they'd say. Abandon all hope all ye who enter! The three of them would lure men into the town for the sole purpose of bringing them to their deaths. You can stare at me mean all you want, but I'm tellin you that Eliza, Ophelia and Clara were harpies from hell in those days. The Wheel controlled them, Ezekiel. Like drugs control junkies, the Wheel controlled them. You heard Lady Ophelia tell you how evil Clara is, and that's true! Only Clara Washington had done what the other two had only conspired—she made a deal!

"The Wheel of Fortune they called it back then. A man's fate was written upon the Wheel, or so it was said. A man decided who he was going to marry, where he was going to live—his lot in life by what ever the Wheel said. And the three of them defined what the Wheel said, Ezekiel. They decided who married, who owned land and who rented. They decided everything back then.

"Cypress had so many deaths an murders back then that it won't funny. A man's life won't worth the ink on his birth announcement. They would kill a man jest to see him die. They was all fascinated wit death, Ezekiel. It won't jest the Evangelist that stained the Wheel wit blood. The three of them did that. An I hafta tell you that they daddies didn't kill each other. The three original judges was sacrificed to the Wheel by they daughters. That's right! I'm tellin it true!"

"How do you know that? Who would be alive now to confirm that story?" I asked. Old Lady Ophelia's story was hard enough to swallow, but this was just too incredible to be true.

"The Evangelist kept a diary of all occurrences, Ezekiel. It's in a big book that she wrote her spells and witchery in.

"Now, bout your daddy. The three of them were trying to get pregnant. The Wheel tole them that the first one of them that had seven straight sons would inherit the Wheel's full power. I don't know how to say this nicely, so I'll jest say it. The three of them slept with so many men in those days it's a wonder you ever saw them dressed! Now I know a man is subject to getting his teeth knocked down his throat for speakin ill of someone's dead momma, but the truth is the truth!

"You don't believe me? Well, chew on this! Who do you think Lukie's parents are? Clara and your dad! That's right, Ezekiel, Lukie is your half brother! He picked up your dad's strength and Clara's evil. That's also the reason why she wants all of your mother's children dead!"

I slammed into him and held him by the throat. This time Patrick didn't try to stop me.

"My father loved my mother! He worshipped the ground she walked on. Old Lady Ophelia told it right! He laughed at her and he didn't touch that bitch!" I seethed.

"Ezekiel, you are right about one thing. Your father did love your mother. But he was with the Evangelist, too. They had Lukie before J.B. was born. Now you look me in the eye an you'll see I'm not lyin."

I slowly released him, sensing that he was telling me the truth. "Then why did Ophelia lie?"

171

"She didn't lie, Ezekiel. She just tole you the story from the middle."

"She said my dad laughed at her and didn't touch her!"

"And she was right! Your daddy never cheated on your mother. This happened before they started courtin'! That's why Clara swears your mother stole Uriah from her!"

I stood back, stunned. I looked at One-Leg and George. They knew this all the time, but didn't tell me.

"Seven straight sons, Ezekiel. It didn't matter by how many men. Your momma loved your daddy, Ezekiel. Don't let me confuse you on that, but before they got together she was jest as wild as Ophelia and Clara. You wanna know how wild? She was in jest as much of a hurry to get the power as Clara was and she'd do anything to get it. Including murder."

"What's that supposed to mean? What are you saying?"

"Jim Bruce died on March fifteenth, over two dollars in a crap game. The story goes that he had to shoot a guy in self defense."

"Yeah, so? I already said that! I saw what happened when I stepped on that corner!"

"I know, the black lights. Hell, we all know about that. But do you know who J.B shot that day?"

"No."

"Well, his name was Clem. Ring a bell?"

"No," I answered. The name didn't ring a bell and I didn't know the person that J. B. shot from Adam. Not that it would have mattered if I did; it as self-defense, justifiable homicide.

"Clem was one of the Evangelist's sons, Ezekiel."

Buford stared at me as if I was a retarded child that managed to crawl out of bed and embarrass dad during a cocktail party. The look on his face insulted me. I was the one with the education. I was the one with culture and refinement. *He* was the Neanderthal.

"So?" I replied snottily. "I was unaware that someone as evil as the Evangelist could bear children. I thought she was born sterile, you know, just to kind of even the odds. If this guy Clem was her son, my brother did him a favor. Besides, it was self-defense. Clem pulled first."

"Ezekiel," One-Leg said somberly. "You're missin the point. Your mother sent J.B there to kill Clem, as revenge for your father's death. It was tit for tat—"

172

"And it kept goin. So many deaths. So many funerals," George whispered, clutching the locket around his neck.

Cypress is known for its beautiful funerals...

"So! My brother kills her son, in self-defense and she takes umbrage to it! So she places a curse on the rest of my brothers to get back at them—"

"No, Ezekiel." This time Patrick spoke. "As George told you, tit for tat. Your family and hers were set against each other. She blames your mother for destroying her chances of achieving the Wheel's full power. The Evangelist's sons killed your brothers and each of your brothers either directly or indirectly killed one of the Evangelist's sons. They did this at their mother's behest, Ezekiel. She ordered each of them to murder. I know how this sounds, but it's true. You have to accept this, you have to beat this."

"Ask me who my daddy was," Buford said.

"Now, Buford. Maybe it's best to water his liquor," One-Leg interrupted.

"No! It's time for it all to come out! Ain't that right, Patrick?"

"That depends, Buford. I think we've heard enough for now. Why don't we get out of this tunnel and back into the sunlight. Things always look better in the sunlight."

Buford gave Patrick another hard stare that Patrick returned in doubles. There was an icy, ridged moment between these two behemoths. They stared at each other like fighters making their way to the ring.

"Let's go, Buford," One-Leg said. "Let's get out of this tunnel and then we can find out what happened to Lady Ophelia."

We started walking again and I kept thinking about Buford's words. Lukie being the Evangelist's son made sense. The twisted evil in Lukie's mind could have only come from Clara. Lukie being my father's son was too farfetched to imagine. My parents had the type of relationship that I've always dreamt of. There was no way my dad had any outside children—especially a demonic walking abortion like Lukie.

"Look, Buford. I know there are probably plenty of rumors and old wives' tales that have been circulating for years about my dad. I forgive you for believing them, but they're just not true. My parents had seven children together and none apart."

George said, "I know it's a hard thing to fathom, Ezekiel. Your dad was a *good* man. A real good man, but it's true that he and the Evangelist dated a long time ago. Hell, you hafta remember that Cypress Point is a small town. Hell, everybody hopped somebody's fence back in them days!"

"Let's put this nonsense behind us and concentrate on the task at hand. We have to remember who the true enemy is here, gentlemen!" Patrick said.

"There's some steps here!" Tamara said running to them. They led to a manhole cover. We were right under the street. I could hear the traffic overhead.

Buford went up the stairs first. It would take an awful amount of upper body strength to open that manhole. Buford opened it as easy as opening a window. I could hear the cars whoosh by.

"How are we going to get out of here? The cars are coming by too quickly!" Tamara said. Buford climbed down and found a pole lying in the dirt. He shoved it through the opening. I heard a car screech to a halt.

"That answer your question, girlie?" Buford chided.

"There's no need to be rude to her, Buford!" I said as I climbed the steps. The driver of the car had stopped about a foot away from the manhole's opening. It felt good to step out into the street. I don't know how long we were in that tunnel, but it seemed like days.

"What the hell is wrong with you! I could have been killed! You don't stick something up out of the street when somebody's driving!" the driver said hotly. He exited the car and was standing over the manhole, shouting down at me. I climbed out and ignored him.

"Get back in your car and forget you saw us, unless you want your shadow tied into a pretzel!" Buford ordered. The man huffed, got back into his car and sped off. We hurried out of the street and onto the sidewalk. Traffic was bustling.

"What time is it? What is it, rush hour?" I asked, remarking about the heavy traffic. Just then, the car that had sped off made a U-turn back toward us. Other cars jumped the sidewalk circling us and in an instant we were surrounded. At least a dozen men had shotguns aimed at us. They were waiting for us.

"You might wanna put your hands up real high, Boofuss. Less you wanna get shot."

It was Lukie, standing in the doorway of the building right behind us. He moved with such silent speed that he was standing right next to me before I could react. My heart skipped a beat as every nerve in my body went numb. The men with the shotguns took our weapons and pulled us roughly to the cars. Two men had aimed their shotguns at the front and back of Buford's head. He slowly raised his hands. We were caught!

Caught!

Boochie Collins wore a Smokey the bear hat and a tin star pinned to his chest. He strutted like a peacock and spat in George's face. George lunged for him and someone clocked him across the back of his head with the butt of a rifle. George fell in a wet heap.

They put Tamara and I in one car, One-Leg and Georgie in another. Patrick was placed in one car along with Buford. My head reeled thinking about what they planned to do to us.

"Listen," I said to the driver. "I can give you money! All you have to do is let me go!"

"I'd advise you to shut your mouth an not open it again. We don't give a whit about your fancy money," the driver said.

"What's your names? I mean, I don't even know you guys! What beef do you have with me? What have I done to either one of you?"

"Boy, I don't have the time to 'splain all this to you!" the driver said. "You bout the dumbest thing to hit Cypress Point in a long time. I'm Doug Hollands and this bulldog sittin next to me is Cliff Dixon. You kilt my son this mornin." He pointed his pistol at my nose and cocked the hammer back.

"*I'm gonna see if a man kin live wit a bullet in his eye,*" Doug Hollands whispered.

"This is going to be a real pleasure watching her holiness teach you a lesson!" Cliff quipped. At the mention of the Evangelist's name, Doug Hollands lowered his weapon.

I remembered the names from Lady Ophelia's story. They were henchmen of the Evangelist. For a moment I hoped maybe they were cops, or just bounty hunters. That way maybe they could be bought. But these men cared more about carrying out the Evangelist's orders than monetary gain.

175

I sat silent, trying not to cry. The car's windows were heavily tinted, obscuring my vision. They didn't want me to know where we were going, but I had a good idea. They were taking me to her. She probably wanted me locked up until March 15th, just another form of her torture. If I didn't get out of this car soon there would be no escape.

"They're not going to kill you. Even she said you have to die March 15th," Tamara whispered. I guess she thought that would make me feel better, but it didn't.

"You'd be surprised how much pain a man can survive, Molly!" Doug said. He waved a pistol close to her face and leered at her breasts. "Maybe we should pull over a minute, Doug! Molly here looks game for a little fun! Ain't that right, Molly?" He stuck his hand down Tamara's blouse and I instinctively punched him in the face.

"Don't you *ever* touch her!" I screamed. He looked shocked that I had the audacity to strike him.

"You gonna regret that one, boy. The Evangelist only told us not to kill you. She said we can do whatever else we wanted to. I should've told you that Cliff here likes boy-meat."

I saw the blow coming but I couldn't move out of the way fast enough. The butt of the gun caught me just below the ear. I heard Tamara scream and then the black water of unconsciousness washed over me.

—   —   —

Consciousness returned slowly, painfully. I swam out of the wet darkness of sleep onto the unfortunate shore of reality. I was strung up, hanging by my bound hands. My arms ached and my fingers were numb. My face felt swollen and bruised and I could barely move my head. My ears felt clogged and a sharp shooting pain kept stinging me in the neck.

I refused to open my eyes, so sound came in first. I slowly became aware that Patrick, Buford, and Tamara were screaming my name. I was scared now. Really scared. For a moment there I thought I was dead and that the nightmare was finally over. Now I realized it had just begun.

It took several blinks for my eyes to adjust to the light. Through the watery glare I saw Patrick, Tamara, George, One-Leg and Buford all tied up and suspended from an overhead pipe—the same way I was. They were all screaming at me, telling me to wake up. We were in the basement of the funeral home. The preparation room, where the bodies were eviscerated. I looked down and saw my shirt was drenched in blood.

"Stop screaming. I'm woke," I gasped. I had never been in so much pain. A few of my ribs were badly bruised and I knew I had a pretty bad concussion. I could tell from the Tamara's face that I must've looked as bad as I felt.

"Are you all right, Mr. Johnson?" Patrick asked.

"For a man of your obvious intelligence, Patrick that was a very stupid question. I'm about as far from being all right as Pluto is from the sun. Just tell me that you have a way out this—" I coughed and a clot of blood shot out of my mouth. I was bleeding internally.

"Now that we have confirmed you are still alive, there is yet hope."

"Hope is overrated, Patrick!" I winced in anguish.

"The giant called Lukie brought us down here and strung us up. You were the last to arrive. You've been out for hours. I'm not sure, but I think the sun has risen, making this March 14th."

"No, it can't be. We weren't here that long. The most it could be is March 13th."

"You're wrong, Mr. Johnson. It was March 13th when I arrived in Cypress Point. It was dusk when we left to find Lady Ophelia. We were in that underground tunnel the duration of the evening. We emerged right before daybreak. Today is the fourteenth."

I wanted to argue but I had to trust that Patrick was right. It seemed that time was moving at a more rapid rate. This was undoubtedly the Evangelist's doing. She just couldn't wait for the big showdown.

If it really was March 14th then I had one day left to live. I would have never guessed that I'd spend my last twenty-four hours strung from a sewer pipe, badly beaten and bleeding internally.

"Quit feelin sorry for yerself! We gotta work together to get outta here before Lukie comes back!" One-Leg hissed. "Your daddy won't nobody's punk an I know you ain't."

"How? How can we get out? The way we're tied up the more we struggle the tighter the knot becomes!" Tamara shot back.

"Patrick, I'm real sorry I got you involved in this craziness. I know my apology doesn't mean anything, but I never meant for this to happen. Not to you, not to One-Leg and George, not to any of you."

"One-Leg is right, Mr. Johnson. We're not dead yet. Where there's life there's hope."

"I jest hope I gets to kill Boochie," George whispered. "Gawd in heaven, jest let me kill Boochie." The left side of his face was a swollen pulp. His left eye was bloodshot and there was a deep gash across his left temple.

"Ezekiel, what I said back there in the tunnel, about our mothers. I know you don't want to hear it but it's true. I'm your half-brother. Uriah was my daddy, too."

I didn't reply. I didn't want to believe it, but I knew he was right. If my dad fathered Lukie then anything was possible. I wished he hadn't said that. There are certain things that are just best not known.

The door opened and Lukie walked in with a conceited strut. Behind him, Doug Hollands, Cliff Dixon, and Boochie Collins followed.

Lukie groped Tamara's breasts and darted his tongue around her ear. "We could have some fun first, Molly. I know you like to have fun." The salacious look in his eye was enough to turn my stomach. I felt so bad for Tamara. Being beaten and tortured was one thing, but being raped was a physical and spiritual degradation.

"*Please, please don't—*"

"You will not speak, Molly. You will jest do as you told," Lukie sneered as he continued groping her. "*Have I made myself clear?*"

"Yes," Tamara whimpered.

He stepped back and opened the door, revealing the Evangelist just standing there smiling. Clara walked in and stared at me with a look of triumph. She had won. She paid no attention to the rest of them. Her focus was squarely on me.

The fox finally snared the hare.

"Let me have them, ma'am! Let me have them!" Lukie pleaded.

"Not yet, Lukie. I'm gonna let you have them. I'm gonna let you have them front ways and back ways and some ways that even you ain't thought of!" Clara smirked. Boochie roared with laughter. He stared at Tamara and licked his lips.

"When the hell did you start likin girls, Boochie? I mean, besides your hairy ass momma?" George asked.

Boochie took off his Smokey the bear hat and sat it down on one of the steel tables. "Boy, I had jest bout enough of you callin my momma outta name. Now I can finally put boot to that flabby ass a yours." He walked up and pointed his gun at George's head.

"Now, whut was it you said bout my momma?" he smirked.

"Well, let's see…" George said, thinking. "Which time are you talkin bout? The time when I banged her so hard every time she burped she tasted me, or the time when me and One-Leg tag-teamed her so long she had trouble walkin for a week?"

"Or maybe the time I had her on all fours howlin at the moon!" One-Leg broke in.

"Oh yeah," George remarked. "I plumb forgot bout that time! No wonder she's so hairy! Boochie, you gotta be more specific if you want me to—"

Boochie pounded on George's head with the butt of his gun. The dull thuds reminded me of when my mother would beat a steak with a special hammer to tenderize it. George stared at him defiantly, not mumbling a word until he fell into the waiting arms of unconsciousness.

"C'mon an gimme mines, too! C'mon, Boochie!" One-Leg screamed "You punk ass! George ain't the only one that banged your nasty momma! C'mon an gimme mines, too!" One-Leg was handcuffed by his hand to the pipe. The remainder of his amputated arm swung in impotent frustration at Boochie.

"You want yours so bad? *Clap for it!*" Boochie said, huffing and out of breath from beating George for so long, he turned and walked out of the room. Doug Hollands and Hugh Dixon walked out after him, laughing.

"He still beat you, Boochie! He still ten times the man you are! You'll never be nuthin more than a punk ass! You caint beat me an I only got one arm!" One-Leg hollered after him. I strained to see if George was still breathing, but I couldn't tell. His chin was slumped down in his chest, but from the depressions in his skull from the butt of Boochie's pistol, I knew if George was still alive he was in desperate need of medical attention.

As we all were.

"I swear, Boochie! I swear on everything I am that I will kill you! I swear on my name! I swear on my *word*!" One-Leg said trembling with rage.

The Evangelist took all this in stride. She paid no attention to the vicious beating that George had taken, or to One-Leg's rants. Her eyes never left me the entire time.

"You keep an eye on our guests here. I gotta few things to take care of." She walked over to me and brutally squeezed my crotch. I winced in fresh pain. "There's a certain funeral I have to prepare for. Lukie, make sure our guests are comfortable. And don't do anything that I wouldn't do!" She laughed and walked out of the room. Leaving us alone with this sick pervert.

Lukie smiled like a kid who had just discovered he'd been left alone in a candy store. His attention was still on Tamara. He started undressing her and I shut my eyes. Partly out of respect, but mostly because my mind was shutting itself down. I refused to stay in that room. I refused to witness the horrors I knew were coming.

"Please, Lukie, please don't!" Tamara whined.

"I thought I done told you, Molly! You don't speak! You jest do!"

"Leave her alone, you bastard!" I heard myself say.

"Why don't you jest be quiet, Ezekiel. I'll get to you next!" He turned and continued to undress Tamara. He had her blouse wide open and he ripped her bra off. Her nipples darkened and stiffened as if a cold wind woke them. He yanked her jeans down to her knees and began to fondle her private parts. I shut my eyes again, this time mumbling a fervent prayer.

"*Please don't, Lukie. Please stop!*" Tamara whined.

"Leave her alone, Lukie! If I was loose I'd buss yo' ass!" Buford screamed. This got Lukie's attention.

"You wanna play wit me, Boofuss? Cause I'll play wit you! I'll play wit Molly later and then I can play wit you now!" He said this with glee. Like a child telling a playmate which game should be played first.

"C'MON, LUKIE! C'MON! YOU! SICK! FUCK!" Buford screamed. Lukie really got excited now.

"I'll play wit you, Boofuss! Oh hells yes, I'll play wit you!" Lukie untied Buford's hands from the overhead pipe and my heart soared. We had a chance! A chance! Buford wasted no time. He attacked Lukie like a man berserk with rage. He rained

180

pulverizing blow after blow on Lukie's head. Buford hit Lukie with a shot that I swore would have knocked out a bear, but it barely dazed Lukie.

"Get him, Buford! Keep hitting him! Kill him!" I screamed, ignoring the caustic pain in my side. We had a chance! All Buford had to do was knock Lukie out and we could escape! Lukie reeled from the blows and Buford kept swinging, forcing the perverted brute to his knees.

Keep swinging, Buford! Kill him! Oh God, please kill him!

"You play real good, Boofuss," Lukie said, rubbing his jaw. "You play real good. My turn now." Lukie stood and swung one blow. A left-handed haymaker that caught Buford flush on the chin lifted him up off the floor and sent him sprawling across the room. Buford landed with a dry hard thump. Lukie picked him up, threw him over his shoulder and tied him back up to the overhead pipe.

My heart sank.

"Boofuss didn't really wanna play. Now I gotta show him the rest of the game." He walked over to the cabinets that held the mortuary instruments. He pulled out a book, a large bowl and a bottle of liquid. "You jest hang there for second, Boofuss. I'll be right there in a moment. Won't be too long, Boofuss. You jess wait for me. I'll show you how to play."

Buford hung unconscious, oblivious to Lukie's words. Lukie kneeled and took off Buford's pants, underwear, shoes and socks. He splashed the liquid on Buford's privates, his legs and then poured the rest into the bowl and placed Buford's feet in it. He stood and opened the book.

"I will now read from the Book of Pain, first chapter, first verse." He fished in his pocket and pulled out a lighter. By now, Buford had finally begun to come around. *"And thy feet shall be held to the fire, and thy stones shall know the flame."*

"No, Lukie! *No!*" Buford screamed, but it was too late. Lukie lit the liquid and I watched mortified with disgust as bluish green flames licked up Buford's legs. The smell of that flammable liquid coupled with the searing odor of burnt flesh overwhelmed me. I coughed violently—spasms of pain wracked my body.

"May the Lord bless the bleeding of his words, and sanctify them in our hearts." Lukie shut the book and closed his

eyes as if in prayer. He held the book above his head and waved it, the way the old ladies in church would wave the bible when the sermon got hot and heavy.

"You see how to play now, don't you, Boofuss. I'm glad you wanted to play, Boofuss. Real glad." There was no anger or malice in his voice. He was simply stating a fact. This was all a game to him.

I heard two loud popping sounds like gunshots and I vomited as I realized it was Buford's testicles exploding in the flames. The skin on his legs blistered and crackled as the flames danced up and down his body in bluish tongues of fire.

Buford howled in what must have been excruciating pain. I had never heard that sound made by a human being. It was a wail of ultimate suffering. That man burned and cried—*begged* for death. His screams pervaded the smoky room and were only matched in intensity by Lukie's peals of laughter.

I shut my eyes tightly and tried to drown Buford's screams out of my mind. Lukie's laughs were a cacophony of madness. Tamara's whimpers seemed to excite him. He turned his attention to her.

"It's too hot in here, Molly. I needs to take all your clothes off now…" He fondled her again, roughly squeezing her breasts and buttocks. His eyes were cold flints of madness. The front of his trousers stood out as if covering a tent pole. He licked her face. Tamara retched in disgust.

I felt so bad for her.

"Put him out, Lukie. Put the fire out," Patrick said calmly.

"Whut did you say?" Lukie turned and eyed Patrick suspiciously.

"He's dead, Lukie. You can put the fire out now."

Patrick motioned to the fire extinguisher hanging on the wall. Lukie took it and doused the flames. Buford was now a charred husk. The only parts of him that were recognizable were his arms, which were still tied to the pipe. His face was a hard peeled leathery shell. His legs looked like Slim-Jims. The smell in the room was a horrific toxic mixture of chemicals, smoked flesh and burnt hair.

"You happy now, mista?" Lukie asked Patrick. He walked over to him and stared at his huge abdomen. The expression on his face grew from a scowl to wide-eyed amazement.

"Wait a minute! Wait. A. Minute. Gawd-damn a bear! Good-googaly-goo ain't you a big one!" He caressed Patrick's stomach slowly, almost lovingly. "I'll be danged and hanged! Whut you eat to get this big? A whole cow?" Lukie roared with laughter as he grabbed a hand full of flesh and seemed to marvel at the sheer size of it.

"Whut's your name, sow-man?"

"Patrick."

"Well, Pat-*trick* let's see whut tricks you can pat! You gotta belly bout big as a trunk of a car! *Good-guga-muga* you a big one! I'm gonna have real fun wit you, horse-boy!"

"You like to have fun, don't you, Lukie."

"Yeah! I like fun a lot!"

"Do you like games, Lukie?"

"Yeah," Lukie looked confused for a moment. Patrick's attitude and demeanor were so calm you'd think he was speaking to a toddler. I was sure he had a plan, but I wondered where he was going with this. Lukie was so unstable he was likely to kill Patrick in mid-sentence and not give it a moment's thought.

"I think I have a game that you would like. Do you want to play with me, Lukie?"

"Well now, Mr. Fat-Man, that all depends. I don't like my food talkin back to me."

"Oh, I'm sure you'll like this game, Lukie. You don't even need to untie me for us to play. I ask you a question and you answer it. Then you ask me a question and I'll answer it. The first one who gets a wrong answer loses and the loser has to do whatever the winner says. Deal?"

Lukie stared at Patrick trying to decipher his calm and nonchalant manner. He was completely unnerved at this turn of events. I was in absolute awe of Patrick. Did anything rattle this man?

"I...I don't know, Dino-boy. You might have a trick so—"

"*Now, Lukie*! You have all of the cards stacked in your favor! After all, you have the book with *all* of the answers in it! Plus you have me at a disadvantage because I don't have my book! Not to worry, because I know Lukie always plays fair. Doesn't he, Mr. Johnson? Doesn't Lukie always play fair?"

"Yes," I stammered. "Lukie is known to always play fair!" I had no idea what Patrick was up to, but the fact he was up to *something* meant there was a chance that we wouldn't just lay down and die without a fight.

"If Mr. Johnson says that Lukie plays fair, then Lukie plays fair! I like people who play fair, Lukie. It's important to the game, don't you agree?"

"Yes...that's why Boo-fuss lost. *He didn't wanna play fair.*"

"But you always play fair, Lukie. Let's play the game, Lukie. Let's play it now."

"Well," Lukie shifted from foot to foot uneasily. I saw then that the book in his hand was a coloring book with a leather cover that read, *Holy Bible*. "No tricks, Hippo-boy! Or I'll cut your *stomach* out through your ass!" He poked Patrick in his backside and hissed at him.

"Then I take it you want to play, Lukie?"

"Yeah, Pig-boy. I'll play."

"Good. You can go first and ask me a question."

Lukie held his book tight and smiled. "Whut's on the thirteenth page of this book in my hand?"

"A drawing of a man and a goat. The man is... *courting* the goat."

Lukie gasped in shock. Patrick was right.

"Now it's my turn—"

"How you do that? How you knew that, Flabby-boy?"

"I guess I'm like you, Lukie. I must have the same book. Only real smart people have that book, Lukie. Now, it's my turn to ask you a question."

"Go head. Lukie always play fair."

"In the jungle the lioness is chasing the zebra. The lioness wants to feed her cubs. The zebra wants to live. Whose prayer does God hear?"

Lukie stopped, dumbfounded. He searched his book and scratched his head. After a few moments he shrugged that he didn't know the answer.

"Well, Lukie, you lost this round but there is still a chance you can win. Why don't you go ask the Evangelist? I'm sure she knows. She knows everything."

Lukie shook his head. "Then the 'vangelist'll be mad at me, Dookey-boy!"

"No she won't, Lukie. She'll be *glad* that you went to her! She has always told you that if you didn't know something to ask her, right?"

"Yes, but—"

"But you didn't ask her before you burnt up Buford, did you?"

"No, but Boofuss didn't play fair —"

"I know, but I did. And she specifically told you not to do anything that she wouldn't do. And you know she would never break the rules. You go ask her the question and come back and tell me what she says. I'll wait here for you. Take your book with you, in case she wants you to write down the answer. The Evangelist will be happy with you, Lukie. She wants to see you succeed. She loves you."

"*She loves me*," Lukie frowned and bit his lip in confusion. He shuffled back and forth, like he had to use the bathroom. Patrick stared at him coldly. Finally, Lukie relented and left the room. I exhaled a silent prayer of thanks.

"Thank God! But how do we get out of here?" Tamara gasped.

"I've been studying this knot and I think I've got it figured out." Patrick managed to wiggle his fingers into the knot and work it open. He was free.

Free!

Chapter X: The Ides of March.

"Hurry, Patrick! Before he comes back!" I rushed. We were all excited now. Patrick had bought us a reprieve from torture and death. He moved with silent steady grace undoing first my bonds and then Tamara's. She hurriedly pulled up her pants and tied her torn blouse as well as she could to cover her breasts. I rushed over to George, I lift his head and drew in a pained breath when I saw him. The pupils of his eyes were grayish and his forehead was dented in a series of half moons from the impact of Boochie's gun. A bloody string of drool hung from his swollen bottom lip.

"I saw that black cloud, Ezekiel. I saw the angel of death an I axed him to come back jest a lil later. Jest a lil later. I told him if'n he came back a lil later he could have Boochie's ig'nant ass an then I'd come wit him gladly. He said that'd be fine wit him. He took Buford and he said Miss Adira and Miss Adina waitin for me. He ain't such a bad guy after all!" he sighed as I untied him. I don't know how he managed to stay alive—more less *conscious* with head injuries like that. I ripped a towel that was laying on one of the steel tables and made a bandage out of it, wrapping his head. Patrick freed One-Leg from his handcuff using a sliver of metal from Buford's charred belt buckle.

"We must hurry before Lukie returns," Patrick said.

We stepped out of the room into the hall. Everything was so quiet and serene that you'd never guess the horrors that had just occurred. *"We have to hurry! It won't take that monster long to get back!"* Tamara whispered. We were so worried about taking a wrong turn and running into Lukie and the Evangelist that we were scared to move.

The hall was a massive labyrinth. There were no marks on any of the doors, no exit signs. We could wander down here for hours and find ourselves back where we started.

I motioned for us to take the left wing of the hall, not really knowing why. I suddenly got this overwhelming sense of déjà vu—that I had been in this hall before. Every breath was a major exertion. Every step I took increased the pain. I wanted to move faster but my body betrayed me. Patrick held me, letting me lean on his massive frame. One-Leg supported George and Tamara was strong enough to move on her own.

"Who are you, Patrick? How do you know so much about this terrible town?" I asked, trying to ignore the pain that wracked my body. I was drenched in sweat and it hurt when I breathed.

"I believe the old woman told you that you will know the answer to all of your questions in due time, Mr. Johnson. Buford told you that you'd better get *Cypress Tough*. It seems to me at this stage of the game you had better take heed. A word to the wise should be sufficient."

"I'm bleeding internally. Tamara is one step from a cerebral salad and for all I know George could be suffering from permanent brain damage. I'd like an answer."

"And you shall have it. In due time."

"She won't have to wait until the Ides of March. If I don't get proper medical treatment I'll be dead in just a few hours."

"That's not true, Mr. Johnson. You're going to be fine. Trust me on that one. You're going to be just fine."

The shadows were long in the tunnel. The light was dim and cast a dingy pallor along the cave walls. I closed my eyes and leaned on the cool rust colored stone. I wanted to sleep so badly. I was exhausted and feverish.

"You're going to have to do better than this, Mr. Johnson. We have to—"

The words were stuck in Patrick's throat as I turned and saw Boochie adjusting his Smokey the bear hat standing boldly, blocking the hall.

"Shoulda known that haid a yours was too hard for the butt a my gun, George. I shoulda put a bullet in that tub stomach a yours. I came back cause I forgot to give One-Leg here his lumps. Together you two butt muffins make half a man. Guess I shoulda sent both a you bum-asses to hell. Oh well, there's still time for me to fix it. Get ready to see them two ole lesbian skanks. Tell them Sheriff Boochie Castor says hi."

Boochie aimed his pistol at George's stomach and pulled the trigger. I cringed, preparing for the report, but there was nothing but the dry clicking of an empty chamber. Boochie repeatedly fired to no avail. Either the gun was empty or it jammed.

"*You can't win like that, Boochie. You an me gotta tangle this one out. I'm gonna take you to meet the man,*"

George said sleepily. He walked toward Boochie with a half smile half sneer and stood directly in front of him. One-Leg walked up and stood beside George.

"*Let me do this one here, One-Leg. Let me take this bitch to the man.*" George tried to push One-Leg back, but he'd have none of it.

"Now, now, George. You know I cain't leave till this here prick either gives me that drink he promised or the two dollars I spent on the extra strength douche to clean his momma's ass out wit."

"*Suit yourself,*" George shrugged. Blood seeped through the towel, leaving a red ring around his head. "*Long as I gets to kill him first.*"

"Ya'll go head," One-Leg said to us. "Me an George here got this. Don't worry or fret none. After me and George finish wit this here sissy we gonna finish wit Boochie's momma. By the way, Boochie—you promised me a drink. Where is it?"

Boochie backed away as George and One-Leg slowly walked toward him. The color drained from his face.

"*Boochie,*" George whispered, and I could hear murder in his voice. "*Whut I am gonna do to you today should not be done to a farm animal. Today I pays all past due debts. Yes sir, today I give the devil yo' ass!*"

"Y'all keep back! You hear me? Y'all keep back!" Boochie whined. His eyes grew wide and his voice shook in horror. I looked up and saw what had him so spooked. A dark cloud had settled right above George and One-Leg's head. It looked like a swarm of angry gnats. I stared in stark amazement as the swarm unfolded and began to take shape.

"Look away, Mr. Johnson!" Patrick ordered, pulling me and Tamara away. "They can handle the sheriff. We must keep moving!"

"We can't leave them!" I said to Patrick.

"We must! That's death hovering over them! Believe me, it doesn't discriminate!"

"*The good news, Boochie,*" I heard George say as we were leaving the hall. "*Is that it won't hurt too much longer.*"

"The bad news—" One-Leg continued.

"Is that it'll hurt for the rest of your life!" they both chanted.

"*C'mon, Boochie. I got some gold! I got some ole Jew's gold for ya!*"

I heard Boochie scream and then their voices faded as the dark swarm covered the three of them. We ran through the halls in a blind panic. I swore I could feel something following me, something sucking all of the air out of the hallway.

"That was Death over them!" I gasped, trying to ignore the stitch in my side and woefully painful ribs. "George was right! Did you see it, Patrick? It looked like a giant black cloud of —"

"Don't speak on it again, Mr. Johnson! Don't speak on it and keep moving. The fact that we all saw it means that we have to—"

"—Die, Fat-man!" Lukie suddenly appeared and viciously plowed into Patrick with the force of a battering ram, hurling him into the wall. Patrick slumped to the floor in a massive unconscious bulk of flesh. My heart almost leapt out of my chest the way he hit the ground. He seemed so still, no movement. Not even the slow methodical rising of his chest to show me he was breathing.

You could be bringing that man here to get him killed!

A deep sense of grief and remorse came over me. First Slim Ron, then Buford, One-Leg and George and now Patrick. It was just as much my fault as Lukie's. I looked around to see if I saw that black swarm but I didn't. The feeling of grief was quickly replaced by the severity of the situation at hand: Lukie towered over us like a volcano about to erupt. I would have to mourn them later, or join them.

Even in the low light I could see Lukie's gigantic lips drawn back in a deranged sneer, revealing large teeth that looked like fangs. He was happy when he killed Buford. I couldn't imagine what he would do while angry. We were in real trouble now.

"I axed the 'Vangelist bout you an she said jest kill you, Pat the Trick! Now that that's done, Lukie can have some fun. Startin wit you, Molly! Then I'll play with Ezekiel an then I'm gonna cut up the fat man an bring the 'Vangelist his haid an stomach!" He looked at Patrick's bulk and rubbed his chin. " *I might needs me a wheel barrow though…*"

"Lukie! It wasn't my idea! Patrick made us leave!" Tamara blurted. She tried to hide behind me, but I could barely stand. Every breath felt like a sharp hot knife poking me in the ribs.

"Git naked, Molly. Git naked right now an maybe I won't play wit you like I played wit Boofuss."

Slowly, almost catatonic, Tamara began to undress. The blank look of defeat in her eyes told me that she had resigned herself to what was to come. The game was over. The bad guys won. Her eyes were empty. She had drawn deep into herself, creating a mental sanctuary.

He's going to rape her right in front of me!

I struggled to get to my feet. My head felt too heavy for my body.

"When he starts with me, you get out of here, Ezekiel," she whispered. *"Maybe you can find the way out now."* I saw the salacious look in Lukie's eyes. He bit his bottom lip in anticipation of what he had planned to do to her. And she was going to let him. She was going to let him because I couldn't protect her.

"No! Put your clothes back on, Tamara."

"You best do right, Molly. You best do right or I'll cut you first an then I'll have fun wit you! Or maybe I'll burn you first! Which one you want, Molly? Lukie got a lot of ways to play!" In his left hand he held the lighter he had used to burn Buford, in his right he held something that looked like a skewer.

"Blood and fire, Molly. That's all we got 'tween us now. *Blood and fire.*"

Patrick lay behind us; his giant frame kept us from backing up. Lukie filled the tunnel in front of us. We were trapped. I could feel Tamara's heart hammering in her chest. I couldn't tell which one of us was more afraid.

"There's no way you could be Uriah's son," I said flatly.

"Ezekiel, you jest be glad I don't make you git naked too. Now stand aside and let me and Molly play, and then I'll play with you like I did Boofuss."

"There is no way my father could have made anything as grotesque as you. My father was an honorable man. A good man. You must be the bastard child of a circus animal! That's it, isn't it, Lukie? The Evangelist lifted her skirt for one of the monkeys in the carnival and nine months later she shit you out!"

"You best shut up, Ezekiel! You jest better shut up talkin like that or I'll have to make a whole new game jest for you!"

"Admit it! A man as decent and as good as Uriah Johnson could never have made something as hideous as you!"

190

"You best shut your mouf right now, Ezekiel!" Lukie's body trembled in anger. He looked like he was about to explode. I was winding him up like a jack-in-the-box and any moment now he would pop. "You don't know whut you talkin bout! You jest best shut up!"

"My brothers and I never had to rape a girl, Lukie. You do because that's the only way you can get a woman! How many times did you play with the Evangelist, Lukie? You burn her feet, too?"

"I'm warnin you, Ezekiel! I'm gonna fix you real good, pretty boy!" Lukie stomped his feet and marched in place, his face beet-red in anger and...

Fear?

"Yes, Lukie! Pretty!" I teased, running my hand through my hair and blinking flirtatiously. "Just like all my brothers! My real brothers! We were all pretty because of our father! Uriah Johnson!"

"*He...was my dad...too!*" he whined like a spoiled child. He stomped in place and hammered his solid fists against the walls. Clumps of dust fell. I could feel the dull vibration of the punch through the stone.

"What are you doing?" Tamara whispered. "You'll make him so mad he'll kill us!"

I ignored her and continued. "No, Lukie. He wasn't your dad. Your dad is probably drunk somewhere disgusted with himself for screwing that whore you call a mother! That is of course, if he's actually a man. For all I know your dad is probably one of the dead bodies Clara keeps tucked away! That's the only way she can get a stiff one!"

"*I'LL FUCKIN KILL YOU!*" He screamed and charged at me. His eyes were red flames of anger. He swung with the skewer in hand. I barely moved out of the way in time. Lukie was like a man berserk now, swinging wildly. Adrenaline coursed through my veins like hot magma. I somehow managed to avoid his blows and as he lunged again I caught him by the hair and using his momentum slammed him headfirst into the stone wall. I backed up, pulled the tattered baseball out of my pocket and threw it with everything I had in me. It was the fastest fastball I'd ever thrown. I had never thrown a baseball that hard before. Not even Petey on his best day would've been able to hit it. It flew so fast I could see the air split around it.

The flap of cowhide looked like a cape pulled taut around a superhero's neck.

The ball did not spin, it *flew* straight as if hurled from a cannon.

The ball hit Lukie in the face and I heard his nose splatter with a dull crunch. He dropped the skewer and we both leaped for it. I managed to snatch it first. Lukie kicked me in the ribs and my body shook in flaccid waves of pain.

"*You gonna day it, right befo' you die,*" Lukie garbled as he spat out teeth. "*He wa' my fadda, too. You gonna day it!*" He dove on top of me and I barely managed to hang onto the skewer. I plunged it into his throat with all the strength I had left in me. Lukie stood and clutched his neck in an attempt to stop the gusher of blood. I scrambled to my feet ignoring the pain and overwhelming fatigue.

"*Let's play, Lukie,*" I whispered as I stabbed him again. This time I caught him in the chest. I pulled the skewer out and repeatedly punched him with it. I was drenched with his blood.

"*You... play... real... good, Ezekiel. Real good,*" he gurgled. His eyes rolled back in his head, his tongue hung from his mouth like a limp rag. His body fell with a sickening thump.

David had slain Goliath.

"*You-you did it! You killed him! I can't believe it! You killed Lukie! I can't believe it!*" Tamara said. I turned and saw she was clutching her side. Her face was an ashy grayish color.

"Are you okay?"

"*Yeah, I just got cut a little bit when he first came at you. I didn't move fast enough. I can't believe you beat him!*"

"Let me take a look at it." It was a deep puncture wound, just below her left breast. Blood steadily poured out of it like a faucet. "We're going to have to get you to a hospital, Tamara. Can you stand?"

"*No...I don't think I'm meant to leave here, Ezekiel. I think this is it for me.*"

"Don't talk like that! We're gonna get out of here and see that Knicks game! Remember? I owe you a six pack of Budweiser! Tall cans!" I tried to apply pressure to the wound, to at least slow the bleeding, but it wouldn't stop. Tamara was bleeding to death right in front of me and there was nothing I could do about it. Out the corner of my eye, I saw Patrick's enormous frame move ever so slightly. He was alive!

"Patrick! Patrick, wake up! Wake up!" Patrick slowly stirred, holding his head. "Get over here! Tamara's been stabbed! She's bleeding badly! I can't stop the bleeding! Help me, Patrick!"

"Is that...is that *Lukie*?" Patrick asked as he crawled over to Lukie's body.

"Forget him! I need your help here! She's dying, Patrick! She's dying!"

"How did Lukie die?" Patrick asked, inspecting the monster's body.

"I killed him! Now will you help me?" The bleeding showed no signs slowing. Her life's fluid was steadily seeping out of her. Tamara was barely conscious now.

"So much blood. I can't believe you actually beat Lukie in hand-to-hand combat! What did you stab him with?"

"Are you crazy? This woman is laying here bleeding to death and all you can think of is that perversion of nature there? I stabbed him with this skewer! Satisfied? Now think of something to help Tamara!" I pressed hard, trying my best to stop the bleeding.

"There's nothing we can do for her, Mr. Johnson. The wound is near her heart. She'll be dead very soon. My, my, my. Look at Lukie now. You really did a number on him and you were barehanded and wounded!"

"Patrick, you are starting to scare me. I mean, you've been freaking me out since I met you, but now you're really starting to scare me." I was shocked at his nonchalant manner. I had sensed that neither he nor One-Leg or George cared much for Tamara. They seemed to regard her as beneath them. But Patrick's blasé attitude was so cold and inhumane you'd think he was referring to an old couch that had to be discarded. There was a gleam in his eyes, a hard obstinate look that both unnerved and reminded me of his sudden violent reaction to George.

"*Who are you, Patrick?*"

"*The Wheel is about to turn!*" Patrick said with a puzzling smile.

Just then there was a great rumbling sound, like an earthquake. I looked around in shock as the hall shook and the floor became unsteady. I watched in amazement as the wall shifted and moved with the ease of a revolving door. A gaping hole was now opened in what was solid stone a mere moment ago—a hole that led to the highway out of Cypress Point.

"Let's go, Mr. Johnson! Providence has smiled upon us! The Wheel has turned toward the exit! We need to leave now!"

The rumbling grew louder, like giant metal gears grinding teeth.

"She'll *die* if I leave her!" I screamed. Tamara was in shock. Her skin was blanched and pale.

"*You'll* die if you don't!" Patrick said as he pulled me toward the opening. That strange secretive look still plastered on his face. I struggled and pulled against him. He was now part of the problem.

He scared me.

"Then I'll die, Patrick! I can't leave her like this! I can't leave her in this godforsaken place to die! Not after seeing my brothers the way I did!" The bleeding had slowed down considerably, but the pressure of my hand was all that kept the wound closed.

"*Go, Ezekiel. You have a chance to get out of here,*" Tamara whispered, barely audible. Her voice was weak, but unafraid. She had come to terms with dying. "*You can beat her, Ezekiel. You can win if you leave now.*" She touched my face and managed a delicate smile. "*I'll have to pass on that six pack.*"

"She's as good as dead, Mr. Johnson. Think about what you are doing, man! There isn't anything in this town worth staying here for! The people here are crazy! Infected with a sickness of the spirit that cannot be cured! This place is as damned as Buford said it was. There is nothing here for you, Mr. Johnson! Return to New York City! Return to your life! Come with me now! I can't promise you another opportunity like this one! The Wheel has turned toward the exit! We need to go now!"

"You go! If I leave her she'll die! I can't let that happen! It wouldn't be right, Patrick. There is good in this town, you just need to dig to find it and keep an open mind! Besides, I-I love her!" I didn't realize how I felt about Tamara until that moment. Leaving her was inconceivable. We would either flourish or perish together.

"Love. Such a strange emotion," he chided. "If you're sure about this course of action I must leave you to the skein of fate, Mr. Johnson." Patrick turned and walked through the doorway and right before the portal slammed shut he said, "I hope you know what you're doing."

"That...was really dumb...and really romantic, Ezekiel. You had a chance to go! You should've taken it!" Tamara gasped. The bleeding slowed, but I dared not move my hand.

"You're going to have to help me here. I need for you to hold your hand right here while I try to find something to tie around this wound." I placed her hand over the bloody hole and pressed it tight, hoping she had enough strength to keep pressure on it. I ripped Lukie's shirt off him and made a bandage. Tamara's skin felt cold and clammy to the touch. Her complexion was a milky candle wax color.

"Did you really mean that? I mean the part about loving me?" she asked as I picked her up.

"Yes. I really meant it."

"Good, because I love you, too."

I carried her as best as I could, mumbling a prayer for a miracle. I stumbled and almost dropped her a few times, using the wall as a brace. Twice I thought I was about to pass out from fatigue and fever, but I managed to stay awoke. My legs felt like boiled pasta, but I held on. I bit the inside of my cheek to keep me focused, using fresh pain to handle the constant sharp tear in my torso. I had no idea where I was headed or which way I should turn when the medallion around my neck stood straight out like a divining rod, pointing which direction I should take.

The Wheel affects virgin women and children different from men, and women who have lost their maidenhead.

The Wheel! Maybe there was a chance it could save Tamara! Excited with the prospect of saving her I moved quicker, ignoring my own injuries. I struggled to remember everything that I was told about the Wheel. Whenever I came to a fork in the hall the medallion would point left or right and I would take that route.

"Tamara, you just hold on! I'm going to find the Wheel! It'll fix us, I just know it!"

"How-how will you find it? So many people searched and died. Let me go, Ezekiel. Save yourself."

"No one can fully hide the Wheel if it's sought," I said, remembering Lady Ophelia's words. "This thing that One-Leg gave me seems to be leading me! I just hope it's to the Wheel and not to *Clara*!"

Tamara grew heavier in my arms, but I dared not stop to rest. While my injuries were severe, they were nothing in comparison to hers. I struggled on; blinking back tears trying to purchase hope with faith.

I was just about to collapse from pain, muscle failure and sheer exhaustion when I saw the strangest light blinking unnaturally in the distance.

The medallion led me to the Wheel.

Nothing that I was told could have prepared me for what I saw. The Wheel was something beyond the comprehension of the wisest man. I was overwhelmed at the magnificence of it. I understood Lady Ophelia's ranting when she said that the three judges tore themselves to bits over this thing. Compared to this, gold was as worthless as sand.

A wheel. Such a simplistic yet so complex a design. Infinity. No beginning. No ending. A wheel. Forever turning. Forever spinning. I thought of Ophelia's words, how the Wheel wasn't from this plane of existence.

There is a place where light meets shadow, where the line between reality and illusion is blurred. This is where life and death kiss. This is where you will find the Wheel.

And I now stood in that place.

An incredible light pulsed off it, radiating energy. I put Tamara down and walked toward to it. Drawn like a magnet. The nearer I got to the Wheel the brighter the light became. I could feel my insides mending, healing. I could hear voices. Low, whispery, but they came in clear and unobtrusive. Thousands of voices, overlapping, chanting, elated.

Voices welcoming me, telling me to come closer. A joy arose in me, unlike anything I've ever felt. My body shook and trembled with waves of indescribable ecstasy. The closer I came to the Wheel the closer I wanted to be. The light lifted me off my feet and carried me to it as if I were a newborn baby. The light scratched and tickled me. I surrendered myself to the Wheel and it did the same for me. I crossed a vinculum that I somehow understood was the outer Wheel. This was the portion that the three judges saw. That the three daughters saw. But I was special. I was going to see the inner Wheel.

The Wheel *within the* Wheel.

Chapter XI: A Wheel within a Wheel.

There was a thrumming sound that throbbed and shimmered with waves of silvery energy. I was now right below the light, suspended in mid air. Wisps of colored vapor caressed me. I could feel each strand of my hair stand at attention, every pore within my flesh became aware.

The Wheel carried me closer. I understood things with a frightening clarity. The outer Wheel was something like a roulette wheel. It had notches that turned and opened doors. That's what Patrick meant when he said the Wheel had turned toward the exit. It was like a combination lock lining up its cylinders. The eddy of this thing turning caused unnatural tornadoes to pop up with no warning. No one could predict where the notches would stop when the outer Wheel halted its spin.

What I stood in front of defied all attempts of description. I had no frame of reference, nothing to compare it to. I stared at it and realized why so many men went crazy beholding its beauty.

I don't know how long I hovered over this thing, I sensed time was irrelevant to it. I was entranced. Nothing else mattered.

[*WHAT DO YOU WISH OF US*?] It asked me, but there were no words. I simply understood. The Wheels were sentient, intelligent beyond mortal reckoning.

{The young lady has been wounded—}

[*HAVE YOU BROUGHT HER FOR SACRIFICE*?]

{No. I want her to be healed. Her wounds are life threatening.}

[*IS THIS ALL THAT YOU WISH*?]

{ I need to know why I am supposed to die on March fifteenth.}

What happened next was a bizarre fusion of memory and communication. I saw the three judges standing over the Wheel on March fifteenth, so many years ago. They had agreed to share the power, to use the Wheel for good, but their daughters had another plan.

Buford was right. Ophelia only told me part of the truth. Clara, Ophelia and my mother, Eliza got them inebriated off newly brewed wine, laced with virgin menstrual blood, they then seduced the three men into an incestuous orgy. They fell upon the three judges in the dead of night and murdered them while they slept. Each was guilty of patricide.

Every drop of their blood was used to drench the outer Wheel. They burned the flesh in a sacrifice to the Wheel and made an altar from the bones.

The idea was to corrupt the Outer Wheel until it gave access to the Inner Wheel.

Seven sons. The first one of them to bear seven sons would gain passage to the Inner Wheel. For only the seventh son could get past the outer Wheel. And the only day the Outer Wheel granted passage was March 15th.

The Ides of March.

The three of them would lure men to their beds in hopes of becoming pregnant. If the men weren't fertile enough, or prove virile enough they would sacrifice him to the Wheel.

Clara proved to be the most promiscuous of the trio, enticing and entangling the most men. She became pregnant first. She gave birth to a stillborn son. Sensing that Ophelia and Eliza killed her firstborn, she became paranoiac and maniacal, vowing revenge.

And that's how it started.

These three women who were supposed to be like sisters, murdered each other's children for years. All in an attempt to keep the other from gaining the Wheel's power. The Outer Wheel was immersed in the blood of so many men that its light went from glossy silver to deep violent burgundy. The blood ate away at its luster until it became porous, honey-combed, with millions of silver veins. The Outer Wheel sat atop the petrified bones of tens of thousands of men.

So much death and carnage.

My mind staggered at the wanton and prurient slaughter these three performed with impunity. They approached men with as much regard as the worker in a slaughterhouse treated cattle.

They were invulnerable. Their whims were instant law, and death was meted out at an instant's notice for the slightest infraction. The town worshiped them as seers and soothsayers. A person could be put to death by jugular incision for just *thinking* against the trio.

The Wheel held me immobile while this disgusting scenario played out in my mind's eye. I tried to search for any logical rationale to justify my mother's actions, but there was none. I tried to deny it, to say that the Wheel was lying, but I knew that wasn't possible.

The Wheel was incapable of lying.

The three of them shared their unholy grip on the town with an evil equanimity. Each just as guilty as the other two, no act too vile or perverse. They had bartered their souls to the Wheel in search of knowledge and power.

Then, they met my father.

Uriah Johnson was the seventh son of a seventh son. His grandfather, my *great-grandfather* was the seventh son of a seventh son. This uncanny lineage traced back to ancient Africa, where my father's ancestors were regarded as powerful warriors, with strength that mocked the limits of human ability.

The Wheel had shown each of them that this man could fulfill the quota of seven straight sons.

Clara lured him into Cypress Point with the promise of a good job. It was her intention to use him just as she had done the rest, for one of the cardinal stipulations the three of them vowed was to never fall in love.

But she did.

She tried everything to woo my father, but he ignored her advances and spurned her openly. The more he spurned her, the deeper her desire was for him. She was not used to being told no. The Wheel could perform many miracles, but it couldn't make a man fall in love.

That part of Ophelia's story was right. Only the night she got Uriah Johnson drunk off that witch's brew he *did* sleep with her, and the result of that unholy abominable union was Lukie.

Suddenly, I was surrounded by the vision of a little boy sitting in a chair, terrified beyond imagining in a huge expansive room. A monster of colossal proportions loomed over him, teasing and taunting, taking depraved pleasure in scaring the child witless. My heart went out to him. I wanted so badly to rescue him. To kill the monster and tell him that he never had to be afraid again. One look in that child's eyes was enough to tug at anyone's heartstrings. Who could harm a child in such a heinous manner? Who could take such glee in frightening a poor little boy?

The little boy was Lukie.

The monster was Lukie.

That sweet innocent little boy was locked in the body of the monster all of this time, crying to get out. And I killed him.

Lukie was *my brother! I killed my brother!*

—It was self-defense! I had to! Look what he did to Buford! Look at what he was planning to do to Tamara and maybe even me! I had to kill him! I couldn't leave him alive because he might have followed me and I was wounded. I had to kill him. It was justifiable homicide! I had to...I had to!

Just as my mother felt she had to kill Clara's children...to protect her own. *Lukie killed Buford, and I killed Lukie.*

I am the last of Uriah's sons.

I was suddenly awash in shame and humiliation, overcome with conflicting emotions. The idea I could mourn Lukie was ridiculous, but I did. I had seen too many deaths, beheld too much violence.

I'm not naïve enough to think someone as psychotic as Lukie could have been rehabilitated, but I do believe that if he had been born to any other woman he could have had a different life.

The Wheel continued with its strange vision.

After the birth of Lukie, Ophelia tried her hand at wooing my father. She had taken up nursing, and for many years she was the town's mid-wife and doctor. Ophelia had arranged for my dad to hurt himself on the job. A piece of lumber struck him across the shoulder and left an eight-inch gash on his arm. Ophelia patched him up and then brazenly offered herself to him. Her advances became so bold that she would knock on his door in the middle of the night. My father succumbed to her overtures and she gave birth to the lumbering giant named Buford.

My father did not love either of these women. He slept with Clara once and never again. The same with Ophelia. For reasons even the Wheel could not fathom, he had fallen head over heels in love with my mother. His love for her was true and not the result of a spell or incantation.

Ophelia bowed out gracefully. She would either miscarry or give birth to stillborns, time and time again. This is what drove her crazy. She had corrupted her womb with such malevolence that no seed could grow there. She accepted this fate as punishment for meddling in the natural order of things.

Clara on the other hand claimed Uriah was her man and that my mother had broken the pact by falling in love with my father. She refused to believe Uriah had fallen in love with my mother naturally, and she refused to let her feelings for him die.

Thus, began the feud.

My mother, sensing Clara's thirst for revenge, set each one of my brothers on a mission of murder. They each were required to kill one of the Evangelist's sons before the Evangelist's sons could kill them. A sort of gruesome First Strike.

The Evangelist had six sons, all by different men. She tried to keep their identities a secret, to protect them from my mother. It was the Evangelist driving that Electra 225 that day. She was trying to protect her son, Clem.

This broke my father's heart when he discovered his wife's machinations. It caused him to have a stroke with her refusal to turn from this vendetta. She kept claiming it was Clara forcing her hand to murder. That she had no choice in the matter. She would tell my father that all mothers in nature, both man and beast were programmed to protect their young at all cost. My father's strength wasted away, but his love never did.

The vision faded and I realized I was crying. Never would I have thought the woman I grew up calling Mommy would be capable of such acts. That this loving and nurturing soul could harbor such a cold and vicious side. She had no qualms about killing Clara's children. The fact that she struck first without being provoked had no bearing on her decision. In her mind it was justified.

No wonder Clara hates me so much! I can't blame her!

Just then, the Wheel beckoned me to look deeper into the strange light. I did and saw there was another wheel beyond the second. I peered beyond that and saw a third, then a fourth and so on. It stretched out into infinity. Like the image two mirrors would reflect into each other.

But a mirror's reflection is an illusion.

This is what drove them crazy. This is what caused the insane lust for power. They spent their lives trying to get past all of the Wheels. They wanted to reach the center of the Wheel's power, but the Wheel had no center. Why couldn't they see that?

Two wheels, one inner, one outer. The inner wheel reflects the outer and the outer wheel reflects the inner, thus giving the illusion of depth. Even a child could see this! Why couldn't they?

Because they never got this far! They never got past the first Wheel!

I stifled the urge to laugh. What had happened was too simple to be true; the three of them were awed by an illusion. They had been wowed by a magician's trick and believed it to be true. From the vantage point of the first wheel this thing must indeed have appeared to be infinite.

If the Wheels are the mirror images of each other, then they must be opposite! The Outer Wheel the equivalent of Death and the Inner Wheel the equivalent of Life.

They believed the Wheel to be all-powerful, but it wasn't. The fact that the Outer Wheel could be corrupted by blood was proof of this. I remembered Ophelia's story about the three judges.

This is why I was able to get past the first Wheel, because of the medallion and because I am the seventh and sole survivor!

The Wheels turned again with a loud violent humming sound that reminded me of fingernails being raked across a blackboard. My skin erupted in thick gooseflesh and my teeth were on edge. The light above and below me grew white hot, and the medallion around my neck floated toward the light over my head. The chain pulled and bit into my neck. The medallion disappeared into the blinding white light. I reached to grab it and instead, I clutched what felt like a foot. I pulled and found myself staring into the eyes of a frightened little boy.

Suddenly my head felt as if it was about to explode. Memories deeply buried sprang to the surface of my consciousness. I remembered everything in that moment. I stood face to face with my younger self. This is what happened to me when I fell through the hole. The day I trespassed into her yard after the baseball.

That day was March 15th.

{*Ezekiel, are you okay*?} I thought and I could hear it echo all around me. My thoughts were being carried by the strange thrum. I could speak to myself telepathically.

{Petey! Help me, Petey!}, the little boy thought, and I heard it like he had screamed into a bullhorn. We were both covered in the light, bathed in its eerie glow.

{Petey isn't here, Ezekiel, but you don't have to be afraid. I'm not going to hurt you!}

{*Where am I? The light's too bright*!}

{We're in the Evangelist's basement, remember? You went in the yard to get the ball for Petey.}

{Who-who are you?}

{You don't know me, Ezekiel, but trust me. I am here to help you.}

{I don't know what you're talking about, Mister. I want to go home! I'm scared and I want to go home!}

I could feel the fear and the rage radiating off my younger self.

{Calm down, Ezekiel. I have something very important to tell you! You have to listen carefully to everything I'm about to say!}

{I wanna go home, Mister! This is the Evangelist's house! She'll get me if I stay down here too long!}

{No, she won't. I promise you. Listen to every word that I say very carefully and never tell anyone about this...}

I proceeded to tell him everything. How to finish school, what colleges to apply to, and most of all, the essay that would get him out of Cypress Point and into New York. I told him who to avoid on the streets and who to align himself with. I gave him a blueprint for life.

My life.

Through some strangely wonderful anomaly, a hole must've opened in Time, allowing me to see and interact with my nine-year-old self. This is how I was able to make it out of Cypress. The information I gave that small boy afforded me a fighting chance to beat the Cypress Curse. It was suddenly all there, as I remembered meeting a man in the light as a child. A man who told me that wonderful things were waiting for me once I got out of Cypress. A man who instilled within me a burning desire to achieve in the face of overwhelming adversity.

A man I desperately wanted to grow up and become.

I stood there, staring into the eyes of that child—the child I was and was not, feeling a sense of astonishment.

I remembered my mother beating Petey with an extension cord for letting me go into the Evangelist's yard. She was hysterical screaming at him, "*You could a let her take it all! You could a killed my baby and let that bitch win!*" she sobbed as she beat Petey until he passed out.

I remembered my head ached for over a week after I got home. I remembered how schoolwork seemed so easy after the headaches went away. I remembered the looks of amazement on my teachers' faces, as they scratched their heads in wonder at my newfound intelligence.

The humming grew louder, drowning out the mental voices of the little boy and I. The cavern shook violently and I knew the Wheel was turning again. This time I could hear clicks. The inner wheel and outer wheel weren't turning in sync.

I looked up and saw a man grab the little boy around his waist and pull him out of the light. The man was One-Leg. He had both arms and his skin was clear and healthy with no shine or waxy complexion from years of drinking. Instinctively I took the chain from around my neck and passed it to him. One Leg looked into my eyes and I knew then what scared him so badly that he took to drinking rubbing alcohol.

The light became blinding as we separated.

<u>Chapter XII</u>: **The hour of reckoning.**

When the rumbling of the Wheel ceased and the light died down, I found myself standing on the death corner. The same corner my brothers died on. It was now twelve o'clock, March fifteenth. Tamara lay on the ground beside me, her wounds healed, but she was unconscious.

The streets were deserted. The air was still. Nothing moved. Not one sign of life, other than Tamara and I, and she lay so silent I wondered if she was really alive. I could hear my heartbeat pounding in my ears.

This was like the showdowns in the old westerns I used to watch as a child. I stood wondering why the Wheel transported me to this terrible place at this appointed time, when it hit me.

This is how my brothers died...

No matter where they were on March 15th, at high noon the Wheel put them on this corner.

There was no escape.

J. B., Richie, Danny, Tom, Henry, and Peter. Murdered. Right here on the same corner. Their blood cried up to me for vengeance, and not only them—all of the souls that lay in anguish at the hands of this insane woman. All of the life-skeins cut short by the capricious whims of the Evangelist.

Anger burned within me. After all I had been through, all I had seen, she would still subjugate me to this. I stood as still as the wall behind me. My eyes fixed and locked on the street.

Let her come. I'm ready.

Across from me, in the middle of the street, a black dot hovered in mid-air slowly growing larger. The black pinprick of darkness doubled then tripled; expanding until it was an imminent gaping chasm.

The black lights.

The shadow that the blood soaked Outer Wheel cast on the Inner Wheel. The reason why a Cypress Point man's shadow was his best companion.

You will know everything in the proper time, Ezekiel...

Oddly enough, I was no longer afraid. It had come down to this: the last moves in a game of Chess. Either I would win or lose. It was that simple. This was game seven of the World Series, the NBA Finals, and the final seconds of the Superbowl rolled up into one. It was a tight game, but I was determined to win.

"Ain't no punks in my family," I said to the black light.

I remained motionless as the shadow of death eclipsed everything around me. My brothers died on this corner. Their life's blood had spilled and emptied right where I stood. I imagined the bewilderment each of them felt.

They used to tease and berate me for being the smallest, the weakest. But I am no longer small or weak.

"I am Uriah's son."

Within the black light I saw a gray-silhouetted figure, slowly writhing. The wind picked up, swirling around me in gusts of fury. The figure stepped out of the blackness as if it were a simple doorway. I took a deep breath and held it in anticipation.

I was ready to face her.

"The seventh son of a seventh son."

The black lights obscured her face, but I recognized her white robes. Two other hooded figures were behind her, slowly climbing out of the pulsing black hole that throbbed like a poisoned wound in the middle of the street. There was still no traffic, no movement—not even a window from one of the nearby buildings raised to see what was about to happen.

Death would claim someone this day.

And I was determined it would not be me.

"Uriah was my father. He raised me to respect death, but to revere life."

The two other figures were now right behind her, all three of their faces shrouded by the darkness of the black lights. The three slowly moved toward me, as silent as a breeze. I stared at her, wondering who her two followers were.

Doug Hollands? Cliff Dixon?

"The appearance of the wheels and their work was like unto the color of a beryl," she said. "And they had one likeness. And their appearance and their work was as it were a wheel in the middle of a wheel. You know where that comes from, don't you, Ezekiel."

"Yes," I answered. "The prophet Ezekiel wrote it in the bible."

Her eyes were the first things to come into view. They were as white as her robes, pupils and all. She slowly glided toward me with the two silhouetted figures behind her.

"I sent you through the valley of dry bones. I tested you and tested you and yet you remained. This much I will give you; you are an admirable opponent. Tell me, Ezekiel. Tell me what the Wheel showed you." There was a ghostly hollow echo behind her voice. Her words reverberated in my mind, canceling out all other thoughts.

But her lips never moved.

"I asked the Wheel to heal Tamara. Lukie had stabbed her in the heart and she was bleeding to death. The inner Wheel healed her."

"Toy with me no longer, Ezekiel. Tell me what I wish to know or I will mar you. What did the Wheel tell you?"

Her voice had a sickly sweet tone to it. The way a child would imagine a witch sounding in a fairy tale. The mist around her and the other two grew thicker. The rest of the street was a hazy blur. The breeze had picked up, but Clara's robes flowed against the wind.

"It showed me what you did to it. I saw how you and Ophelia and my mother seduced and killed your fathers. I saw how you lured men to their deaths. I saw how you three spent generations murdering each other's children. I saw how the three of you destroyed this town."

"You think to sit in judgment over me, Ezekiel? You think that you are qualified to counsel me?"

"I think that the three of you came upon something you had no way of understanding and you polluted it with your ignorance! What right did you have to play with so many lives? You're sick beyond belief, Clara! You—"

"SILENCE!"

The wind howled when she spoke. Her voice boomed like the ocean's tide. My head swam and it took me a moment to gain my bearings. I stood quiet. It wouldn't do to antagonize this woman.

"I have seen *worlds* and *wonders* beyond number, Ezekiel. The theme of the universe is survival! The Wheel gives me the power over *death*!"

She said death like it was something to be venerated and worshipped. I shuddered in revulsion thinking of all the men she murdered. This woman killed with a hedonistic fury. There was no end to her epicurean bloodlust.

"Wake up, Tamara," she said.

Tamara bolted and stood as if shot out of a cannon. I reached for her hand and she gently pulled away from me with an odd look on her face. "I'm so sorry, Ezekiel! I told you to go when you had the chance!" She kissed my cheek and walked over to the Evangelist. Clara touched her forehead and Tamara knelt in front of her.

"Tamara, what are you doing? What are you doing?"

"You understand, don't you, Ezekiel? I had to do as she said! She's my mother!" Tamara said.

Clara pushed her aside and kept gliding toward me with the two figures in tow behind her.

"She hated me for being born a girl, Ezekiel. She had six sons and her seventh child was a girl. She hated me, Ezekiel. I am the reason she didn't inherit the Wheel's power! This is the only way I could win her love, Ezekiel. You understand, don't you?"

"Your mother? Oh, *no-no-no*!" I stammered, shocked. "It all makes sense now! Now I know how she was able to find me! You led her straight to me, didn't you! That's how she jammed the cell phone and the laptop. I saved your life, Tamara. I could've let Lukie have his way with you. I could've left with Patrick and let you die! You said you loved me, but I guess the fruit doesn't fall far from the tree!"

"I didn't lie about that, Ezekiel. I do love you. You-you don't understand! Can you imagine what it's like being hated by your mother? Can you imagine being Lukie's sister? Being told that you're nothing but a Molly girl, having a molesting fiend for a brother! Can you imagine that?" She ran up to me, staring deep into my eyes, pleading for understanding. I looked past her, not taking my eyes off her mother.

"You don't have to die, Ezekiel! Just give her what she wants and we can still leave! Just give her what she wants! That was the promise I made to her. I told you I came here to save the living—you, Ezekiel! I came here to save you!" She tugged at my arm, begging me. "If it was your life she really wanted she could have killed you at any time! Think about it! She just wants what you have! Give it to her and I swear on the Wheel that you can leave here alive!"

"What about George and One-Leg? What about Buford? Did you sell them out as well?"

"NO! Think! She never touched them! I know this sounds stupid, but she never *harmed* you! Lukie went too far, but *she never harmed you!* Do you think I would have put myself in Lukie's hands—that I would have endured that *sick bastard* touching me again if I didn't love you? I won't let her hurt you, Ezekiel! She never planned to hurt you! "

"Yeah, because she was waiting for March fifteenth! So she could sacrifice me to the fucking Wheel as she did all of my brothers!"

"Then why are you still alive? Why am I standing here telling you that I love you? That you don't have to die and I won't let you die! Tell her what she wants to know and break this stupid curse!"

"So…what? You Uriah's daughter?"

"No, Ezekiel. You met my daddy; that old bum, Pickle. He was cursed for not giving her a son."

The Evangelist forbade me to ever see my love or my baby again. No reason. Just that it was God's will…

"Figures. Just figures!" I threw up my hands in disgust. "Well, forget that! Just let her kill me instead of what she did to that poor bastard."

"She won't kill you, Ezekiel. I need for you to trust me now, more than you ever did! Please*, just trust me this once…*" she whispered, sotto voce. I stared at her, wondering what she meant. Something made me want to believe in her. Even against all evidence to the contrary.

Clara came no closer. The two shadowy figures remained in the background. Tamara held my face and forced me to look into her eyes—eyes that bored into me with love and fealty. I wanted to believe her, but I couldn't let my guard down.

"What do you want from me, Clara?" I asked. I remained motionless, unflinching, and desperately trying to remain unafraid.

"Tell me what the Wheel told you, Ezekiel. Tell me what happened when you reached the center of the Wheel and I'll consider letting you go. How many Wheels did you pass to reach the center? What is the total number of them?" She moved a yard closer and so did the two figures behind her. Her robes flowed around her and her feet hovered above the ground in a misty haze of silvery fog.

The other two figures moved to her side now, their faces still obscured by the shadows. The three of them floated about three feet off the ground.

"You, Ophelia and my mother have corrupted the outer Wheel for nothing. The infinite number of wheels is an illusion. You were seeing the reflection of the inner wheel. It was like two mirrors reflecting each other. You ruined the outer wheel and destroyed the synergy they had with each other."

A bolt of force pinned me against the brick wall. Hot desiccating pain seared across my chest. A thin black spear of light slowly pulsed from her fingertip toward my head.

"You lie, Ezekiel! You want to see what happens when someone plays me for a fool! Now tell me what happened when you went into the White Light!" she spat, almost hysterical.

"My liquor's proof, Clara. I'm telling you the truth," I mumbled, trying to ignore the pain. The black spear of light etched closer and closer to my head. I was pinned so tight that I couldn't move. I could see Tamara pleading with her mother to stop, but all I could hear was Clara's voice.

"I'll give you this one last chance, Ezekiel. One last chance to redeem yourself and tell me the truth. Oh, I can make this last a good long time, smart boy. I can strip you naked and have you howling at the moon. I can crush your testicles and leave you a eunuch. Now you tell me!"

"I'm telling you the truth!"

"*Ezekiel saw a wheel within a wheel...*" She began to sing and I could hear her voice all around me, as tinny as a child's toy xylophone.

"*Within a wheel—*

...within a wheel...within a wheel..." this part echoed, striking the core of my psyche like the Chinese water torture.

The black light came closer, mere inches from my forehead. The whiteness of her gown blinded me. I could feel pieces of my sanity tear and float away. She was inside my head, probing, searching—ripping my thoughts to shreds. I could feel her stomping out my will power.

"I am...the seventh son...of Uriah and Eliza Johnson." *God, the pain is so great. Focus, Ezekiel! Focus!* I shut my eyes and tried to force her out of my mind.

"Ezekiel saw a wheel, within a wheel..." her voice was so sing-songy. A child's nursery rhyme. The last three words echoed into infinity.

—*Within a wheel, within a wheel, within a wheel...*

Her voice was now damp flat notes that rubbed and grated the frayed ends of my coherence. That voice became everything, overpowering all thoughts. I fought back with every vestige of my strength, shielding the secrets of my intelligence.

"Uriah...was the seventh...son of...a...seventh son." She was searching my memories. Invading me. Violating me.

"Ezekiel saw a wheel within a wheel." If she kept singing I would soon join her in reciting that phrase and it would be the only thing I would ever be able to think or to say. I would be insane. *This* is what she did to Radar.

"That's enough, Clara. That's enough."

My eyes popped open in shock at hearing that voice. The person on the left of Clara stepped out of the shadows. The face was visible to me now. I shut my eyes again and willed the person away. There was no earthly way this person could be standing in front of me. This was another one of the Evangelist's tricks. It had to be.

The person on her left was my mother.

I opened my eyes again and saw Ophelia step out of the shadows on Clara's right. The three of them were dressed in the same white flowing robes. They hovered in mid air, just feet away from me.

This was too much for me to bear. It would have been more merciful for Clara to just put a bullet between my eyes and be done with it. I reached out to touch my mother, to see if she was real or a phantom when I heard a cacophony of voices in my head.

— They were witches!
— *Your mother died with your name on her lips.*
— Evil bitches!
— *You must complete the plan your mother and I conceived so long ago.*
— Bred in the stove of hell!
— *I'm going to break you, smart boy. I'm going to stretch the limits of your sanity and have you beg me for death.*
— She'll die if I leave her!

— You'll die if you don't!

I collapsed, holding my head, trying to make the voices go away. The woman before me was not my mother. She couldn't be. She was not the woman who poured kisses over skinned knees and elbows and rocked me to sleep when the bad dreams came. This was not the woman whose waist I held as a child and inhaled deeply, treasuring the smell of her apron.

"Get up, Ezekiel. Clara, I think the boy is telling the truth. He probably can't remember what happened."

It was her voice, her face. It was even her scent. But how could this be the woman my father fell in love with? How could this be the woman who bore seven sons for him? The woman who raised and nurtured me. The woman who took me to church, taught me right from wrong—standing here side by side with the Evangelist!

"He remembers, sister. Let me probe him just a bit longer. I promise you we will learn his secrets," Clara urged.

"We grow tired of waiting, Clara." Ophelia said. "We cannot afford to tarry any longer."

The three of them loomed over me, shoulder to shoulder. "Let me try," my mother said. "Ezekiel, Tamara is right. You don't have to die. I made a truce with them to save you. It's the first truce that I've made in ages. I did it for you. I did it out of my love for you, but you have to work with me here, or I won't be able to help you."

Once in New York, my company published a series of articles about women who killed their children. Filicide is the term for it. One woman in New Mexico thought her child was possessed by Satan and boiled the baby in hot oil to exorcise the devil out of it. Another woman in Iowa believed that her baby would be taken to heaven by angels, so she threw the child off the roof of a building.

"How could you join forces with the woman who *murdered your children*?"

"There is too much at stake here and not enough time to explain to you, Ezekiel. You have to tell us what the Wheel told you. If you ever trusted me, I need for you to trust me now. I sent you the pie case and the baseball, Ezekiel. I knew you would need them. You have to believe me! The cycle is ending, Ezekiel. *The Wheel is about to turn!*"

She spoke quietly and calmly, yet I was able to detect the naked terror in her words. My mother always had a way of putting her best face on when trouble struck. She was always the rock of the family, guiding us. Leading us. My father would constantly joke that she was the boss of the family, and although said in jocularity, we all knew it to be true. This same woman, who taught me to remain proud and to stand upright no matter what my circumstances now stood before me with piercing eyes.

"How could you stand next to her, knowing what she did! What about my father! What about his memory? Who mourns Uriah Johnson and his six murdered sons? Ophelia told me that you were dead—maybe this is just another trick of Clara's...playing with my head!"

"The charade was necessary, Ezekiel. I had to make sure you would play your part accordingly," Ophelia said. "I know what you think of us, but the chicanery was unavoidable. We needed to make sure you sought the Wheel. We must know what happened to you when you stepped into the White Light! Time grows short for us, Ezekiel!"

"When you stepped into the White Light none of us could detect where you went," Clara said and for perhaps the first time she spoke to me with no bitterness in her voice. "It happened once before when you trespassed on my property. We need to know where you went! We need to know how you found the way out of Cypress and more importantly how you found the way back here!" she continued hotly. "We must learn what you know, Ezekiel. We must survive at all costs!"

"Even at the cost of your own children? What kind of monster kills its own child?"

"That is why you must tell us, Ezekiel. In order to stop the killing! Clara has lost sons, as have Ophelia and I. Let the grief and hatred—the *murder*s stop with you! Heal these wretched souls and bring peace to this troubled land!"

Her words were soft and drenched with emotion. The three of them begged me with their eyes. I reeled in confusion. Was this real? And if it was, could I trust the women in front of me?

I stared at them. The three of them seemed so alien to me at that moment. This was all so incredible, but my mother was right. Here it was March 15th and I was still alive. Maybe the only way my mother could save me was to make a truce with Clara.

Your mother needs you...

"Is this how my brothers died? Did the three of you set them up like this?"

"No, Ezekiel—" my mother said.

"Your answer, Ezekiel. Quickly," Clara broke in. "The truce between the three of us depends on your answer. Ophelia has yet to mourn Buford and I have yet to mourn Lukie."

If this was real and there was a way to save not only myself, but countless others—if there was a way that I could stop the killings, then wasn't I bound by humanity to do that, regardless of the cost?

"Tell them, Ezekiel. Tell them and I promise you all will be well. Take me for wife, combine the blood line. Ophelia shall stand as godmother to our children. This will be the peace." Tamara held me tightly, her lips fluttered against my neck. I could feel the blush of her cheek, like a low flame on my skin. I could smell her sex. I wanted to devour her in one bite. Her scent was intoxicating, as succulent as pie.

Boston Crème Pie…

"*I know how confused you are right now*," she moaned. "I know how you must feel. Believe me when I tell you I love you. Trust me. Trust your heart this once and I promise you will never regret it. I will strive to make you a good wife. I will give you *sons,* Ezekiel. You will sit at the head of all tables. The Inner Wheels shall bow before you and your name will be written in the stars forever." Her hands caressed the small of my back and slowly worked their way down in small circular motions. Her voice was thick and husky with carnal desire. She took my hand and placed it on her breasts.

Trust me this once, her eyes said.

A fire ignited in my veins. A primal, feral, *sordid* want overtook me. I needed her, but only her. No other woman would suffice. My manhood swelled to painful proportions and all that mattered was that I took her. I desperately needed releasing, and she alone could release me. My need for her was ravenous.

Insatiable.

"*I will give you sons, Ezekiel. I will give you all that you wish, devoting myself to you and only to you forever more. No woman born of flesh could ever have more love for you than I. When your heart is light I will share your laughter, and when your mood is somber I will share your pain.*" She placed her hands on my swollen groin and deftly massaged me. My knees buckled and threatened to give out from under me. "*Give me*

214

your love and heal me. Heal this wretched soul, Uriah-son. I shall worship you, as your father worshipped your mother."

I bit her bottom lip hard, drawing blood, but not caring. I grabbed her roughly by her hair, entangling both hands in her locks. She was *meat* and *milk*, born and built to sate my hunger.

"Take me, Ezekiel. Take me as often as you wish. Take me for wife and I shall give you sons."

The flame of desire engulfed me and I was blinded by my total wanton lust. My tongue explored the deep recesses of her mouth. All I could taste was Boston Crème Pie. She returned my kiss with a heat like a blast furnace, vigorously massaging my crotch.

I held her tighter, and no matter how tight I held her it wasn't tight enough. I wanted her, but not just for release right now. Not just for sex.

I wanted her to give me sons.

Suddenly I was overcome with a vision of her, womb swollen and in the throes of labor, birthing my children. I saw her growing old with me, as we watched our progeny mature. It was all there, my future laid out in front of me.

The woman before me was *my* Inner Wheel.

The Ying to my Yang.

The smell of Boston Crème Pie was unmistakably overpowering now. I pressed my nose against her neck and inhaled deeply. Her back arched, molding her chest with mine. My hands splayed in a vise-like grip on her firm buttocks.

Is this love, or lust? I thought. Is this what my father felt? I remembered how I felt when she lay bleeding. It was at that moment that I realized Tamara was the one who kept me sane. I never could've made it without her.

"Fill me with your seed and I shall give you *sons*, Uriah-son."

Her voice was as sultry as Sade's and God she smelled so good! And was it my imagination or was she just so much prettier now! Her breasts looked so firm in her torn blouse, her waist so small and pinched. She was as alluring and as tempting as forbidden fruit.

I panted so hard I could barely catch my breath. My mind swarmed with various ways of taking her. I wanted to mount her so badly, to rut like an animal in heat. I wanted to rip off her clothes and run my tongue over every square inch of her skin.

She put my hand between her legs and clamped her thighs closed. "*All for you and only you. Yours forever and ever. Till death do us part.*" Her voice and scent were a powerful aphrodisiac. My libido increased to a frenzied height.

I inhaled deeply, relishing her scent. Dazzled by her sensuality. I was *hot* for her. A heat that burns in the marrow of the bones and simmers.

And then, out of the fog, "Your answer, Ezekiel," Clara ordered. I was too enthralled with Tamara to speak, so I merely nodded. Tamara's tongue fluttered ever so lightly around my throat, leaving a scintillating tickle that sent all of my nerve endings into overload.

"Answer her, Ezekiel. *Answer her and we can be alone and I promise you she will bother you no more.*" Her voice was so soothing, like the sound of drizzling rain on a spring day falling on newly blossomed flowers. Like a butter-smooth silk suit, perfectly tailored and swathed on my body.

I turned to answer Clara, anxious to get her out of my face so that I could be alone with Tamara. The three of them stood quiet, breathlessly waiting to hear what I had to say. Even the wind stopped blowing.

Just then, the sound of a car screeching broke the grim stillness. I turned and saw Patrick jump out of the fully restored Mercedes with a look of wild panic in his eyes. This time there was no mistaking it, he was larger. Much larger. His girth almost blocked the car entirely and he was even taller than I remembered. Lukie would have definitely needed a wheel barrow to carry his carcass.

He stood defiantly staring at them with a smirk that froze my blood. His clothes had changed also. He now wore an all black no-collared suit with a wide brimmed hat that immediately made me think of an old eighteenth century undertaker.

The three of them turned in unison—no, that's not right. This is what happened; one moment I was looking into their faces and in the next instant, I was staring at the back of their heads. Their bodies did not turn. They simply went from front to back in less than the blink of an eye.

"They turned not when they went," I mumbled, quoting the book of Ezekiel.

They slowly, methodically floated toward Patrick. Their robes eerily danced against the ever-increasing wind. The sky darkened as thick purplish storm clouds amassed.

They hummed an odd tune, matching each other perfectly in tone. The wind moaned in response. Patrick stood glaring at them, his massive chest heaved up and down and it seemed with each breath he drew he somehow became even larger.

"I thought you said Lukie killed him," my mother remarked.

"Well, it seems the Wheel will have a sacrifice after all!" Clara shrieked with laughter. "Although I am anxious to see how it reacts to being soaked in gravy instead of blood!"

"You should have left when we offered you the opportunity, Patrick. Now your flesh will be ours." Ophelia said. "I claim his eyes and tongue! Retribution for his lack of respect when he entered my hall!"

"And you shall have them, Ophelia! I just want his skin, heart and lungs! Such a *large* man will provide ingredients for many a spell! Stake your claim, Eliza!"

"Well," my mother, Eliza said, hovering over Patrick's head like a bird of prey, "It's been so long since we've done this together. I've always been partial to a man's spine. I claim his spine as my own!"

"So much flesh on one man! So much skin to drape myself in!" Clara chimed. "I shall make a gown of your skin, Patrick. I shall make wine bags out of your lungs!"

"We shall make soup of your blood," Eliza said.

"And sausage of your manhood and bowels!" Ophelia added.

"*And the Wheel can have your soul!*" they raved together, laughing maniacally.

Patrick dared them to come closer, beckoning them with his hands. He growled and puffed out his chest, the way a cat would swell to try to intimidate an attacker.

"*We are not children now, caretaker of death! You will find us a most formidable adversary! Prepare to be sacrificed!*" They chanted together, their voices indistinguishable, blending perfectly. The wind carried their song like an acoustic amplifier and I felt my insides roil and tumble. The pitch of their voices was a sharp hot needle prickling my brain. I covered my ears to block out the raucous sound.

"Who is he?" I asked aloud. The answer came from within and yet without.

The answer came from the Wheel.

[*It was he who seduced the girls to kill their fathers and dance before the Wheel. It was he who first stained the Wheel with the taste of human blood. He has been banished from Cypress Point for over a century, until you invited him back. He will kill the three of them and then he will try to kill you to gain the power of the Wheel...*]

Him got the looks of Foreigner!

Him from CYP-press Point. Him turnin home!

The hair on the back of my neck stood at rigid attention. My testicles shriveled and numbly nestled themselves in my abdomen.

The shit had hit the fan.

<u>Chapter XIII</u>: He has ciphered it…

The three lingered over Patrick, swiping, spitting. They circled above him like hawks about to swoop down on an unsuspecting hare. He hissed angrily and kept trying to pull them down. I watched in dumb horror as it finally dawned on me why everyone was so afraid and appalled by Patrick's appearance.

Foreigners aren't allowed in Cypress.

He was the reason why the Evangelist didn't want anyone to leave Cypress Point. She was afraid that someone would unwittingly bring Patrick back! I now knew this, because I shared some kind of arcane inner voice with the Wheel.

"Let them do this! It's the prophecy!" Tamara said as she grabbed me, holding me back. I had not realized it then, but I was heading toward the fight. It was instinctive, seeing my mother getting ready to fight set off an automatic reaction.

"Listen to me, Ezekiel!" she rushed. The smell of Boston Crème Pie was gone, but she was still just as enthralling to me.

"I know what happened when you went into the White Light. There was a little girl hiding from Lukie in the corner of the cellar. She was awestruck at seeing a man carrying a bleeding lady to the Wheel.

"The little girl, she liked to stay near it because the Wheel was the only place the monster couldn't get her. This little girl…she prayed that someone would come and save her from the monster. Someone kind and strong and brave. Someone smart like the people she would read about sometimes in the books. She prayed that someone would kill the monster. She prayed for you.

"She watched all of this from the corner and she heard everything the man told the little boy in the White Light. The bleeding lady saw her and told her what to do. The little girl had a medallion that she managed to chip off of the Wheel. She kept it for good luck and to keep the monster away from her. She threw it into the White Light, Ezekiel. She did it because the bleeding lady told her to.

"I have loved you from the first time I saw you, Ezekiel. From the first time I saw you fall into the cellar, into the waiting arms of the man you are now. The bleeding woman told me to take care of you. I asked the Wheel to show me the way out to get you. I lied and told my mother I could bring you back here for her, but I brought you back for your destiny. Trust me this once, Uriah-son and I promise you will never regret it. Do you trust me?"

I looked into her eyes and knew at that moment how my father felt about my mother.

"*With all my soul*," I replied, trembling from a place so deep within me I didn't know it existed.

Tamara grasped my hand tight and stood by my side. The sky darkened as clouds churned helplessly before the swirling winds.

"Did you know all of this was going to happen?' I asked.

"No! Like you I couldn't remember and then when you took me to the Wheel it all came back to me because I saw myself as a child just as you did! I can remember some of the things the Wheel told me now. Like I can remember what it told me is about to happen now and how you have to make a choice, but I don't know what that choice is or what you have to do."

I squeezed her hand tighter. Her hand in mine felt like the last piece to a completed jig-saw puzzle. It had never occurred to me how she was able to leave Cypress Point or why she was on the same plane as me. Our lives were intertwined in ways I could yet imagine.

I was watching the end and the beginning.

Ophelia swung at Patrick and caught him hard across the face. He stumbled back against the Mercedes, his cheek ripped like an opened zipper. Clara wasted no time as she swooped in. Her fingers, spread like talons, tore a flap of flesh off of Patrick's scalp. Blood sprayed the Mercedes in a crimson arc.

Patrick grabbed Ophelia by her gown and viciously swung her into the Mercedes. Her head went through the windshield, leaving jagged shards embedded in her scalp like a broken crown of glass. Her gown was drenched in blood. Patrick held her by the throat, lifting her bleeding body high above his head.

"The times for games and charades are past. Give me the secrets of the Wheel, or this slattern dies first!" Patrick seethed. Obviously he saw no reason to remain civil.

My mother and Clara lunged at him and Patrick hurled Ophelia into them. The three of them quickly regrouped and attacked him again. Clara tore into Patrick's side, leaving a foot long gash across his abdomen. My mother clawed at his eyes. The four of them fought with a frenzied rage and I stood petrified watching blood splatter and sinew rent from bone. It was like watching animals tear into each other. They laughed and screeched with every blow they struck, savoring the sight of so much blood and torn flesh. The dark cloud of death hovered over them, covering them like an impenetrable thick black mesh, preventing me from joining the fight.

Patrick threw Ophelia through the black net. She landed hard, her body twisted and broken. Her skin dry and peeling. She looked so old in that moment. Older than anyone living had a right to be. Like she had ducked death one time too many.

"Ezekiel, you have to remember what was on the disk! We cannot defeat him alone!" she gasped and a black cloud seeped from her lips as she spoke. I turned and saw Clara land in a similar heap of broken bones and spent flesh. They both struggled to get to their feet, to get back into the fight.

My mother was left alone against Patrick. I ran up to them but I could not breach the black cloud that covered them. I watched in abject horror as he tossed her aside like a sack of trash. The three of them stood uneasily, their robes bloodied and torn covered in what looked like strands of black thread.

Patrick looked even worse; he had large chunks of muscle ripped from his body, but there was no blood. Just a rust colored suppuration that oozed out of his mangled flesh. Though judging from the severity of his wounds I imagined him to be in excruciating pain, he laughed as if someone had just told him the most deliriously funny joke.

"Ezekiel, you must remember! You must remember!" they chanted.

"It's too late, changelings! The Wheel is turning," Patrick gloated and it was true. The ground silently split and I could see an incredible light pouring out of the aperture. My eyes burned, but I couldn't look away. It was like staring into the sun. The Wheel rose out of the fissure like a magnificent Phoenix and hung about a half mile high in the air. I managed to shut my eyes, and the light still blinded me.

The wind whined like a banshee in heat. Dust and debris swirled around me in a dangerous maelstrom. I searched my memory for what was on Ophelia's disk. I remembered her telling me that when the time was right I *would* remember. The disk, it was shiny, silvery. It had a strange writing on it, characters that looked like hieroglyphics drawn by small malnourished children.

But what did they mean?

The harder I tried to remember the more I kept drawing a blank. I searched Ophelia's words for a clue...

The message on it was given to me by the Wheel itself. No one, not me—not Clara, not even your mother could cipher it...

I remembered the shapes and strange patterns of the markings. I remembered suddenly being bombarded with information, but I could not remember what the information was.

"This is the moment where all will be lost or won, Ezekiel. You know in your heart what must be done. This is your destiny," Tamara whispered to me. "All you have to do is believe in yourself and remember what the Wheel told you. If you don't he will kill us all."

"I'm trying like hell to remember, Tamara! Don't you think I want to remember? I keep coming up with nothing! Just a bunch of dumb symbols that don't mean anything!"

"They *do* mean something, Ezekiel. You have to stop thinking so hard! The answer is staring you right in the face!"

The wind increased, threatening to suck the air out of my lungs. Grit got in my eyes and for a moment I was blinded with nothing but the sound of the storm in my ears.

You be better than good at it! You hear me, E. J? You bout the only one with a real chance, so you be better than good at it!

I will, J.B! I promise all of you that!

Time seemed to slow down, as I finally remembered the strange writings on the silver disk.

"I remember what was written on Ophelia's disk! Here is wisdom! *Let he that hath understanding reckon this:* The first Wheel is the earth spinning on its axis!"

"I command you to stand silent!" Patrick shrieked and for the first time I saw him rattled. He struggled to get to me, but the wind now blew against him, holding him still.

I ignored him and continued, "The second Wheel is the moon spinning around the earth! The next is the earth spinning around the sun, and then the sun spinning on its axis. The next is the solar system spinning in the galaxy, and the galaxy spins through the universe, and it all spins on a wheel in the palms of God's hands!"

The wind shrieked so loud it sounded like a high pitched whistle. My head trembled from the vibrations. I could feel my eyes shake in their sockets. There was a whirlwind of debris swirling under the Wheel in an inverted vortex.

Then everything stopped.

Tree limbs, bricks, concrete blocks, car parts, broken street lamps, torn awnings, dirt and rocks all hung, suspended in mid air. I looked around in utter shock. I touched one of the concrete blocks; it must've weighed at least a couple of tons, yet it gently spun in place like a toy top. The Mercedes sat straight up in the air on a ninety-degree angle. Tamara and Patrick were motionless, frozen stiff.

"*This is where life and death kiss,*" I said in awe. Time had stopped. This was the space between the Wheels. I felt my chest and couldn't feel my heartbeat. I was now *in between* heartbeats.

Dead time.

"*Come to me, Ezekiel. Let me share something with you before I leave this plane of existence...*" Clara whispered in a croaking voice. I hesitated, not sure if I could trust her, but she smiled and beckoned me closer. "*Come, Uriah-son. I will not—I cannot harm you now.*"

I went to her. Her body was as still and as cold as a mannequin. The only sign of life was in her eyes, and this was the first time I ever saw anything in them other than pure hatred. I knelled down to her and put my ear to her lips. Her breath was a ragged chipped thing rattling in her chest. She was dying and we both knew it.

"*Beware the Wheel, Ezekiel. It is a treacherous thing. Tell me ...although I have no right to ask, tell me what happened when you stepped into the White Light.*"

I told her.

"*Then the joke has been on both of us! Since you have been so honorable I will share something with you, seventh son of Uriah and Eliza: I did not kill your brothers. Your mother and Ophelia finally realized this when Patrick returned and they sought me out for the truce. Truth to tell I am glad I was able to make up with my sisters. I can't tell you how much I've missed them over all these years. You will take care of Tamara for me?*"

She truly loves you. She will make you a good wife. Give you lots of sons, Ezekiel."

"I'll take care of her," I said, understanding that Clara was dying and this was her last wish. But what did she mean, she didn't kill my brothers? If she didn't then who?

Who?

"Then with my last breath I pass all of my knowledge on to you as I join my sisters in death. Blessed art thou, seventh from Uriah to survive the Ides of March. May your seventh son—my grandson sit at the head of all tables, for you will not..." She sighed and I saw the same black cloud trickle out of her mouth. She was dead and I knew then that my mother and Ophelia were dead also.

Their faces looked like porcelain masks; hard, cold. My body shook as all they knew about the Wheel passed on to me, the knowledge was great but was incomplete.

Everything was still. The Outer Wheel remained motionless, but the Inner Wheel turned upright until both looked like a giant gyroscope.

The Inner Wheel gleamed with a light that was so incandescent it made everything look like an X-ray. It looked like a huge platinum ring. Slowly the inner Wheel spun, pulsating with tremendous energy. The debris crashed to the ground with a thunderous clatter.

Time started again.

I saw their faces and robes become as hard and still as stone, then hairline fractures appeared in their features. Bits and pieces of them began to break off and float to the outer Wheel, becoming part of it. The bits and pieces became dust, and flowed to the Wheel until the three of them were no more.

Our mothers and Ophelia were dead.

All that was left now was Patrick.

Patrick...

The shit soaked fan was now on high speed, blowing right in my face.

Chapter XIV: The Sacrifice

Patrick stood on the other side of the chasm, pacing back and forth like a boxer who couldn't wait for the opening bell. Black vaporous strands wafted from his mouth and nostrils like sentient smoke. There was a fierce cold anger in his eyes. Patrick looked like a man who had seen death up close and ate it. He walked the edge of the rift, frustrated he couldn't reach me.

"He can't cross the gap!" Tamara said, with a tinge of awe in her voice. "He can't cross the Wheels, Ezekiel! Don't you feel it?"

I did. Through the knowledge I had inherited from the three of them, I knew Patrick's history. And I wished I didn't.

—   —   —

Patrick started out human enough. He was a medic in the Civil War, a scholar who'd joined the military because he truly believed in what he was fighting for. The abolishment of slavery and a country united in its ideals. On the battlefield he proved himself a brave and dedicated healer, administering salve and first aid to the wounded regardless of race. Once the war was over Patrick played physician as well as undertaker. He was well suited for both positions since he was equally obsessed with both life and death.

When Cypress Point was first found by former slaves and former soldiers, Patrick was among them. The story Ophelia told me was true. Cypress Point was just about the closest thing to Utopia at that time.

And then Patrick found out about the Wheel.

It started innocently enough. A small Native American boy had fallen out of a tree and fractured his skull. Patrick wrapped the boy's head as well as he could and monitored him, but there was little hope for the boy's survival. The other Natives in the village assured Patrick that the boy would be fine once they took him to see the Natives' judge.

Patrick insisted to them that there was nothing humanly possible that could save the boy. His head wounds were too severe and he had lapsed into a coma.

Death was imminent.

But yet the tribe's people seemed more concerned with placating Patrick than showing any sign of grief. He was taken aback at the nonchalant attitude of the parents and tribal members. Patrick watched and followed from the shadows, curious as to why such a close-knit group would treat one of their children so blasé. He noticed whenever they spoke of the child they did so in whispers, and always when they thought no one was around.

Patrick skulked in the shadows eavesdropping and picking up bits and pieces, wondering just what *The Wheel* was and what power it had.

He watched as they set the stones for the Medicine Wheel, the *Sacred Hoop,* as they called it. The setting of the stones was the tribe's way to alert the Wheel that it was needed for a peaceful purpose. The tribal judge carried the boy to the Wheel, and Patrick kept a safe distance, lurking like a thief in the shade.

Patrick remained hidden in the cave, watching in wide-eyed awe as the judge beseeched the Outer Wheel to open and give access to the Inner Wheel to save the child. The Outer Wheel acquiesced, accepting a sacrifice of fruits, corn and grains, soaked in the blood of a slain bison.

Even after the child stepped out of the White Light, hale and whole, Patrick did not reveal himself. He remained hidden in that cave with no food or water, staring at the Wheel for three days before the Outer Wheel acknowledged him.

Thinking that the blood sacrifice the natives made was the reason the Outer Wheel proffered it's gifts, he promised it *gallons* of the scarlet fluid in return for its favor.

He promised it *human* blood.

At first Patrick saturated the Wheel with the blood of the dead. Women who had passed giving birth, men killed from disease or accident. The deceased were drained of every drop of the ruby liquid. Their veins emptied, sucked dry as surely as if they had been bitten by a vampire.

This aroused no suspicions among the town because blood draining was a normal step in the embalming process. Though morbid, he was not yet *damned.*

But then the Outer Wheel would no longer accept blood from the dead. It wanted to taste the warm throbbing pulse of the liquid from the living. He was forced into the ghoulish task of supplying fresh victims to the Wheel in exchange for knowledge.

Patrick, a teacher to the three judges' daughters, thought their menstrual blood would be sufficient to fool the Wheel. In theory it should have worked, but what Patrick did not anticipate was how quickly the three girls adapted to the Wheel.

The Wheel affects virgin women and children different from men and women who have lost their maidenhead...

The onset of puberty, the girl's virginity and innocence, coupled with the trio's seemingly inherent ability to wield the Wheel's power, waylaid Patrick's plans. The girls became more powerful than him almost immediately. And so Patrick resorted to trickery to deceive the girls.

He told them that their fathers held the key to the *Inner Wheel* and try as he might he could not convince the patriarchs to trust their daughters with the secret. Like the aged old serpent in the Garden of Eden he kept beguiling them with the *potential* they could wield. He goaded them to push their powers further, to near impossible limits and when they failed at the given task he assured them that if their fathers would only share with them the secrets, they would achieve power beyond their wildest imaginings.

Clara was first to take heed. And on a warm day in the middle of March Patrick explained to them exactly what they had to do...

"It may seem to you that what I say is wrong, but it is in the bible! Read the story of Lot! When his wife passed on after disobeying God's holy edict, Lot's two daughters gave him wine to drink, and when he was drunken they lay with him a fortnight until both conceived and were with child! Now, I am not saying that you have to bear the fruit of the judges' loins, but you should sacrifice your maidenheads to the Wheel. In return for such an august gift, I am sure it will grant your every desire!

"God wants you to do this! Why, if He didn't He would not have sent the Wheel to you by me! And look at you! One black, daughter of a man born into slavery; one white, a daughter of a man sworn to fight to end that terrible injustice, and the daughter of an Indian. Whose land and country has been usurped to say the least! Why, with the power of the Inner Wheel at your disposal, anything will be possible! You could heal this wretched land and bring peace to this troubled world!"

It took hours of Patrick's badgering until the three of them finally relented, believing that if Lot did it then the bible condoned it. Patrick concocted the *Witches' Brew*. Wine laced with virgin menstrual blood to give to the judges and he brewed another potion for the girls—one that made them insane with the thirst for bloodletting and heightened their sexual desire. A drink that bore an uncanny odor of Boston Crème.

What happened that night was an unholy abomination against all the laws of man, nature, and God. In the morning the girls awoke from the drunken stupor to find themselves deflowered and their fathers mutilated. Their memories spotty, only bits and pieces of the horrific acts would allow themselves to seep into their minds' eye. Although the specific events would escape them for years, one thing they knew for certain.

Patrick tricked them.

And the Inner Wheel was angry.

The Inner Wheel.

The Wheel that meted out life and blessings. Rage flooded the girls' hearts at Patrick's betrayal and their beloved fathers' deaths. They attacked him in unison, but he was ready for them. In the end the three turned to the Outer Wheel for help and that's how the deal was made.

In exchange for banishing Patrick the girls promised the Outer Wheel that they would replenish it from time to time in human blood. They undertook this repugnant task, justifying their actions that Patrick was the greater threat, and if he should ever unlock the Outer Wheel to gain access to the Inner Wheels (for even Patrick did not know that there was just one Inner Wheel then) all of Cypress Point and perhaps the *world* could be destroyed at the hands of this nihilistic despot.

But there was another Quid Pro Quo; *something for something*.

The Wheel banished Patrick for a distinct amount of days. He was prophesized to return and take his revenge on the three. The only one who would be able to stop him was the seventh son of a seventh son.

Me.

Patrick wailed and my insides turned and tightened into a wet knot. The sound pierced the wind and twisted every nerve in my spine. I gagged and had to fight back the hot bile that burned the back of my throat. He shook like a dog trying to dry itself. Clumps of flesh fell from his form and landed with a shrieking hiss. What was left clinging to his massive shell was a perversion of life, as pus filled squirmy things dribbled and writhed around his cadaverous frame. I watched as the thing known as Patrick shook off its last semblance of humanity.

The Mercedes warped and morphed into a black horse pulling a hearse.

"Nobody sends telegrams anymore!" He shook and changed into the man behind the Plexiglas with the beard and no mustache. "*Cypress Point. That's all it says. From Cypress Point. No zip-code, no state or nothing! Just Cypress Point! Hey, mister...where is that?*"

He shook again and changed back into himself.

"*I'm going to teach you about pain, Ezekiel. I'm going to teach you about fear. Just when you think you can't be anymore afraid, I'm going to double and triple your fear. I'm going to break you, smart boy. I'm going to stretch the limits of your sanity and have you beg me for death!*" Patrick said, but it was Clara's voice. He shook again and the ground around him mildewed with mold and rotten growth.

"*Do you know what a Colostomy Bag is, Ezekiel? It's when you have to push through your side because your asshole's been torn out!*" he shrieked again in her voice. He shook once more and contorted into the thing that destroyed George's diner. It was Patrick all along. It was Patrick, not Clara. Patrick! Feeding me memories. Scaring me. Tricking me as he did my mother all those years ago. He had been in Cypress since I arrived! Since the time he shook my hand in the airport and followed me.

I now saw his true guise. What he had become after so many murders and blood sacrifices.

Tamara screamed so loud my head rang like a school bell. Neither of us were prepared for what we saw. Where the Wheels were splendid to behold Patrick was the complete opposite. He was apotheosis of pain and suffering. The epitome of wrath. His *body* for lack of a better term was a mockery of the form God breathed life into. I stood, absorbing the memories of the Three as I understood exactly what I had done.

I brought the Foreigner to Cypress.

It was Patrick who dug up my brothers' graves so I would find them. It was Patrick who manipulated us all!

"I may not be able to hurt you, Seventh," he croaked. "But I can certainly hurt her. Surrender the entrance to the

Wheel and I will let her leave here. Refuse and she will join your mother and her adopted sisters in the Valley of Dry Bones."

"The only thing I will surrender is the path out of Cypress! You are barred from this land forever! Leave now, caretaker or die!" I said without thinking. The words just poured out and I trembled as I realized that was exactly what the three of them told Patrick when they banished him.

"You can not trick us, Caretaker as you did our mothers! Leave this land! The Wheels abhor you! They block you!" Tamara said. I realized then that I was in the fight for my life. That there was still a chance—even with the Evangelist and Lukie dead that I could still die on March 15th.

"No matter what he says or does, Ezekiel you cannot let him get to the Wheel!" Tamara cried. "He'll destroy everything! He can't get to them with you blocking the entrance! No matter what, do not move!"

"The circle is complete, Seventh!" Patrick shrieked. "You have to make a choice! Either you can let me enter and find the true secrets of the Wheels and save this trollop, or you will watch her die!"

Patrick screamed again and it sounded like a thousand panes of glass crashing. The air itself seemed to shatter as the tremor throbbed through everything. The sky blackened like a huge bag of soot and my body went limp as I watched black hail fall at his command. The ebony pieces hit the ground and unfolded like evil bits of origami. The black hail swarmed around Tamara and stuck to her like a second skin. She screamed in pain and I ran to her, trying to pull the loathsome creatures off her, but my hands passed harmlessly through them. She continued to scream and I was helpless to aid her. The black hail continued to cover her, wrapping around her like an obstinate cocoon.

She was now totally covered. Her screams were muffled shrieks, terrified prayers for breath. She was suffocating right in front of me and there was nothing I could do.

"What is she worth to you, Seventh? How long can the sow hold her breath? In a few moments they will begin to eat through her skin! Move out of the way and you will save her! What does this town matter to you? You can take your woman and leave here!"

The black hail created an impenetrable mesh around Tamara. It molded to her features and hardened like a sentient sarcophagus. My mind raced for a way to save her. I stood on the verge of panic, futilely clawing at the black webs. Tamara was dying right in front of me.

"There is nothing you can do, Seventh! Why deny yourself? Take this whore and flee! Let her give you sons in the new city of York! Forget this town and its wretched inhabitants! Don't make the same mistake your father made!"

"Release her, Patrick! Do it now and leave and I won't destroy you!"

"You have less than a minute, Seventh! The time for games has expired. Move out of the way!"

Patrick had me in a bind. If I moved to save Tamara I would give him access to the Wheel and with its power he would murder everything in sacrifice. If I did not move Tamara would die in my arms.

You hafta let go of all your schoolin, Ezekiel...

I finally understood what One-Leg meant by that statement. It wasn't my education I had to surrender, it was my arrogance. My cocky attitude that I was so much better than everyone else in the town.

"There's a third choice for me, Caretaker! One that solves both problems!"

"What! What are you going to do?" Patrick shrieked.

I beseeched the Outer Wheel to give me access to the Inner Wheel.

The Inner Wheel lay flat, totally hidden by the Outer Wheel, but the Outer Wheel opened a portal that showed me not only the Inner Wheel but beyond!

I felt myself being pulled up into the white light again. This time I could clearly see the Inner Wheel. It opened for me fully, revealing to me all of it's secrets. I saw then, in that moment how wrong I was. The Inner Wheel was just another door to *another Wheel!* And there was another Wheel behind that one! And another! And another! Each more powerful and more beautiful than the one before it! The Wheels showed me colors, shapes and sights never before witnessed by any of the living. The more Wheels I passed the more of them there were to pass!

Clara was right! One-Leg was right! If not for my arrogance in being better educated I would have certainly seen this!

I was up to the Seventh Wheel, so anxious to see what was beyond this one. Indescribable ecstasy flooded every cell in my body. I stood on the cusp of it, knowing in my heart what I had to do and praying for the strength to do it.

I felt like a man standing a yard away from heaven and being told that he could not enter. I knew then how the biblical prophet Moses felt when God told him that after all his work, he could see the Promised Land, but he would never step foot in it.

I took a deep breath, closed my eyes, thought of my father's love for my mother, and made my choice.

[*Banish the Caretaker,*] I mentally told the Outer Wheel, [*and I shall bring you sacrifice!*]

"Whose prayer does God hear, Patrick? The lion's or the zebra's?" I said, mocking him.

"You fool! You simply prolong the inevitable! Those three slatterns could not keep me away and neither can you, Seventh! I'll be back! I'll be back, Seventh!"

"Not in my lifetime you won't!" I shouted.

Patrick screamed again but this time his pain and frustration were genuine. The Outer Wheel picked him up and dissected him as he hung in midair. I watched as his skin and hair were peeled away layer by layer, then his muscle, veins and nerves, until all that was left was bone. The Wheel crushed his skeleton like an eggshell and absorbed his dust.

[No further shall you come, Seventh. You have reached your worth. Our bargain is complete.]

I was back outside. Standing by Tamara. The black mesh covering her fell away, landing in harmless obsidian flakes and crumbling on the ground.

"Do you know what you did, Ezekiel? Do you realize what you gave up?" she asked me.

"I know. And I would do it again."

Epilogue: The Circle is unbroken

It's been seven years since that fateful day in March. Tamara and I are married and we have six sons. She's pregnant with the seventh. I never made it back to New York City and I very rarely catch a Knicks' game. Oh sure, there are times I miss it something awful, but when those spells hit I just look at my sons and the woman who bore them and I am content with my life.

Cypress Point took a lot of rebuilding after the earthquake. With the Evangelist gone, Tamara inherited a great deal of money and after I was elected to the head of the City Council, we used it to reconstruct the town. George's Diner was remodeled and is now run by one of his nieces. We renovated the library and built a new school. I even managed to start an adult literacy program.

The Molina Houses now have day care and a drug treatment center. We've opened medical clinics, crisis prevention seminars, and I've started work-study programs. It feels good to walk down the street and see the positive labor come to fruition.

Pickle (who after intensive research I discovered was named Hosea) sang beautifully at our wedding. I managed to have him cleaned and doctored up, but after two decades of living on the streets he was too far gone to cure everything that ailed him. He died happy though, seeing three of his grandchildren. We named our second son after him. Our firstborn we named after my father, Uriah.

I had the death corner demolished. The entire block is now flatland and off limits to residents. The Wheel is buried deep beneath it in a hollow cave that only I have access to. This was to ensure no one would have a homicidal breakdown from being in such close proximity to it.

I love Tamara. I mean that. I love that woman the way my daddy loved my mother. Deep down inside I think that's all I've ever wanted and I have to be grateful now that I have it.

A man has to have something to hold on to.

Sometimes she'll catch me looking despondent, thinking about what lie just beyond that Seventh Wheel, and she'll say my head is made of glass because she can read my mind. She'll stop and hold my head in both of her hands, making sure I stare deep and hard into her eyes, and she'll ask me, "Are you feeling any regrets today, Mr. Johnson?" And I'll look into her eyes, eyes that saw so much pain and suffering, yet had the capacity to reflect so much love.

"No, Mrs. Johnson," I'll answer her. "Not even for a moment." And it's always true.

I often ponder certain paradoxes that the Wheel created. What if I had never answered that telegram? What would have happened to me if I had never returned to Cypress Point? Or if I had left when the Wheel first showed me the way out?

I figured out many things about this town in the last few years, like why all of the canned food has generic labeling on the packages. Cypress Point can only be accessed when the Outer Wheel opens; food delivery trucks are waylaid into this town by a wrong turn. The Evangelist would then bag the food and sell it to stores and restaurants. The Wheel decides exactly what is needed. The Wheel decides who enters and who leaves.

Another interesting point is the death of my brothers and this is perhaps the hardest thing that I have learned to come to grips with. That fateful day I fell into the Evangelist's yard as a child, I was so scared and so angry at Petey and all of my brothers for their bullying ways that I subconsciously wished them dead.

All of them.

The fact that this all occurred on March fifteenth cannot be a coincidence. The Wheel thought that I was making sacrifice and so chose to take them one by one. Thus it was I who caused their deaths. I've ceased to wonder about the irony of my most hated enemy becoming my mother-in-law. God it seems is not only cruel, but He also has a sadistic sense of humor.

Now that I've become a father, I've come to understand my daddy all the more. The love he had for my mother and his children. The sacrifices he made to keep his family together. The hope and trust he placed in me to fulfill my destiny. Which in some haphazard fashion I guess I've done.

I am hoping that my seventh son will have access to the Inner Wheels since they no longer hear me. Once I had Patrick banished and consciously offered to make sacrifice, I had corrupted myself in the Inner Wheels' eyes. Only the Outer Wheel hears me, which relishes human flesh and blood from time to time.

So now, I am required like my mother, Clara, and Ophelia before me to lure unsuspecting men and women to their deaths at the Wheel's behest. I try to be very selective and only pick the basest of people, those with no morals or scruples— rapists, murderers, whores, pedophiles, drug dealers and such. This creates a catch-22 because the Wheel learns what it absorbs.

There are tales whispered in bars, taverns and truck stops in all of the small towns surrounding Cypress Point. They tell stories of a strange town off the beaten path that's filled with an evil history and woe betide any who don't take heed to the road signs.

Stay away from Cypress Point, they say. Men enter never to be seen or heard from again!

Tamara makes sure that each and every one of them receives a proper burial.

Cypress is known for its beautiful funerals.

THE END